ALSO BY MA

Memories Live Here

Altered Past

PARALLEL MINDS

PARALLEL MINDS

CHERL
BOOK 3

MARC SHEINBAUM

ROUGH
EDGES
PRESS

To all the great people I had the pleasure to work with…
Especially those trying to do the right thing.

PARALLEL MINDS

CHAPTER ONE

DAN BARRY ROLLED out of bed and padded to his bathroom to wash up and get the day started. Sure, it was fifteen minutes before six a.m. But he and Nicole had learned the night before they had the day off. The forecast was spectacular—mid-seventies all day with bright sunshine—and Dan had a great idea for a new hike he wanted Nicole to experience in the Big Sur. After all, how many times to you get a surprise vacation day?

Dan pulled up a pair of sweatpants, went to the kitchen, and started the coffee maker. He cracked four eggs into a bowl and added a touch of milk and vanilla extract before chopping up red and yellow peppers.

"Hey," a voice said softly.

Dan turned. "Hey, yourself." He beamed as he held out the bowl. "Hungry?"

To Dan's surprise Nicole Ryder shook her head. Despite her incredibly lean figure, she never turned down a delicious meal.

"Come on," Dan insisted. "I'm making my egg white frittata." He nodded toward the refrigerator. "There's multigrain on the second shelf. Put in some toast."

Nicole was quiet as she squinted under the bright

kitchen lights and opened the refrigerator. Dan thought she seemed nervous.

"You need to relax, Nicole," Dan said as he emptied the eggs into the skillet. "They'll figure out what's going on. Naveen will probably want us back at our workstations by noon so we should enjoy our little break while it lasts."

Naveen Gupta was their boss at the Sway Corporation, the project manager overseeing the artificial intelligence project known as CHERL. Every employee had been told to stay away from the system until further notice as Sway's cyber security team was investigating a potential breach.

"Grab some coffee," Dan told Nicole. "This will be ready in a few minutes."

"I forgot to brush my teeth," Nicole said. "I'll be right back." Before she turned away, Dan thought her eyes looked a little watery.

Something bigger than the company lockdown had to be on Nicole's mind, he thought. Maybe she felt the emotional vestiges of the previous evening, when they had been even more passionate with each other than usual. Every time Dan thought their love making had reached a new crescendo, Nicole surprised him by leading him to a new place. And when they were done, Nicole had clung to him so tightly he could hardly move, as if she was afraid to let him go—scared he might not return. But the idea was foolish. From the moment he set eyes on her three months earlier, Dan had fallen madly in love. He knew she was the one. Dan was sure they would spend the rest of their lives together.

Until the door to his apartment burst open.

"What the—" Dan started, but he was tackled to the floor, overpowered by a husky man in a dark suit.

"Stay down, fuck face," the man said as he pressed the side of Dan's face into the floor.

"Dan?" he heard Nicole call out from the bathroom.

"Who the hell are you?" Dan managed, his heart pounding.

"Official action," the man said. "Stay still. We're not here for you."

"You're cops?" Dan stopped struggling as he heard his bedroom door being smashed in, followed by the sounds of a struggle. "Nicole!" Dan called out.

"Quiet, asshole," the man holding him down said.

"This is a mistake!" Dan said. "You're in the wrong place." He heard a thud coming from the bedroom followed by a clicking sound Dan recognized as some type of handcuffs. Seconds later Dan could see the cop walking Nicole past him and into the hallway.

"She didn't do anything," Dan said, his voice muffled by the weight of the man pressing on his back.

But seconds later, the man finally stood up and said, "Stay the fuck down," before walking out of the apartment.

Dan slowly rose but struggled to maintain his balance. His head felt as if he'd been hit with a hammer. He staggered to the door and looked down the hallway, but they were gone. He touched his cheek and winced at the pain from the golf ball sized welt. After stumbling back to the kitchen, Dan removed an icepack from the freezer and held it against his face. He sank into a chair, trying to clear his head.

This had to be a mistake. What could Nicole have done? He removed the cell phone from his pocket and was about to call the police when the doorbell rang.

"What the…?" Dan shuffled to the door. Two men in black suits stood in the hallway, their FBI badges clearly visible.

So were the pistols pointed at his head.

Dan removed the pack from his face and said, "Did you assholes forget something?"

"Get on the floor!" one of them shouted.

"Again?"

———

AFTER READING Dan his *Miranda* rights, the two agents he'd been handed off to outside his apartment building had remained silent as the sedan made its way through downtown San Francisco traffic. Dan still had no idea why he and Nicole had been arrested within minutes of each other. The sedan pulled past an Enterprise Rental Car office and came to a stop in front of The Federal Building. The car door opened and one of the agents, a tall, Black man named Spencer York, reached in and said, "Let's go." The welt on Dan's face was still pounding as Agent York escorted him through the glass doors of San Francisco's FBI headquarters and into an elevator. They exited on the eighth floor and shuffled Dan past a wall-sized display of newspaper clippings from infamous FBI cases. Agent York walked him into a small room and lowered Dan into one of the three chairs surrounding a metal table. There was a glass partition on the far wall.

"Before I call in the DA," Agent York said as he took a seat opposite Dan. "Do you want to tell me where your girlfriend is?"

"Are you serious?" Dan responded. "I thought *you* had her."

A bespectacled agent entered the room, folded his arms, and was about to sit in one of the chairs when York said, "Don't get too comfortable, Agent Kata. It appears Mr. Barry has no intention to cooperate."

"That's a shame, Agent York," Agent Kata said. "I guess we should get the process started."

"What process?" Dan said. "I didn't do anything!"

Agent York rubbed his chin. "Hey, how much time did that last perp get for espionage?"

Dan's shoulders shuddered. "Espionage?"

"At least thirty years," Agent Kata said as they walked to the door. "And there's never any parole for spies."

"This is crazy! I'm not a spy!" Dan said, his heart now pounding. "Nicole is not a spy!"

"Then why won't you tell us where she is?" Agent York asked.

"Because I don't know. Two cops...at least I thought they were cops, came and took her five minutes before you guys showed up." He pointed to the bruise on his face. "How do you think I got this?"

The agents exchanged glances before York asked, "Did you get a good look at them?"

Dan shook his head. He knew he should call a lawyer, but he didn't know any. And he wasn't about to call his father in New York and get him all worried. Not until Dan understood what was happening.

"Okay," Kata said. "Then let's start with your girl-friend. What's her real name?"

"Her *real* name?" Dan shook his head. "What do you mean? She's Nicole Ry—"

"Cut the bullshit," Agent York said. "The real Nicole Ryder lives in Sante Fe, New Mexico."

"What?" His mouth went dry again.

"Your girlfriend was nothing but a hoax," York said. He placed a picture in front of Dan, showing an attrac-tive but professional-looking blond woman. "This is the real Nicole Ryder. She worked for Aztec several years ago, but she's taking time off to raise her baby." York paused, raised his eyebrows, and smirked as he asked, "He's not yours, is he? The baby, I mean."

Dan slowly shook his head, his heart still pounding.

York nodded and said, "I didn't think so."

Dan swallowed hard as Kata chimed in, asking, "How much did she pay you?"

"Huh?"

"Are you trying to tell us you gave a spy a copy of the CHERL system specifications and got nothing in return?" Kata looked at York, who was suddenly distracted by something on his phone. "I hope he at least got laid, don't you, Agent York?"

"A...spy?" Dan whispered.

The FBI agents exchanged glances again. "He expects us to think he didn't know," Kata said.

"The DA won't believe him," York responded.

"They won't waste their time..." The FBI agents continued their banter as if Dan wasn't in the room. He watched their mouths move, but his ears rung as if someone had set off an alarm.

Nicole wasn't real? She was a spy? His mind flashed back to the night at his apartment when he first introduced Sway's newest engineering hire—the woman Dan would fall in love with—to his colleagues on the CHERL project team. "I've never even seen CHERL's design specification," Nicole had told them, claiming to want to learn more about the artificial intelligence system. "I have no idea how the data is used to make CHERL recommend what she does."

"I guess there's no harm in lending you my copy for a few days," Dan remembered saying. Minutes later they made love for the first time. Now, as his memories lingered on images from that night—of the woman he thought was Nicole Ryder—wrapped in his arms, Dan said to the agents, "She didn't...give me anything in return for the documentation."

But for the first time since he had been arrested, Dan wasn't certain he was telling the truth.

CHAPTER TWO

THREE YEARS LATER...

"AS LONG AS Alina Petrova is out there," the FBI assistant director said, "Russia is always going to be a threat."

Special Agent Lucas Foley watched the steely-eyed image of Domingo Compo from the secure video conference room of the FBI's field office in downtown Chicago. Lucas wasn't sure why he and Special Agent Rob Dennison of the San Francisco bureau had been invited to meet with the head of the FBI's Counterintelligence unit, but Lucas did know that the broad-shouldered Compo was correct in his assessment of Petrova. In fact, Lucas knew everything there was to know about the dangerous Russian spy that had worked undercover in America three years ago.

He knew that Petrova, who had impersonated an AI engineer inside the Sway Corporation, could play the role of a beautiful seductress. After all, Lucas had interviewed all the victims of her "Sugar Baby" scheme, where Petrova executed elaborate ransomware attacks against both private and public companies. And he had seen the tantalizing photos and surveillance footage.

Lucas also knew Petrova could portray a brilliant programmer and artificial intelligence engineer. He had read the FBI lab's description of the sophisticated code the Russian built to search for information about her mother.

And Lucas knew Petrova could kill like a professional assassin. He had seen the bludgeoned skull of the Rojas Cartel member she murdered in order to steal thousands in cash, and he had read the CIA's conclusion about her role in the Alexi Romanoff termination.

"We believe Petrova delivered a deadly nerve agent that took out the former KGB agent who ran the rogue Russian cyber hacking ring. We have conflicting intelligence as to why Romanoff was eliminated. Some report the Kremlin was angry that Romanoff lined his own pockets with millions of insider trading profits. Others say Petrova had a personal vendetta."

Lucas knew that both accounts were probably true.

"And let's not forget," Director Compo continued. "She has espionage in her lineage," Compo paused, his glare directed at Lucas as he said, "Isn't that right, Agent Foley."

"That's correct, sir," Lucas said as he felt a sudden cramp in the leg damaged years ago during his last undercover drug operation. While the bullet wound had healed, Lucas Foley's relationship with the bureau's top brass had been frosty at best. While half of the agency thought Lucas was a hero for discovering Alina Petrova's mother was a Russian mole who had risen to the highest levels of the FBI, the other half thought Lucas had made a serious blunder by confronting "Assistant Director Sonia Gilroy," leaving the Russian no option but to take her own life without revealing the network of spies supporting her rise within the bureau.

Unfortunately for Lucas, he knew FBI Assistant Director Compo fell into the latter group. While Lucas was allowed to remain in his position as a cyber security agent within the Chicago bureau, he had come to accept that his chances for advancement were limited.

He hoped the invitation to today's conference call meant something had changed.

"Has there been a break in the case?" Agent Dennison asked.

"No. But there is a new urgency coming out of the White House."

"Why is that?" Lucas asked.

"For years, President Wainwright has been hearing about Sway's artificial intelligence invention recreating great leaders from the past. He has been asking for this CHERL system to be installed in the Oval Office. The president has even picked out the leader he wants. But the National Security Administration wants proof CHERL can operate without cyberattacks—given the Russians hit Sway twice in the past four years. Many within the NSA believe as long as Alina Petrova is in circulation, they can never allow CHERL anywhere near the Oval Office. But there's only just so long they can stall the president. The NSA wants us to pull out all stops to find Petrova and…neutralize her."

"What do they think we can do that hasn't already been done?" Dennison asked.

Compo leaned forward, his face practically filling the screen. "We've uncovered encrypted messages she exchanged with her former American boyfriend."

"Dan Barry?" Lucas asked.

Compo nodded. "This exchange occurred a while back. Their messages seemed innocuous but our decoding team believes she's been softening Barry up for something. She either plans to recruit him or convince him to join her wherever it is she's disappeared to."

"Do you think Barry will lead us to Petrova?" Lucas asked.

"He hasn't until now," Compo said. "But we plan to provide an extra…push."

Dennison asked if he should assign local agents to tail Barry in San Francisco.

"Barry moved to New York earlier this year to be closer to his ailing father," Compo said. "The Manhattan bureau has been monitoring everything about his life. Our Quantico guys say our predictive models are flashing signals that his father's situation is about to deteriorate."

"What does that mean?" Lucas asked.

"I'm sure Special Agent Lummis and her team will provide you with all the details. They've conceived an operation. It's complex and things could get…messy."

Lucas waited for Compo to elaborate about potential complications. Instead, Compo said, "If we're successful, Barry will have little choice but to do exactly what we ask."

"What do you need from us?" Dennison asked.

"You both know the Petrova case and the events at Sway better than anyone. I'd like both of you to be part of the daily debriefs. Provide your expertise and background from what you learned about Alina Petrova and Dan Barry."

"Whatever you need, sir," Dennison said.

"Speaking of Sway," Lucas said. "A few years ago, they were trying to use their AI to track down Petrova. I provided Sway's lead scientist, Dr. Josh Brodsky, with information from our case files, anything the bureau's compliance team approved. It's always been a long shot, but should I check to see if Brodsky's made any progress?"

"Good idea," Compo said. "Sway should be motivated to help. After all, this entire operation revolves around the White House installing their CHERL system. But be careful what you share. I don't want civilians knowing about our operation."

"Brodsky's not exactly a civilian, sir," Lucas said. "He still holds the top-secret security clearance from the Department of Defense. He would never disclose any government action, especially one that's going after Petrova."

Compo was silent for a few moments, until he said, "Maybe so. But I expect you to clear everything through Agent Lummis. She's in charge."

"When do we find out more about the operation, sir?" Dennison asked.

"I'll leave it to Agent Lummis to bring you both up to speed," Compo said as he stood. "She'll be in touch."

As soon as the video went blank, Lucas slowly rose and took in a deep breath. He thought about Compo's *"things could get messy"* comment again. Lucas had been part of many chaotic situations as an undercover narcotics agent earlier in his career.

What could possibly be messier than going after a drug cartel?

CHAPTER
THREE

"I SENSE YOU ARE FRUSTRATED, *Dr. Brodsky,*" the clean-cut-looking avatar on the computer screen said. *"But Russia is a very large country."*

"I'm not frustrated, Officer Friday," Josh responded. "I've given you everything I have. I'm just trying to get to an answer."

The male avatar responded. *"I will not be able to narrow down the possibilities to less than two hundred women without answers to my questions. Russia has almost one-hundred-fifty million citizens."*

"I understand," Josh answered slowly, choosing his words carefully. "But less than two hundred Russian women have the kind of training in artificial intelligence needed to masquerade as an engineer in my lab."

"That is correct."

"And I've told you my target is probably less than forty years of age—"

"I understand, Dr. Brodsky. But almost all of Russia's AI engineers have been educated over the past twenty years, meaning most are younger than forty."

Josh leaned back from his computer screen and rubbed the back of his neck, trying to think of another approach that might unlock the answer. This latest version of his artificial intelligence creation lacked many of the personality traits he and his team had spent the past five years building into CHERL. Josh actually enjoyed conversing with the emotionless intellect, the AI's unmodulated voice echoing off the walls of the project control room. He had selected the Officer Friday avatar as his tribute to those old *Dragnet* television shows he and his brothers used to watch when they were kids in Brooklyn.

"All we want are the facts, ma'am," the actor Jack Webb used to say in his famous monotone. So that's how Josh had programmed his skunkworks project. "Friday" wasn't designed to be aggressive or brusque. Josh's latest AI recreation didn't contain the data elements needed to exhibit empathy or compassion. Officer Friday wasn't built to forge a personal connection with Josh, who for now, would be the sole client.

Over the past three years, Officer Friday had become Josh's personal passion project, an AI "super-sleuth" that modeled the best techniques from the greatest detectives and investigative journalists in history. After another massive investment to upgrade Sway's cyber security, Josh and his team resumed building and installing CHERL's re-creations in the C-suite of corporate America. But Josh kept a very small, elite team working on Officer Friday, hoping to help the FBI track down Nicole Ryder's impersonator and to prove that the spies who attacked Sway were no longer lurking in the shadows, waiting to hit CHERL again.

Because until Josh had sufficient proof, a CHERL historical recreation would never be installed in the White House. And providing a version of CHERL to the most powerful person in the world remained Josh Brodsky's most important mission.

He originally trained the Officer Friday AI with volumes of publicly available files documenting the approaches used by some of history's greatest investiga-

tors. He included the complete works of David Halber-
stam, winner of a Pulitzer Prize for his penetrating work
on the Vietnam War, and thirty books written or co-
written by Bob Woodward of Watergate fame. Josh
uploaded the case files of the early twentieth-century
police detective Raymond Schindler, who many in law
enforcement referred to as the most brilliant investigator
in American history. CHERL's Officer Friday even
digested novels revealing the scientific method of fictional
characters like Sherlock Holmes, along with every season
of the *Perry Mason* and *Columbo* television shows. AI was
particularly well suited for Holmes's scientific method—
"frame the problem, gather observation points, and
'deduce' or infer a hypothesis," which is then tested
before the process is repeated over and over until the case
is solved. After absorbing this veritable smorgasbord of
investigative techniques, Officer Friday began asking a
series of questions, constantly drilling down and
demanding more information.

"Did she speak with an accent?"

"Was blond her natural hair color?"

"What type of alcohol did she drink?"

Josh provided everything he knew about the beautiful
spy who penetrated CHERL not once, but twice. First by
tricking Josh's brother Donny into sending Josh a
corrupted email that launched a ransomware attack on
CHERL. The spy's malware successfully recorded and
transmitted details of a board presentation Josh was
preparing on his top-secret project:

> Computerized Human Experienced as Real Life
> (CHERL)—"To deliver humanlike re-creation of the
> greatest leaders in world history, the CHERL AI engine
> will infer how these brilliant minds would tackle
> modern-day challenges in selected disciplines, including
> politics, international affairs, business, and science."

By divulging Sway's secrets to her Russian handlers, the hacker set in motion a year-long infiltration of Sway. Impersonating an American AI engineer named Nicole Ryder, the spy managed to get herself employed on Josh's team. Once in place, she secretly fed CHERL with alternative information—data that "trained" CHERL's recreated AI business leaders to promote business transactions earning the Russians over three hundred million dollars in insider trading profits. Before the impostor could be apprehended, she disappeared. Vanished into the night.

Josh loaded Officer Friday with every piece of code the spy had developed during her time as a data management engineer at Sway, hoping AI would identify patterns that might assist with the FBI's investigation. And right after Nicole Ryder's impersonator disappeared, Agent Foley sat for extensive interviews, providing Officer Friday with his personal knowledge of the case.

"What made her dangerous was her incredible power of deception," Agent Foley explained in his first meeting with Officer Friday. "Her real Russian name is Alina Petrova but she used a forged passport and the name Briana Danis to enter the country. Once in America, she had many aliases including Nina Gladway, Deirdre Pescon, Dina Ginero. And, as you know, Nicole Ryder."

Agent Foley claimed the hacker literally had espionage in her lineage, as she was born to two Russian spies named Grigory and Valeriya Petrova, two spies who lived in America in the late 1990s—until Valeriya disappeared.

"I believe searching for her mother was Alina's prime objective," Foley concluded. So Josh trained Officer Friday with the powerful hacking programs the spy used to crack into systems throughout the United States, including a program she called her "AI Scout" in an audacious search for her mother.

"THE SUSPECT COULD NOT HAVE CREATED *her scout program and hacking tools unless she was a legitimate expert in artificial intelligence,*" Officer Friday had deduced.

It had been three years and in all that time, despite the vast trove of information and all his efforts to perfect the AI super-sleuth, Josh still had no meaningful hypothesis on Alina Petrova's whereabouts.

It was time to return Agent Foley's phone call and tell him the same.

CHAPTER
FOUR

DAN BARRY CHECKED the time as he exited the Penn Station 34th Street subway station. He had fifteen minutes to walk two blocks to WompleTech's Manhattan headquarters, plenty of time before Julius Etchell's mandatory noon meeting. Suddenly, Dan heard a loud *bang*. He jumped out of the way of oncoming pedestrians and pressed his back against the side of an office building. He squeezed his eyelids shut as his heart pounded. When he finally opened his eyes, he saw an old-fashioned delivery truck rumble down 7th Avenue, backfiring several times as it crossed the 33rd Street intersection. Dan drew in a deep breath and exhaled as he shook his head. Moving back to his cacophonous hometown had not been the best antidote for his newfound anxiety disorder.

But he hadn't moved to New York for the calm.

By the time Dan entered the conference room, his ten coworkers on WompleTech's AI team were already helping themselves to slices of fresh pizza arranged on the table. Various flavors of still and sparkling water were neatly placed along the credenza, next to the commemorative plaques and company awards. Dan grabbed a paper cup and poured some lemon-lime. He read the inscription on a plaque placed beside the ice bucket.

"Congratulations to WompleTech for being named one of America's best places to work!"

"Dig in, Dan," Anita Barkley said, motioning for Dan to join her. His bubbly coworker was enjoying a slice covered in pepperoni.

"It's okay," Dan said. "I already ate." The truth was, he wasn't the least bit hungry. Something didn't feel quite right about this impromptu gathering. Etchell held monthly "grab and learn" luncheons, where one member of WompleTech's team would present their latest AI enhancements. Agendas were always sent out to make sure everyone was prepared with insightful questions. But no advance email had been received today.

The door opened and Etchell entered, his eyes lowered as he walked to the head of the table.

"Hey, boss," Barkley said to Etchell as she chewed on her slice. But Etchell still hadn't raised his head as the door opened again. Susan Whittier, WompleTech's head of Human Resources entered, followed by her assistant, Glenda Parson, who was carrying a stack of papers. Carlo Falcone, another of Dan's coworkers, slid next to Dan and whispered, "Oh shit."

"What's going on?" Dan whispered back.

"I think we're about to get screwed," Falcone said.

Dan suddenly felt lightheaded.

"Please," Whittier said solemnly. "Will everyone take a seat."

Only three engineers lowered themselves into chairs in the now tense conference room. Dan and the others remained standing.

"Very well," Whittier said. She turned to Etchell. "Julius, do you want to kick this off?"

The department head was grimacing and still hadn't made eye contact with anyone. He shuffled his feet before finally looking up. With a clearly forced smile, he said,

"I'm really sorry. I know this is crazy. But it wasn't my call."

Dan felt as if he'd been kicked in the stomach as the sound of murmuring filled the conference room. Etchell cleared his voice and said, "This is a tough situation. It seems to be about survival of our company. We have to make sure we can continue...I mean, we're burning through a lot of cash and...well..." He looked at Whittier, his eyes pleading for her to bail him out. "Unfortunately, this team is deemed to be discretionary right now."

"What the hell does that mean?" Falcone said loudly.

"Calm down," Whittier said. "You're all getting good packages."

"Packages?" a Chilean woman named Florencia asked, her voice quavering. "I left my job in Miami four months ago to come here!"

Dan leaned against the conference room table and stared at Etchell, but the department head was suddenly more interested in reading something on his phone. Dan couldn't believe this was happening to him, again. Three years ago Dan thought he was set for life. He was a member of the most dynamic and advanced artificial intelligence team in the world.

But that was before he met Nicole Ryder. Or at least, the woman who *said* she was Nicole Ryder.

The woman Dan had fallen in love with. She'd used him to blend into life in Silicon Valley—mix in with his friends and coworkers. And she'd exploited their relationship in order to gain access to the system specification for Sway's top-secret project, which showed the Russians how to manipulate CHERL.

Dan had been arrested by the FBI, suspected of collaborating with the woman who'd stolen Nicole Ryder's identity. While he was quickly released—he was never officially charged with committing a crime—word of his involvement spread throughout the Valley. Being known as the boyfriend of a spy was enough to tarnish Dan's reputation, at least on the West Coast. No one from Sway ever vouched for his integrity or came to his defense. And Sway fired him "for cause," for sharing the specifications with "unauthorized personnel."

For almost three years, the only work Dan could land in the Bay area was short-term AI engineering contracts —sporadic programming gigs doled out by small consulting firms that never disclosed his name to clients. Longing for the stability of a steady income—and wanting to be closer to his father who had been suffering with heart disease—Dan decided to seek out a full-time AI position in New York. And the move paid immediate dividends. A former classmate introduced Dan to the head of AI engineering at WompleTech, a New York based commercial real estate company that was leveraging artificial intelligence in their valuation process.

"Julius Etchell is desperate for AI talent," Lester Chang had told Dan. *So* desperate that the "episode" at Sway never came up during any of Dan's interviews. At the time, Dan's instincts told him getting this job had been too easy. But after falling for a fraudulent lover, Dan stopped listening to his broken instincts. But as he was about to lose another job again, he wondered if he would ever find another company that didn't care about his history.

Whittier called out each of their names and handed them their individual severance agreements. Moments after Whittier gave him his letter, Dan was staring at the second paragraph.

The equity grant WompleTech awarded to him when he was hired four months earlier was canceled. His severance payment, a mere two weeks of salary. In two weeks, Dan would have no way to pay the monthly rent on the two-year apartment lease he had just signed.

Not to mention his father's growing hospital bills.

CHAPTER
FIVE

THE DRIVERLESS SEDAN pulled up to the bag drop at the Beacon Hill Country Club in New Jersey. Louie Brodsky exited the back seat just as the valet approached.

"Mr. Brodsky!" the cheery attendant said as he opened the trunk and removed Louie's bag. "Nice to see you again. Beautiful day for golf."

"Thanks, Terry," Louie said. "But we're not playing today. Ed and I are just going to hit some balls."

"Ah, that's too bad," Terry said.

Not really, Louie thought. Sure, the sky was blue and the breeze was soft. But five hours on a golf course with Virtual Bank's CEO was about two hours too long for Louie, especially when Edward Chamberlain insisted on following up with an hour or two at the club's watering hole. The truth was, Louie didn't have patience for his boss's slow style of play. Louie could never find any rhythm during the tortuous, five-hour marathon, during which Louie would have to endure stories about his CEO's favorite courses ("You haven't lived until you've played Whistling Straits"). And Chamberlain loved to pine on about the spin rates of his favorite golf balls. Unfortunately, a golf club *was* the best place to get Ed's attention. Louie knew that, as did the rest of the bank's leadership team, each of whom kept a spare set of sticks in storage at VB's New Jersey headquarters for their monthly visits. Thankfully, today his CEO had asked Louie to meet at the country club's driving range to discuss an investment in a new mortgage system, meaning their time together would be limited. Because as much as Chamberlain loved the game, he hated practice.

Terry placed Louie's bag on an electronic golf caddy, and a few keystrokes later the caddy was following Louie down the pathway. It wasn't long before Louie heard the familiar "thwack" and Chamberlain, finishing his typically off-balanced swing, came into view.

"Hey, Ed," Louie called out as he approached. But Chamberlain was already focused on his next ball. So Louie grabbed a 9-iron from his own bag before his electronic caddy even came to a halt. He stepped up to the mat to the left of his boss, took two warm up swings, and proceeded to hit a ball that nestled a foot short of the one-hundred-twenty-yard flag. Chamberlain's next shot sliced badly to the right as Louie hit a high arcing shot. This time his ball landed slightly to the left of his target.

"Damn, you're good," Louie said to himself.

Too bad his boss wasn't more competitive—and a better golfer. Louie enjoyed having little target practice contests, seeing who could land their ball closest to the yardage marker.

"Ten bucks a shot," he might have wagered. Although Louie's serious gambling addiction was a thing of the past, he still craved the competition. On occasion, he'd logged into his sports betting app and wager on a few games. But nothing as serious as when he was losing thousands of dollars every week. Louie had his gambling under control. But he still ached for *that* feeling—the feeling that came whenever he'd win.

After a few more balls sailed through the air, Chamberlain finally spoke. "I've had a conversation with the board, Louie."

"Did they sign the requisition?" The fifty-million-dollar mortgage system had a large enough price tag to require board approval.

"I'm done," Chamberlain said.

"What do you mean?" Louie asked as he hit another ball. "I just got here."

"Not with practice," Chamberlain said as he took a slow backswing. "I mean, I'm out."

Louie stopped mid-swing.

"The board has asked me to retire at the end of the year."

"What? Geez, Ed. What happened?" Louie's sixty-two-year-old boss was only three years into the five-year employment agreement he'd signed when Virtual Bank merged with Atlanta-based Peachtree Commerce.

"They claim it's time for new blood," Chamberlain said as he placed another ball on the tee. He mis-hit another shot, dribbling the ball into the dirt.

Louie leaned on his nine-iron. "I can't believe it."

"Yeah, well. Believe it." Chamberlain took another swing and added, "Let's just say the board and I don't see eye to eye."

"I'm flabbergasted," Louis said, but the truth was, he wasn't. The promised synergies between Virtual Bank's digital assets and Peachtree's traditional "brick and mortar" branches had yet to materialize. While the combined bank was in better financial condition, Chamberlain never could find a formula for reigniting the growth engine. And *growth* was what investors demanded from the renamed Virtual Bank. As chief financial officer, Louie had advocated for additional acquisitions to fill VB's product gaps. But Chamberlain always worried about a looming economic downturn that never materialized.

"Besides," VB's CEO countered whenever Louie

identified opportunities both large and small, "the prices are too high." Now, as Louie took a few practice swings with his five-wood, another thought entered his mind.

If Chamberlain was out, would Louie be next? Was that why his boss had asked him here today? Instead, when the CEO smacked another shot and held his posture, Chamberlain said, "A few directors would consider *you* for my job."

"Me?" Louie felt a jolt of energy surge through his body. The same surge he used to feel when dealt a strong poker hand.

"Are you going to hit any more balls?" Chamberlain asked without turning around.

"Um…sure," Louie said as he used his club to position a ball on the mat, but he was still trying to absorb Chamberlain's words.

The CEO job.

"Despite my diminished clout, I think I can get everyone behind you," Chamberlain said as he waved his club in the air. Louie's mind was racing. This wasn't the first time they had discussed the possibility of Louie succeeding his boss. But Louie assumed his candidacy was just part of the obligatory "succession planning" conversation—a bureaucratic show of "good governance." But now, was this opportunity truly right in front of him? Louie suddenly felt that ache again. That ache for victory that used to burn inside his chest. He swung at the ball and watched it sail high to the right.

"Nice shot," Chamberlain said sarcastically.

"Yeah, well, I'm a little unsettled right now."

Chamberlain hit a ball clean down the middle of the range. He turned and smiled at Louie. "Nothing to be unsettled about."

"You seem okay with all of this," Louie said. "Aren't you upset with the board?"

"It is what it is, Louie. I knew the score two years ago when I started." Chamberlain hit another ball and said,

"You just need to decide if you want to take a swing at the job."

Louie realized he should be careful how he responded. No matter how well his boss seemed to be handling the decision, Louie didn't want to appear too anxious to take over.

"Er...I guess it is something I'll need to think about."

Chamberlain said, "It's a lot to take on. The demands in your current position are one thing, but trust me—this job will eat you alive."

"I understand."

"Besides," Chamberlain added as he changed clubs, "some on the board are lobbying to start an outside executive search."

Louie gripped the club tightly and faced the CEO. "Which directors don't think I can do it?"

Chamberlain shrugged. "Foster, Kefner, Evans. They think you're more of an individual operator. You'll have to convince them you can lead an organization."

Louie's mind raced as he placed another ball on the mat. He swung but didn't bother watching where the ball landed.

How could any of the directors doubt his leadership? Maybe making him compete for the job was just a test, he thought. To see how hard Louie would fight. To see how far he was willing to go. But Louie knew he could make a compelling case for the decision-makers.

He could *win* the job!

"Take a few days to think about it," Chamberlain said. "But let me know if you want to be considered."

Louie was relieved he didn't need to make an immediate commitment. But he suddenly felt a different kind of sensation in the pit of his stomach.

As the adrenaline left his system, he hoped he could find a way to convince the decision maker that mattered the most.

CHAPTER
SIX

"WHY DID WompleTech need to scoop up the entire department?" Agent Rob Dennison asked from San Francisco. Lucas was wondering the same thing as he sipped on his piping hot coffee. He was sitting alone in the Chicago bureau's video conference room, participating in what he learned would be daily coast-to-coast debriefs.

"It was the fastest way to get him out of his financial comfort zone," Special Agent Tammy Lummis replied from the New York field office. Lummis was the agent in charge of the operation against Dan Barry—and action the bureau now referred to as "Operation Turncoat."

"I still don't understand why didn't the company just fire Barry?" a junior New York agent named Amy Stryker asked.

"Everyone inside WompleTech knows Dan Barry was a top-rated engineer with stellar reviews," Lummis explained. "We couldn't let him be singled out without drawing undue attention. But it turns out, their CEO, Josh Hasbro was under intense pressure from investors to reduce costs, so eliminating the department was actually his idea. Sure, it was overkill, but Hasbro didn't want to miss out on the opportunity to ingratiate himself to the bureau. Especially when we said we might arrange for the IRS to drop his personal tax audit."

"How did you know Hasbro had tax issues?" another New York agent named Sarki Kidane asked. Kidane, who Lummis introduced as a specialist in financial crimes, wore brown horn-rimmed glasses and spoke in a soft, British accent.

"Everybody hides skeletons in their closet, Agent Kidane," Lummis said. "You just need to shine a light in the right spot."

Lucas shook his head. Earlier in the conference call, Agent Lummis provided a broad outline of the plan. Lucas had been part of many operations against drug cartels during his years working undercover. He had witnessed and even caused a great deal of "collateral damage." But Agent Lummis's brief description of the FBI's plan left Lucas feeling very unsettled.

"I've arranged to give you all access to the messages we picked up between Petrova and Barry," Lummis said. "We've seen the bureau's code-breaking analysis, but let me know what you think." She pointed to the screen and added, "Especially you two, Agent Dennison and Agent Foley. You know their history together better than the rest of us."

"Will do," Dennison said as Lucas nodded.

"By the way, Agent Foley," Lummis said. "Did you learn anything from Sway?"

"Not much," Lucas said. Unfortunately, his conversation with Sway's AI expert had been brief. "Brodsky hasn't come up with anything new on Petrova."

"Too bad," Lummis said. "How about further intel on Barry?"

"Only that Dan Barry was a skilled AI engineer who always delivered. Brodsky also said Barry was a real 'gadget geek.' Someone who loved testing out new tech products for the development lab."

"You might have undersold the usefulness of Brodsky's recollection," Lummis said. She silently rubbed her chin. After a few moments, she said, "I think you've provided us with something we might be able to use."

CHAPTER
SEVEN

DAN BARRY RAISED the window shade, and the sun lit up his father's face. Still, his old man did not stir. Neither the beeps from the cardiac monitor nor the tinny blare of the *Price Is Right* announcer coming through the TV remote could drown out the low wheeze emerging with each breath.

"Dad," Dan whispered. Still no movement. Alec Barry's mouth hung open. Dan moved closer, securing the nasal prongs that had slipped from his father's nose.

"Dad!" he said louder.

His father's eyes shot open as he let out a snort. He blinked several times and turned his head away from the afternoon glare coming through the window. Dan moved to the opposite side of the bed and his father smiled. "You're making quite a racket. How long you been sittin' there?"

"I just got here." Dan leaned over, kissed his father on his cheek, and patted his four-day-old stubble. "How ya feelin'?"

Alec Barry licked his lips and stretched his mouth. "All I do is sleep."

Hearing the dryness in his father's voice, Dan opened the water pitcher on the overbed table. It was empty.

"Press the button," his father said. "They never keep that thing filled."

"I know where the water is." He made his way down the corridor to the pantry. When he returned with the refilled pitcher, he poured ice-cold water into a plastic cup and placed it on the overbed table.

"Here, Dad." Dan pressed the controls to lift the head of the bed. "Let's sit you up." After Dan propped up the pillows, his father leaned back, lifted the cup in shaky hands, and tried to drink, coughing after each sip.

"Whoa, whoa, take it slow, cowboy."

"Ahh," his father groaned.

Dan lifted the spirometer. "Are you doing your calisthenics?"

"I'm a regular Jack LaLanne with that thing." His father's gaunt, unsmiling face made him look twenty years older than his sixty-five years. "Forget about me. How you doin'? How's the job?"

"Job's going great," Dan lied.

This wasn't the time to talk about the pizza party subterfuge at WompleTech. Dan hoped to have some job leads before telling his father he was no longer drawing a paycheck. He had spent the past few days reactivating his "artificial intelligence engineers" network. But text and voice message exchanges with former colleagues and college classmates had confirmed how lucky he was to have landed the WompleTech position in the first place. It seemed his "friends" still weren't eager to put their reputations on the line.

"Geez, Dan," said a friend who was well established in a midtown software firm. "I'm pretty sure everyone at my company knows what happened at Sway."

"The background check is pretty rigorous here," said a classmate who worked for a Tribeca robotics firm.

"Maybe you should go back to contract work," suggested another.

Dan had also spent the previous evening programming a "job bot" to scour online career and job boards. By midnight, his "bot" had submitted applications to over forty-five companies, all seeking "New York based artificial intelligence engineers with five to ten years of experience." Dan thought about expanding his search into the surrounding suburbs. But as he stared at his pale, ailing father, Dan knew he needed to be close to the Manhattan hospital.

Dan pulled the covers away. "Your legs don't look very good," he said as he pressed his fingers gently into his father's ankles.

"Is WompleTech training you in medicine?"

Dan replaced the covers and said, "No. But it would be a great way to meet nurses." The truth was, Dan had spent enough time in hospitals over the past few months to feel like a medical expert. This was his father's third trip to Columbia Presbyterian since Dan moved back to New York almost six months ago—each stay separated by two-week stints at a Bronx rehab center to regain his strength. This stay was already on day seven, and it didn't look as if his father would be back in rehab anytime soon.

"When was the last time Dr. Bolan was here?" Dan asked.

"Don't bother the docs. They're just as busy as you are."

"Dad, when did he last look at you?"

His father coughed several times and pointed to the box of tissues at the foot of the bed. Dan handed him a wad which he used to wipe away the greenish-yellow phlegm. Then he leaned forward and took several shallow breaths. "I think that resident was here yesterday," he wheezed. "That kid—what's his name." He cleared his throat again and said, "You gotta get me out of here."

"Let's see what Dr. Bolan has to say."

But as Dan stood by the bedside and rubbed his father's back, he could feel the vibration in his dad's lungs with each raspy breath. His strong, vibrant father seemed to be weakening by the day.

"I'll be right back," Dan said as he walked into the hallway. He proceeded to the nursing command post and rested his arms on the counter. A young woman in scrubs and a floral surgical cap was keying data into a computer.

"Excuse me. Can you tell me if Dr. Bolan is in the hospital?"

Without looking up, she replied, "He usually does his rounds before noon."

Dan checked the time. It was ten fifteen. Maybe the cardiologist would get here soon.

When he returned to the room, his father was sleeping again. Dan leaned against the windowsill and looked out at a police cruiser speeding north on Riverside Drive. Just as he was wondering how he was going to help with his father's growing medical bills, his cell phone rang.

"Is this Dan Barry?" asked an energetic female voice.

"Speaking."

"My name is Paula Calderon. I'm a recruiter with Jingle Finance. We hear you are in the market for an AI engineering position."

Dan quickly scrolled through the names of the companies his bot had applied to. He didn't find Jingle Finance. Maybe his bot had added the company without capturing the name for the tracking list.

"Er…yes, I am," Dan said.

"Our founder and CEO, Milo Galini, is very interested in your background," Calderon said. "Are you available to meet with him?"

"Where are you located?" Dan asked, crossing his fingers.

"We're in Midtown Manhattan."

"Absolutely!" Dan said. "When would you like me to come in?"

"How about tomorrow morning?"

Dan heard a knock on the door. He looked up to see Dr. Bolan standing in the doorway.

"If you could text me the time and place, I'll be there," Dan said.

"Awesome," Calderon said. "We look forward to seeing you."

"Thank you so much," he said before disconnecting and joining the cardiologist in the hallway. "How's he doing, Doc?"

"I want to try a new medication," Bolan said.

"Another one?" This would be the fourth change in his father's medicine.

"We have to do something," Bolan said. "I'm afraid his heart is getting weaker."

CHAPTER
EIGHT

JOSH BRODSKY CHECKED the sound and video quality of the training data supplied by his former contacts at the Central Intelligence Agency. Josh wanted Officer Friday, his artificial intelligence sleuth, to capture every word and intonation coming from the declassified footage. The Officer Friday version of CHERL was set to analyze facial expressions and body language of CIA analysts who could be overly cautious with their words.

"The pattern of these emails and phone calls is disturbing," the CIA analyst identified as Ronaldo Silva said. "Jiang Mi frequently contacts Chinese citizens with ties to the Communist Party."

"We've been watching him since he came to the States," said an analyst, referring to himself as Caleb Ong. "He's attended several technology conferences, mostly dealing with semiconductors. Our surveillance footage is extensive, but so far, a lot of cocktail parties and breakfast meetings with chip designers. Nothing of concern."

"I agree," said a third analyst named Sandra Leigh. "His actions appear innocent. I think we should move on to another subject."

Of course, none of Jiang Mi's activities turned out to

be innocent. This CIA debate had taken place two years earlier, six months before it was discovered that Jiang Mi was in fact, spying for the Chinese government as part of a broad program to steal the latest in America's semiconductor designs. After Jiang Mi was publicly tried and sent to prison, Josh submitted a Freedom of Information Act request to obtain the spy's emails and phone records, as well as the full video footage from the conferences he attended in America.

Josh glanced up at the clock and saw it was five minutes past noon. He had spent the entire morning training Officer Friday. He would execute a new version of his AI sleuth later that day. But now it was time to pivot back to his "day job." He wanted to finish a post-session diagnostic review of CHERL's latest business re-creation.

Having already conducted three separate audits, Josh had surmised that everything went smoothly during the interaction between the CEO of the world's largest oil refinery and CHERL's re-creation of John D. Rockefeller. As with the previous thirty-nine business leader re-creations Sway had executed since the hacking attack on CHERL, Josh found no sign of inconsistencies or irregularities. And no sign of any infiltration or unauthorized changes to his artificial intelligence system.

But as he had learned after discovering the fake Nicole Ryder's deception, high level metrics could be misleading. So, he today he intended to perform a line-by-line review of the Rockefeller transcript when he heard a knock on the door.

"So this is where you're hiding," Jenna Turbak said after poking her head in. Josh's petite boss was standing in the doorway, which led to Sway's massive computer center, known as The Tower.

Josh didn't smile when he nodded and said, "I heard you were coming back early."

Jenna entered and closed the door behind her. "Yeah,

well, Cleo and Callie are settled in. The new nanny is making a huge difference."

"Glad things are going well," Josh said. Jenna had recently adopted her second child from Ethiopia. Sway's executive vice president, one step removed from the CEO's corner office—literally and figuratively—was officially a single mother of a three-year-old and a newborn infant, both girls. Josh wasn't surprised when he'd heard his manager had returned less than two months into her half-year maternity leave. If he had learned one thing about Jenna Turbak, nothing took a back seat to her rocket ship of a career. Not even her growing family.

"What's going on here?" Jenna asked as she glanced at the four open laptops and reams of papers strewn over the front row of the auditorium-style control room.

"Performing another postmortem review."

"Clean as usual?" she asked as she took a seat in the row behind him.

Josh swiveled his chair around to face her and slowly nodded.

"That's good. How many days have you been at it?"

He shrugged. "Three. Maybe four."

Her eyes squinted. "Did quality control raise red flags?"

"Not one." He wasn't about to admit how much of those three days he'd been distracted by tinkering with his AI sleuth.

"You know," Jenna said, "we pay those quality people a lot of money. If we're going to keep them around, at some point, we'll have to rely on their work."

Josh's attention returned to the laptop displaying the transcript of the AI Rockefeller's conversation with Jaspar Phillips, the oil company CEO. "The White House isn't going to accept the word of our QA team, Jenna. We have to prove she's not at it again."

"I can't imagine anyone could break in again," she said. "After all the security we put in place?"

"The Russians never quit," Josh said. But he knew Jenna was right. Sway had invested in a set of extraordinary security measures, actions that very few outside of the defense industry had ever implemented. The CHERL universe inside Sway, including The Tower computer center, had become a cyber fortress. Yet, no matter how much security Sway added, it seemed the White House would never be convinced CHERL was safe enough for the president. In fact, Josh vividly recalled the contentious meeting he and Sway's CEO, Andre Olaf, had with Mike Kaminski, head of the National Security Agency.

"We have too much to lose," Kaminski had said.

"Business leaders have a lot to lose, too," Andre had tried. "Corporate security teams have examined and cleared our improved defenses. CEOs have jumped back in."

"Corporate leaders have short memories, Andre," Kaminski argued. "They're in the business of taking risks and hate the idea of falling behind. That's not how this president operates. And I'm not going to put him in harm's way."

"But America has to lead!" Andre urged. "AI is advancing around the world. It's only a matter of time before other countries will have their own version of CHERL, or something just like it. Allies and adversaries will be using AI to enhance their decision-making. Then *our* country will be the one at a disadvantage. The president will be at a disadvantage! You can't let that happen."

"Don't tell me what I can and cannot do, Olaf. You're the ones who let Russia penetrate Sway and attack your CHERL system. You think the Russians won't find out when your AI is installed in the White House? Imagine what they'll do if they believe they can manipulate your AI again, but this time to influence decision-making in the Oval Office!"

"That short-sighted, pompous ass," Andre had said to

Josh in the limo on the way back to the private jet hangar. But Josh knew the NSA leader was right. Corporate espionage was one thing. There would be no second chances if CHERL was involved in a national security breach.

If Officer Friday couldn't track down the hacker who impersonated Nicole Ryder, Josh hoped three straight years and forty successful—and breach-free—implementations would be enough to make another run at the NSA.

Now, as Jenna surveyed the stacks of papers and computer screens, she said, "Listen, I got a call from Andre's office. He's invited us to have dinner with him tomorrow night. Can you make it?"

Josh knew from experience that Andre Olaf's dinner meetings always had a secret agenda. "What's this one about?"

She stared at the far wall as she said, "I have no idea. I haven't seen him since I've been back."

Josh turned his attention back to the screen showing the transcript from the Rockefeller session. He hated business dinners. But as the years went by, opportunities for direct engagement with Sway's CEO had become few and far between. He wondered what was on Andre Olaf's mind that he couldn't pass through Jenna. Maybe Andre was ready to discuss a follow-up meeting with the NSA.

"I'll be there," Josh said.

"Good," she said before asking, "By the way. How's the team?"

"Swamped, as always. We're about to kick off two new AI leaders."

She stood and said, "Maybe you should hold off for a few days."

Josh stared at his boss. "Why? What's going on?"

She opened the door and was about to leave when she stopped and said, "Look. Andre wants to tell you himself. But you should be prepared."

"Prepared for what?" Josh asked.

As she walked out, Jenna said, "Andre plans to change direction for the CHERL project."

CHAPTER
NINE

LUCAS FINALLY RECEIVED the sign-on credentials to access the confidential case file on the FBI server. According to the FBI's summary notes, two years ago, a counterintelligence agent working in the Russian Embassy reported that "an encrypted communication device" had been delivered to Dan Barry. The FBI's cyber lab used listening scanners and decryption keys to crack into the device, which Dan Barry kept hidden in his apartment. They were able to extract and decipher three separate conversations.

Lucas opened the transcripts and read their first interaction:

Alina: Dan?
Dan: Who is this?
Alina: It's me
Dan: Who?
Alina: Nicole
Dan: Ur not Nicole
Alina: That's the name I used
Dan: How did you get this device to me?
Alina: They still owed me a favor
Dan: Who?

Alina: It doesn't matter
Dan: I can't risk being in contact with you.
Alina: Trust me. Our messages are encrypted.
Dan: Trust you? I don't even know you
Alina: Yes you do
Dan: I only know the FBI thinks I helped you. What do you want?
Alina: To say I'm sorry
Dan: Sorry doesn't help. You destroyed my life
Alina: Please. Let me explain.

BUT APPARENTLY, Barry disconnected before Petrova added anything further. In the second transcript, Petrova started by telling Barry about her childhood and how she always thought her mother had died from cancer. She described how her father revealed he and his wife had worked as spies in America during the 1990s until Alina's mother disappeared. She claimed she offered her services to a Russian cyber hacking team in return for help finding out if her mother was still alive.

Dan: What do you expect me to say about this?
Alina: Say that you understand how desperate I was.
Dan: I understand you lied to me. You used me as a tool.
Alina: At the beginning, yes. But I had true feelings for you. That's why I wanted us to be together.
Dan: You ruined me
Alina: I did terrible things to a lot of people
Dan: How much did they pay you
Alina: I didn't do it for money. They didn't need to pay me. When you are desperate, you do desperate things. Especially if it involves a mother you never knew.
Dan: But you did things to me—to the person you say you loved
Alina: To the person I still love
Dan: Nicole is the person I fell in love with. You are not Nicole
Alina: That is not true. You fell in love with me. Behind the fake name, I was always the real me.

Dan: Then tell me your real name
Alina: My name does not matter—you can still call me Nicole
Dan: No—you are not Nicole—she is real and she exists
Alina: Any name I give you is from my past—it is not my present
Alina: Dan? Are you there?

ONCE AGAIN, it seemed Barry had had enough. It was another month before they communicated again. This time, Barry was the one to initiate contact. And he got right to the point:

Dan: are you still a spy?
Alina: I am not a spy—I only did what they made me do
Dan: did you find her? Did you find your mother?
Alina: Yes—but now she is dead.
Dan: I am sorry—How did she die?
Alina: They found out who she was
Dan: Who
Alina: It does not matter—someday I might deal with them but for now I am done searching the past. I want to build a future. And I want you to be part of it.
Dan: That is not realistic
Alina: But we were in love—we did not fake that
Dan: I am not sure about anything anymore
Alina: I am confused too. But I know I want us to be together
Dan: Are you still in US.
Alina: No. I am far away. Leading a normal life. A life that could include you
Dan: I cannot leave. My father is not well
Alina: What is wrong?
Dan: He has a weak heart
Alina: I am sorry
Dan: Nothing to do with you
Alina: I know you are still upset. But allow me to make it up to you

Dan: I think we should stop now
Alina: I owe you Dan.
Dan: I have to go
Alina: You can call on me if you are ever in trouble—if you ever need help.
Dan: That won't happen
Alina: But before you go. I have something to tell you.
Dan: Yes.
Alina: My real name is Alina

————

EVEN AFTER REVIEWING these transcripts for the third time, Lucas was confused. Assistant Director Compo had said the FBI's decoding team thought Petrova might be about to recruit Barry, but Lucas wasn't so sure. He lingered on her comment, "I want to make it up to you." Was she trying to rekindle their relationship? Lucas even wondered if the devious Petrova had staged these interactions as a means to throw the FBI off her trail.

But if that were true, why hadn't Petrova used the encrypted device in close to a year? Lucas knew Director Compo and Special Agent Lummis had great confidence in conclusions formed by Quantico's decoding team.

Still, he wondered if Brodsky's AI system could tease out a different answer.

CHAPTER
TEN

"HI, *I'm Milo Galini, Founder of Jingle Finance, and I'd like to welcome you to our world. Jingle is a captivating financial platform I created to educate people about managing their finances using a fun and interactive experience. We use gamification to engage users in a way that embeds the knowledge and skill you need to be a confident consumer of personal financial services. Here, you'll learn by interacting and engaging with an enthralling game—come and take a ride on an exciting financial adventure where you will encounter scenarios and earn rewards as you make decisions about budgeting, savings, investing, and buying a home.*"

Dan was so worried about his father's condition that it was difficult to concentrate on the video posted to Jingle Finance's website. He sat at the desk next to the kitchen of his small East Village apartment, replaying the video again and again, trying to absorb Galini's words, willing himself to focus. Dan had to be prepared.

Tomorrow, he was interviewing with Jingle Finance's CEO.

Dan kept telling himself that his dad would be okay. That this was just another setback. After all, his father had been through so many ups and downs over the past few months, and Dr. Bolan had always figured out what to do. His father's cardiologist would come through again.

Dan took a few sips of his lukewarm coffee before pushing it aside.

Okay, he told himself. *Concentrate.*

This time, as he watched Milo Galini, Dan could feel the young CEO's energy jumping off the screen. Handsome and polished with slick-backed black hair and wearing a blue Italian wool blazer atop a crisp, yellow shirt, Jingle Finance's founder was selling hard. Dan watched the clip three more times before moving on to scour every part of the company's website, trying to learn anything he could about the business. And the more he read, the more excited he became.

The idea behind the AI financial management tool was extremely compelling.

Before and during college, Dan and his peers had been put through many worthless financial education programs. He certainly knew people in Silicon Valley—college-educated with advanced degrees, intelligent people earning big incomes—who were clueless about their finances. For those who inhabited the world of hi-tech, it was easy to assume salaries and the value of company stock would only go in one direction. Few bothered to learn how to manage their own money. But as Dan learned from being tossed from high-paying jobs at Sway and now, WompleTech, when the music stops, personal finances take a beating.

Especially when dealing with the skyrocketing cost of his father's illness.

Two years ago, when Alec Barry sold his last restaurant and retired—before his heart started failing him—Dan's father had bought low-cost health insurance. Sure, the premiums were affordable, but the cheap plan had high deductibles and a very high cap on out-of-pocket maximums. As his health deteriorated, and more and more claims were denied by the health insurance company, his father quickly spent down his savings. Dan had been covering the rest of his medical bills ever since, which was why he desperately needed to find another good paying job.

As he continued to prep for his ten a.m. interview with Milo Galini, he decided to sign up for a Jingle account and take the system for a test drive. He uploaded a photo himself and used it to create an avatar that navigated through various "storyboards" of life for a thirty-year-old "professional." Dan advanced the age of his avatar and the Jingle game exposed him to a series of financial roadblocks, requiring him to "play" through each challenge. At the beginning of new life stages, his avatar reset by answering several interactive queries:

"Describe your new financial goals."

"How will your salary change over the next three years?"

"Any job or career changes on the horizon?"

"Will you be adding to your family?"

"Any plans to move or expand your home?"

The "what if" tool allowed Dan to see how different answers to these and other questions modified the outcomes. Dan had to admit the game was nerve-racking but exciting at the same time, more compelling than most video games he used to play with his buddies out west. And as his avatar progressed, Dan felt like he was learning financial strategies he never previously understood. His avatar even built an ideal, diversified stock portfolio, where Dan learned how a one percent "management fee" could eat almost fifty percent of his portfolio gains over time. He learned how to quickly spot hidden, egregious charges in loans and credit card offers. And every path his avatar traveled generated "reward badges" with reminders of how many he needed before real cash was deposited in his account.

But Dan's excitement seemed to dissipate after examining several reports dissecting the limited financial information released by Jingle Finance. He read that the number of people using the Jingle platform had been falling by over ten percent in each of the past three years. These same reviews were pessimistic that the financial education company could turn things around. The last thing Dan wanted was to jump on another sinking ship. But there was little guarantee he'd hear from, let alone land, an AI engineering position with the other companies his job bot had applied to.

So, for now, his only mission was nailing the interview with Milo Galini.

And to get the job.

Dan spent another two hours preparing for how *he* would be the salesman in the room. How he would sell his own work experience in artificial intelligence and answer what were sure to be tough questions about what happened to him at Sway. It was almost three a.m. by the time he finally shut his computer.

He needed to get a few hours of sleep before facing Galini.

CHAPTER
ELEVEN

IT WAS nine forty-five a.m. and the cavernous work area was echoing with conversation, laughter, and some type of rhythmic pounding. As Paula Calderon escorted Dan down the center aisle between people busy at their workstations, the annoying thumping grew louder. When they turned the corner, Dan passed behind the source—a jogger doing a steady pace on a treadmill. A two-foot wide screen was perched on the treadmill's control panel, eye level with the jogger. Dan noticed a thin, silver headband protruding from the runner's wet and matted-down black hair.

"I love that idea," a woman on the screen said. The runner continued to stare at her image in silence as Dan and Calderon passed behind him. The woman on the screen spoke again. "We can make that work. I'll get with my team and get back on your calendar tomorrow."

As Calderon led Dan to a windowless conference room, he wondered if the jogger was viewing some type of webcast—and how anyone in the office without noise-canceling ear pods could concentrate with the pounding from the treadmill.

Calderon smiled. "Milo will be right with you," she said before shutting the door. Dan was about to check his phone to see if any more companies had responded to his job bot when the door opened.

The sweaty jogger from the treadmill walked in, towel and water bottle in hand.

"You must...be Dan," he said, still taking in deep breaths. "I'm Milo."

Dan hesitated before standing. Was the perspiring man in front of him really the same polished guy that pitched Jingle Finance on the company website? Dan extended his hand, but Galini said, "You probably...don't want to do that." Dan self-consciously wiped his own damp palm on his pant leg.

Galini took a long gulp from his water bottle and motioned for Dan to sit. He then lowered into a chair on the opposite end of the room. After carefully removing the thin, silver headband from his hair, he said, "Questions?"

"Excuse me?"

"Questions for me," Galini said, now breathing normally. "I assume you've researched my company, otherwise you wouldn't have applied. You must have questions."

Dan leaned forward and placed his hands on the table. He prepared all night to be grilled about his own experience and the episode at Sway. But as he looked into Galini's impatient eyes, Dan had to quickly reorient himself to be the one doing the probing.

"Well...I reviewed your customer website last night," Dan started. "The platform looks very exciting. Um... how did you come up with the idea for Jingle?"

Galini leaned back, and his serious expression was instantaneously transformed. He smiled like the proud parent of an honor student. "Well, I wanted to create the most extensive financial services platform in the industry. Something that would work for people from every demographic and financial stratum. I'd love to say Jingle came out of extensive product development effort—that I spent two years in the lab—but that would be a lie. Quite simply, I gave the task to a generative artificial intelligence application. Within seconds, AI produced everything I needed to launch Jingle."

"That's incredible," Dan said. He had heard that AI was being used to create new businesses, but not a business model as extensive as what he saw on the Jingle website last night.

"It *is* incredible," Galini said. "I did develop many of the features on my own. The most transformative was gamification. Customers love accumulating points that they can use for real value as they learn. But almost all of our early breakthrough ideas came from AI."

"I have to admit," Dan said, "playing the game was addictive."

Galini banged the table with his hand and smiled. "You played the game! Isn't it incredible?"

"Very impressive."

"An engaging game is critical to the learning experience," Galini continued. "Especially when the game simulates real-life events. We show customers how financial products—credit cards, loans, mortgages—how each affect their lifestyle now and in the future. We even project their income based on education and job history." He paused before adding, "You should keep your account activated, Dan. You never know when Jingle can help you escape from a personal financial crisis."

Dan was only half listening, especially since it appeared that Galini was giving another version of the salesy video presentation Dan had viewed countless times the previous evening. It was only a matter of time before Galini delved into Dan's past. But for now, he sat back and tried to focus on what the founder was saying. Dan had met plenty of entrepreneurs in Silicon Valley. People like Milo Galini loved talking about their businesses.

"That sounds tremendous, Milo." Dan then asked a question he really wanted to know the answer to. "Tell me…how does the company make money?" But Galini waved off the question.

"Nobody cares about revenue for young AI companies," Galini said. "We're in the middle of a land grab, Dan. Success is measured by account growth, not revenue. Nobody cared how much money social media giants made when they first got started twenty years ago. It was all about eyeballs. We'll figure out how to monetize our customers later on. For now, our company valuation will rise again when our number of accounts start growing again. Not dormant accounts that simply sign up and disappear, but customers that *engage* with our platform."

"That makes sense," Dan said. Galini toweled himself off again. Maybe if Dan could keep the CEO talking, he could actually get through the interview without having to explain what happened at Sway.

"What can you tell me about the position?" Dan asked. "What are you looking for?"

Galini leaned forward and placed his forearms on the table. "I built the AI engagement platform you used last night. I recently started building and integrating a new AI program I call Hawk. But I can't run the company and continue the development of another AI system." He looked blankly at Dan, adding, "Although I do love writing AI code."

"Writing AI code is fun," Dan agreed.

"But"—Galini shook his head—"my investors expect me to be the public face of this company." He pointed at Dan. "I'm looking to turn Hawk's development over to someone else, Dan. But not to a programmer who just wants to implement some fancy code."

"I'm not into fancy code," Dan said. "I learned there is only one way to build AI systems. To make them as efficient and streamlined as possible."

"Is that what they taught you at Sway?"

"That's right," Dan said, shifting in his seat, worried about Galini's next query.

"Jingle Finance is not Sway," the CEO said. "We're a small outfit. I don't have an army of AI engineers to throw at Hawk. What I need right now is one great AI engineer. Someone who can bring what I started to life. An AI expert who can rebuild and retrain my system to create successful marketing campaigns—AI that launch promotions to get account growth back on track."

"Marketing?" Dan asked, shifting in his seat. "Doesn't your marketing department handle all of that?"

"They do today, but not very well. That's why our account growth has been dormant. I assume you knew that."

"I did see some reports on the internet," Dan admitted.

"I'm convinced artificial intelligence can turn things around," Galini said. "AI can handle every function our ten-person marketing team is doing. Creativity. Imagination. Planning. Logistics. Execution. Think of it, Dan. If you can help bring our company back to life, the upside for you would be enormous."

But Dan felt his own energy slowly draining away. What did he know about marketing? Perhaps this role wasn't for him after all. Dan was about to ask if Jingle had AI openings in other areas of the company when Galini, perhaps sensing Dan's concern, said, "Now I know you don't have a marketing background. But we've already identified a marketing expert—she's a...freelancer. An outside contractor. I would bring her in to work alongside you."

Dan scratched his head. "I guess that would help."

Galini leaned forward and said, "What I really need is a student of the AI craft. I know people that come out of Sway have a deep respect for what's been done before."

Dan knew that much was true. Learning from the past *was* the secret to Sway's success.

"You were on that CHERL project I've been hearing so much about? Bringing back great leaders?"

Dan straightened in his chair. "Yes. I was."

"I wanted to contract for a Steven Jobs version, but Sway's charging way too much for my small company." He looked away and added, "Maybe someday down the road."

"CHERL's worth it." Dan smiled. "She's a very special piece of artificial intelligence."

"You worked on CHERL for two years?" Galini asked, his attention back on Dan.

"I did. But I also worked elsewhere within Sway for three years before that. It took a while for CHERL's leadership to consider internal candidates. They were very selective about who they—"

"Your leaders couldn't have been *too* selective," Galini said. "Otherwise, they wouldn't have let a spy infiltrate their ranks."

Dan flinched. It seemed Galini was no longer in sales mode.

"I obviously have a lot of contacts in the Bay area," Galini continued. "I've heard all the rumors about you. I need you to tell me what really happened."

Dan inhaled slowly, trying to regain his train of thought, willing himself to remember what he'd practiced the previous night. "*We* obviously let our guard down."

Jingle Finance's founder kept his eyes locked on his candidate as he motioned for Dan to proceed. Dan told the story of how he had first met his coworker on the company shuttle bus. How he was duped into giving her a copy of the CHERL system specifications to help the new recruit get up to speed.

"In my role, I was privy to the full CHERL specifications. Nicole wasn't. I was trying to be helpful, and obviously, I made a mistake. I never knew a thing until she…" Dan studied his hands as he finished. "…until the FBI appeared." What Dan didn't say was how he had fallen in love with the woman who now claimed her real name was Alina. And how, all these years later, he still thought about her. How, despite everything that had happened, after all the havoc she had created in his life, he had never given up on the idea that someday they would find each other again. And if those brief text messages on that device he'd since hidden beneath the floorboard in his closet were real, maybe Alina hadn't either.

Instead, he told Galini, "I was scammed. Obviously, I was too trusting of a colleague." He looked directly at Galini and added, "But I did not knowingly help her."

"I assume a company the size of Sway conducted an extensive internal investigation."

Dan slowly nodded, remembering the two-day interrogation conducted by Sway's artificial intelligence system called PEARL. The Performance-Evaluating Artificial Intelligence Leader had grilled him on every aspect of his relationship with Nicole—how they spent their leisure time, the places they went together, the food they ate, the people they met. The AI performed a full battery of psychological tests, supposedly to assess Dan's motivations, mental health, desires. The two-day session took place in a small, windowless room. He remembered how the cubed, white walls and floor made him feel like an inmate at a psychiatric hospital. He knew the miniature camera lenses buried in the desk were assessing his body language, his facial expressions—matching these visual cues with his words to form an opinion. And a recommendation about what should happen to him.

"While PEARL found no evidence you willingly collaborated with the spy," the official letter from Sway's internal attorney stated, "the company takes cyber security very seriously. Passing the CHERL system specification to an unauthorized employee was a clear violation of data policy, and the company treats all policy violations the same, whether it be sexual harassment, privacy, or security."

"They cleared my name," Dan said to Galini. "But I knew I had no future at Sway." The fact was that Dan was fired "for cause," meaning he received no severance and all of his unvested shares in the Sway Corporation were taken away. Canceled. The only thing his former employer offered was to respond to job reference requests with a simple, "The company separated with Dan Barry by mutual agreement."

Galini stared at Dan as if trying to decipher a confusing puzzle. "What about the feds?" he asked.

"They knew I didn't commit a crime," Dan said. "No charges were ever brought against me."

"And you've been doing consulting work for the past three years?"

"Until I moved to New York to join WompleTech."

"I heard they're having a cash squeeze over there."

"That's why I'm looking for a new position," Dan said.

"And why'd you come to New York?"

"It's home. I was born and raised here." Dan paused before adding, "And my father is not doing well. I need to be close by to help with his…care."

"Sorry to hear that. So…long term…?" His potential employer let the uncomfortable question hang in the air, probing for what Dan's plans would be if his father was no longer around. Dan wiped away the little moisture that had formed in the corner of his right eye and said, "I'm done with Silicon Valley. As I said. This is home."

Jingle's founder grimaced as if another thought entered his busy mind. "My head of Human Capital thinks I'm crazy even speaking with you. She wants to know why would I risk hiring someone with your…"

Dan squirmed in his seat.

"But, you know," Galini said. "Ten years ago, I also got myself on the wrong side of a situation." His eyes grew foggy as his mind seemed to go to another place. After a few moments, he shook his head.

"What happened?" Dan asked.

"The details don't matter. Let's just say my career was almost derailed before I even started. Like you, I made a mistake." His eyes focused, and he looked up at Dan. "I don't know what really occurred at Sway, but I have learned to trust my instincts."

Dan hoped someday he'd be able to trust his own instincts again.

"I've learned to take in the measure of the person before rendering judgment," Galini continued as he rose and extended his hand. "And I know what it's like to be given a second chance."

Dan stood and clasped Galini's hand as the CEO said, "Paula will pull together an offer. I believe every employee should share in our success, especially one who will be so integral to our future. So we target our stock awards to be very meaningful when performance is achieved."

An offer? Was this really happening so quickly?

"I just have one more question," Galini said.

"What's that?"

Galini grinned. "When you can start?"

CHAPTER
TWELVE

"I THOUGHT GALINI DID WELL," Special
Agent Lummis said during the videoconference
debriefing session.

"It is too bad Barry didn't reveal anything new,"
Agent Kidane said. "But I must say. The hidden micro-
phone picked everything up beautifully."

Lummis smiled and said, "Courtesy of our friends in
Quantico."

Lucas wasn't sure he agreed with everyone's upbeat
evaluation of Dan Barry's interview with Milo Galini.
The founder of Jingle Finance didn't really quiz his
candidate the typical topics like work experience,
personal strengths or development needs. But Lucas saw
no upside in offering up his contrasting opinion.

Besides, he was still struggling to digest several unsa-
vory aspects of the FBI's operation. Going after bad
people meant agents confronted difficult choices. Choices
like the ones he encountered when overseeing undercover
sting operations, which sometimes resulted in the "loss"
of cartel informants. Decisions like challenging Sonia
Gilroy, which drove her to commit suicide right before his
eyes.

So now, he had to remind himself that going after

Alina Petrova was no different, as Compo emphasized at the beginning of today's Operation Turncoat debrief.

"The day the Russians sent their spies to live in our country and started manipulating us, screwing around with our technology for their own gain, Russia declared war on the United States of America," Compo had said. "It's been three years, people. We've tried every other route with no success. Dan Barry is our only link. If we want to get Petrova off the board, squeezing Barry is our best hope."

Lucas knew there was no evidence Barry was ever directly involved in any of the Russian's activities. Yet as long as Petrova's former lover could lead the FBI to their high value target, Lucas kept repeating to himself that Barry *was* fair game.

But did the FBI really need to drag Dan Barry's father into their plan?

"I was a little concerned when Milo probed about the Sway case and spies," Dennison said as the agents continued to offer their views on the Galini-Barry interview.

"The Sway case was very public, Agent Dennison," Lummis said. "I'm sure Barry would have been suspicious if Galini never brought it up during his interview."

"Funny how Barry tried to make it sound like he exited Sway of his own accord," Agent Stryker said. "As if his name was cleared."

"Did you expect him to admit he got fired for collaborating with a spy?" Dennison asked.

"Everybody spins their own story," Lummis said. "Even Milo Galini. He spun a pretty good story about his company."

Lucas leaned toward the camera and asked, "What was Galini getting at when he started talking about his own troubled history?"

"That was careless for him to mention, Agent Foley," Lummis responded. "But several years ago, we had

Galini on securities fraud—he was making false state-ments to pump up the value of his previous company. We agreed to make the charges and the evidence disappear—you can't find mention of it on the internet or in his crim-inal background check. In return, we pocketed some goodwill for the future."

"So that's how you convinced him to offer Barry a landing spot," Lucas said. He wondered how many other business executives owed the FBI a favor.

Lummis shrugged. "We didn't need to do any arm-twisting. And this wasn't a one-way street. When we learned Jingle Finance was having money troubles, we arranged for a meeting with a private benefactor—a patriot who the government has turned to over the years, especially for delicate operations involving the Russians. Our financier agreed to provide some short-term bridge financing with the promise of more permanent capital once Operation Turncoat is complete, assuming Galini continues to cooperate."

"Let's just hope Dan takes the bait," Agent Dennison said.

"Don't worry," Lummis said. "Given Dan Barry's very public history at Sway, he won't have any other option."

Agent Lummis went on to cover a few other minor points. Before she adjourned, Lucas raised his hand.

"I read the transcripts of Petrova and Barry's commu-nication," he said.

"Ah, good," Lummis said. "What did you think?"

"While their dialogue seems fairly straightforward, I agree with the decoding team that there might be some hidden meaning." He paused before saying, "What if we supplied the transcripts to Dr. Brodsky at Sway? Maybe his AI can decipher a clue that eluded our codebreakers."

"Negative, Agent Foley," Lummis said. "Those tran-scripts are highly classified and are not to leave our custody."

But Lucas continued to press his case, believing anything that could help locate Petrova—and short circuit the need to continue with Operation Turncoat—was worth a try. "As I explained to Director Compo, Brodsky still holds his top security clearance from his days with the Department of Defense."

"It doesn't matter," Lummis said. "Brodsky's a civilian. And we're certainly not loading classified information into Sway's computer system. Not with their history of breaches."

"But—"

"It's not happening, Agent Foley. My decision is final. Read the transcripts all you want, but those communications are not to leave the FBI's server."

CHAPTER
THIRTEEN

LOUIE DROVE his BMW along Route 15, enjoying the beautiful, scenic road. It had been several days since Ed Chamberlain told him of his upcoming "retirement" from the CEO position at Virtual Bank and Louie was still trying to muster the courage to have the conversation.

This was the discussion he needed to have if he was going to go after his boss's job.

The car navigation system showed he'd be home in fifty-six minutes. Normally he would challenge himself to beat the estimated time showing on the satellite system. But today, Louie drove slowly. He'd need every bit of fifty-six minutes to get his mind in the right place. He tapped an icon on his dashboard display.

"Good afternoon, Louie," came the soothing male voice from his car's sound system. *"How are you?"*

"I'm good, Dr. Wesley," Louie responded. "I mean, well, I'd like to talk something out with you."

"What is the topic this time?"

"A potential change in my career," Louie said as he made a turn and slowly merged onto Route 46. "It seems my boss at Virtual Bank is being forced out of the CEO post."

"Ed Chamberlain?"

Louie nodded toward the miniature camera mounted under his rearview mirror.

"You've had a good relationship with him."

"It's been functional," Louie said. "Ed left me alone to do my thing."

"What does this change mean for you?"

"It means I have a shot at getting his position." Every time he repeated these words, Louie felt the adrenaline course through his body.

"This would be a major step for you."

"Yes, it would. But you know my background. I have the right experience to do the job."

Louie had had countless sessions with this latest version of his AI therapist, so the system was well versed in the arc of Louie's career, as well as his many personal and professional travails prior to taking on the CFO role at Virtual Bank. Still, Louie had never discussed an aspiration to run the entire company.

"You have always done well. As long as you are healthy."

"I've been healthy for years," Louie said.

"Are you worried the pressure might lead to a setback?"

"I'm not. But I know Vicki will be."

"If your wife believes this is so, perhaps it is not worth the risk."

"There is no risk," Louie snapped. "I'm never going backward." He'd left the high-flying Manhattan lifestyle and the cutthroat world of investment banking—a lifestyle, and a gambling addiction, that put him in serious debt and almost cost him his marriage. Settling down in the quiet, bucolic Town of Morristown, New Jersey, was also a tonic for his self-destructive behavior. The stress free, ten-minute commute to Virtual Bank's offices didn't hurt either. He found other outlets, like golf, to assuage his competitive instincts.

Nevertheless, Louie didn't consider his predilection for the occasional wager to be a problem.

"I am not the one you need to convince. Tell me, how do you plan to approach your wife?"

"Well…" Louie swallowed hard. "I'll remind Vicki that it's been three years," Louie finally said.

"It doesn't matter how long, Louie. Vicki knows you will always—"

"I know. I will always be an addict."

"But you are indeed much stronger than when we started these sessions."

"And you've always said part of staying strong is to have other outlets for my…my edge. And to have goals."

"That is correct. It is fine to be competitive. And it's fine to pursue your ambitions. As long as those ambitions don't consume you."

"That won't happen again."

"So you've said. But you obviously don't think Vicki will see it that way."

Louie shrugged.

"When do you plan to speak with her?"

Louie had put this off for days. He knew he couldn't hold off any longer. He had to let Chamberlain and the board know if he wanted the position. Louie glanced at the navigation system and said, "Soon." He would be home in twenty-three minutes. "But I'm still trying to figure out the best way to present the idea."

"You need to accept that you will not be able to manage Vicki's reaction. You should focus on words that put her mind at ease. But you will need to convince her of why you really want—or need—to do this."

Louie shifted in the driver's seat as he gave the therapist's comment some thought. "Well," he finally said, "I'll remind her that I've put a lot of my ambitions on the sideline while I worked on myself. To save our marriage."

"That is a good start, Louie. But she might think that your current job is stressful enough."

"Compared to what I was used to?" Louie shook his head. "Not even close."

"I am also detecting the stress in your face." Louie eyed the camera again as the system continued. *"Vicki will also hear the tension in your voice. You need to remain calm if you want her to believe you are ready."*

Louie took in a deep breath and blew it out slowly. As always, the AI therapy system picked up on Louie's level of anxiety. Throughout his earlier career in the world of investment banking, Louie had no trouble beating his opposition as he negotiated the most complex merger transactions. He absorbed verbal attacks from antagonistic Wall Street analysts, debated and convinced headstrong board members of his business ideas—all without fear. He *had* been a success, winning at almost every level of the business world.

But the idea of going up against his wife sent shivers down his spine.

"Okay," Louie said.

"Remember, you have already rebuilt her trust."

"Vicki and I are in a good place," Louie agreed.

"You have both done an excellent job repairing your life."

"Thanks." Louie cringed. It never felt natural thanking an artificial intelligence therapy system.

After moving from New York, Louie had tried three different "flesh and blood" psychiatrists recommended by his former Manhattan based therapist, Dr. Jacobs. But Louie never trusted them as much as Jacobs. When Louie heard a local hospital was experimenting with artificial intelligence, Louie volunteered to participate in a three-year pilot program.

After all, thanks to his older brother, Josh, Louie had personal experience engaging with artificial intelligence.

"Dr. Wesley" was good at preparing Louie before he engaged in difficult conversations with his wife. But today, artificial intelligence hadn't offered much.

"I'm getting close to home, Dr. Wesley. Anything else?"

"Yes." The system paused before continuing. *"Be sure*

you convey the reason behind your new aspiration. Vicki will need to understand your rationale. Why you seek the CEO role."

Louie didn't interject as the AI therapist continued.

"For example, do you want the CEO job to prove your self-worth?"

"My ego will never be wrapped around a job," he said, which was true. Louie didn't care what anyone thought of him. He certainly wasn't trying to impress anyone with a fancy title.

"Are you seeking power?"

"That sounds like an ego thing again." But even as he said these words, Louie felt a sliver of doubt enter his mind.

"Okay. That's good, but then what is it that's driving your desire for the CEO job?"

"Um…I know I can do a good job?"

"That is not a reason."

"Okay, okay," Louie said as he turned onto the I-287 entrance ramp. "I understand."

Unfortunately, the navigation system indicated traffic was clear. He would be in his driveway in less than ten minutes. He thought about circling his neighborhood so he'd have time to bury the realization that was starting to bubble to the surface of his mind. But that would just be delaying the inevitable, so he headed for home.

Which meant Louie only had a few minutes to come up an alternative to the rationale that was now very clear in his head.

He hoped he could make up something else that would satisfy his wife.

CHAPTER
FOURTEEN

DAN STOPPED at the deli across from Columbia Presbyterian Hospital and ordered a tuna sandwich on whole wheat with honey mustard.

"Honey mustard?" The Hispanic man behind the counter crinkled his nose.

Dan smiled and said, "That's the way my dad likes it." But as Dan watched his father's sandwich being prepared, he thought back to the day in San Francisco when his brown paper bag contained more than just a tuna sandwich.

It had been almost two years since he'd received the cigarette pack-sized communication device at the deli across from his apartment. Questioned the next day, the establishment's owner told Dan the sandwich preparer quit after working there for only that morning. It had now been over a year since Dan last used the instrument to "speak" with his former lover, when she revealed her real name was "Alina." He knew he should have turned the device over to the FBI, but it was too late now. How would he explain why he'd kept the device all this time, hidden beneath the floorboard in his bedroom closet? How would he explain why he hadn't reported three separate conversations he'd had with a woman accused of espionage?

Besides, he couldn't part with the only means he had to connect with his former lover.

"Tuna, honey mustard," the man said as he handed Dan the sandwich.

Dan shook his head, used his phone to pay, and exited the deli.

———

WHEN DAN ENTERED the hospital room, Alec Barry was sitting upright in a chair, pen in hand, marking up the *New York Times* crossword puzzle. "Gimme a five-letter word for 'flip one's lid.' It starts with u."

"Hmmm." Dan moved the tray of dry, uneaten hospital food to the side and unwrapped the tuna sandwich. "Try 'uncap.'"

He raised a finger in triumph. "Thanks."

"Don't mention it. Here." Dan wheeled the table next to the chair. "You should eat your sandwich before it gets cold." His father let out a snort and, after taking a bite, closed his eyes and said, "Oh…that's good."

"Not as good as your sesame-crusted tuna," Dan said.

"Your favorite. I promise to cook for you if you get me out of here."

"Not so fast, Dad."

Dan sat on the edge of the bed and watched his dad quietly savor the meal. Dr. Bolan had done it again. It seemed the cardiologist had found the right medication to equilibrate his father's heart rhythm. But Dan knew better than to get too giddy, knowing from experience how rapidly his condition could deteriorate. Still, he hoped *this* rally would last. The return of his appetite was a good sign, a necessary step before moving him back to the Bronx rehab facility. Hopefully, his father's health would soon be one last thing for Dan to worry about.

Dan pulled out his phone and checked his emails again. Still nothing from any of the companies his job bot had applied to. The only offer Dan had after being laid off was from Jingle Finance, and he was wrestling with what to do. Dan didn't know anything about marketing, and even though the concepts behind Jingle Finance seemed compelling, the company wasn't doing well. At least the salary was close to what Dan was earning at WompleTech, and the offer included five thousand shares of stock in Jingle Finance. But unless the company went public or was sold, he'd have to stay employed by Jingle for four years before he could convert his shares into cash.

Dan promised Milo Galini an answer by the end of today.

His father nodded at Dan's phone. "Work bugging you already?" he said through a mouth full of tuna.

"Not really." Dan still hadn't told his father that he was part of a staff reduction at WompleTech. He saw little value in adding to his list of worries. But now that his dad's strength was back, Dan hoped to solicit some advice.

"I'm thinking about taking a new job," he blurted.

His old man glared at him. "You've only been at WompleTech for four months."

"I know," Dan said. "But listen. I didn't want to bother you with this but…WompleTech laid off a bunch of people this week."

His father placed his half-eaten sandwich on the tray. "What happened?"

Dan shrugged and looked away. "Money trouble, I guess. I thought the company was on better footing. But, I guess, what did I know?"

They sat quietly for a few moments before his dad picked up his sandwich and said, "Is this new job on the East Coast?"

Dan reached for his arm and smiled. "Of course, Dad. I'm not going anywhere. It's here in New York."

The corner of his father's mouth turned up, and he nodded before digging back into the tuna. Dan proceeded to talk about Jingle Finance and the product line. He described his interview with Galini. His dad laughed when Dan described the office treadmill and the sweaty CEO.

"But something's not sitting right with me," Dan said, which was true. There was something about Milo Galini and Jingle Finance that seemed strange.

"Because of the treadmill?"

"Not that."

"What else did he do?"

"Galini didn't do or say anything. It's just a feeling."

"A feeling," he repeated as he rolled his eyes. He took another bite and chewed slowly. After swallowing, he said, "Did he make you a good offer?"

"Good enough."

"You've got to snap out of this self-doubt," his father said sharply. "Everyone's not out there trying to deceive you." He paused before adding, "It's been three years. At some point, you have to start trusting people again."

"This has nothing to do with her," Dan said as he squinted at his phone and acted like he was reading something important. Maybe his father was right. Maybe what happened at Sway left his confidence so damaged that he simply second-guessed every decision he made. But Dan's broken instincts were screaming at him, telling him something was odd.

It wasn't so much Galini's offbeat behavior. Sure, conducting the interview in sweaty gym clothes after jogging on a treadmill in the middle of the office was bizarre. But Dan had seen plenty of eccentric characters in Silicon Valley. Dan did feel his internal radar react when Galini referenced "getting himself in trouble" before someone gave *him* a second chance to resurrect his career.

"Like you," Galini had said, "I also got myself on the

wrong side of a situation." But as hard as Dan searched the web, he found nothing of concern regarding Jingle's founder. Perhaps if Galini had shared more about what happened, that gnawing feeling in Dan's gut would have dissipated.

"Have you applied anywhere else?"

Dan nodded. "But so far, Jingle's the only one that's responded."

"Sometimes the first offer is the best offer." His father paused. "Or…the only offer."

"Thanks for the vote of confidence, Dad."

"I'm not the one who doesn't have confidence in you."

"Maybe it's happening too fast," Dan tried. "Maybe I'm not sure I buy into their mission."

His father let out a short laugh. "Bringing back people from the dead didn't turn out so good for you."

Dan ignored the shot at the CHERL project and asked, "What do I know about marketing?" But he knew he was flailing.

"I know you're afraid of another failure. But you have to move on. From WompleTech and from…that woman."

Dan looked away.

"How many times must we go over this," his father said. "She was a professional, trained to suck you into her orbit. She was play-acting."

But Dan hadn't been play-acting with the fake Nicole. And from the words she used during their encrypted message exchanges, maybe she hadn't been acting either. He often thought seeing her again might be the only way to purge her from his soul. If his father's health continued to progress, maybe that was exactly what he would do.

"You're being irrational." His father's voice sounded gravelly and his eyes suddenly became glassy. Dan stood and moved the table away.

"Take it easy, Dad. Should we get you into bed?"

"I'm fine." He cleared his throat. "Just a little tired."

His dad grabbed Dan's arm and pulled him close. "Listen, I trust you," he said. "If this doesn't feel right, look for something else. But remember, you have a bird in the hand." He let go and said, "Now get out of here. It's a beautiful day. I need to close my eyes."

"Okay, Dad." Dan bent down and kissed him on the forehead. "I'll call you later."

As Dan exited the hospital, the warm sunshine felt good on his face.

Maybe this visit was the push Dan needed. Jingle Finance *was* the only offer he had. He'd heard nothing from those other companies, who might have already done their due diligence on his time with Sway and ruled him out. Milo Galini was offering a solid position—an opportunity to resurrect his career, and a steady paycheck.

"Thanks, Dad," Dan said to himself as he started toward the subway station.

He looked on his phone and scrolled down to Milo Galini's contact information. He typed out a short note, telling Galini how thrilled he was to accept the offer and thanking him for the opportunity. After descending the steps, he stood on the platform waiting for the downtown number two train, remembering the last thing Galini had asked him at his interview. He pulled his cell phone out again and keyed a follow-up message to his new boss.

"I can start on Monday."

CHAPTER
FIFTEEN

THE STREETS WERE quiet when Louie pulled his BMW into the garage of his two-story colonial. He opened the door leading into the mud room and, before he even removed his shoes, smelled the garlic wafting in from the adjoining kitchen.

"Louie?" he heard his wife, Vicki, call out. "Is that you?"

"Yep. It's me." He entered the kitchen and saw his wife placing aluminum foil over a bowl of meatballs. "It's a little early for dinner, isn't it?"

"I made them for tonight. I won't have time to prepare dinner when I get home."

Louie checked the time. He'd completely forgotten that Vicki was attending another afternoon conference at the local Hilton. Since their daughter, Jesse, entered high school, Vicki had become more involved with the local chapter of the League of Women's Voters. But there was no way he could wait until she returned. He had to get this off his chest.

"Ed's out," Louie blurted.

"Out of what?" she asked as she placed the bowl in the refrigerator.

"Out of the company. Out as CEO of Virtual Bank."

"You're kidding me," Vicki said. "I thought he had a few more years."

"Apparently not." Louie brushed his fingers at a spot of tomato sauce on the kitchen counter. "Ed said the board wants him to retire." He looked up at his wife. "Clearly, they don't think he's cutting it."

"Geez," she said as she walked closer to Louie. "Are you worried?"

Louie studied the counter. "I think I have a shot at landing his job."

Vicki stepped back but Louie could practically feel the heat coming from his diminutive wife. "You told them you weren't interested, right?" Louie felt his pulse quicken as Vicki added, "You're not starting this again."

"Starting what?"

"Sinking back into the pressure cooker!"

"It's a big opportunity, Vic. It's my—"

"Opportunity for what?" Vicki asked, her face turning red. "To make yourself crazy again?"

"Vicki, I'm stronger now. It won't happen again."

She let out a sarcastic laugh and said, "Of course not. Do you even know why the board is kicking him out?"

"I told you. They're unhappy with his performance."

Vicki rolled her eyes and said, "What makes you think they'll be happy with yours?"

Louie said nothing as he moved to the sink and washed the spot of sauce from his finger. Vicki was savvy enough to know there were no guarantees in the corporate world. After wiping remnants of garlic and onions from the counter, his wife turned and took his chin in her fingers.

"Louie," she said calmly. "You're finally in a healthy place. Our finances are in a healthy place." She looked around the kitchen. "We've built a comfortable life. In a few years, we'll have more than enough money for you to retire."

"And do what?"

"You'll figure it out." She took her hand away. "Look at me. Three years ago, I was a wannabe living in Manhattan, spending my life and money in that meaningless vortex."

"You've done a wonderful job, Vic."

That much was true. His wife had completely reinvented herself. While it had been Vicki's idea to leave Manhattan, Louie was surprised she enjoyed the suburbs. Gone was the Manhattan socialite who dragged Louie to galas at The Met and Lincoln Center. Vicki had immersed herself in the New Jersey political scene—she was out practically every evening, canvassing for candidates or speaking on issues she deeply cared about, from saving the local Planned Parenthood to passing gun control measures. In fact, while their daughter, Jesse, had only a few years left in the local school system, Vicki had been contemplating a run for a seat on the school board.

"Look, Louie. You hate the corporate bullshit. You say it yourself all the time."

He faced her and leaned on the counter. "Yeah, but it will be different if I'm in the top job."

"Oh, so you can be the one creating all the bullshit?" she asked, her intensity rising again. "All I know is, I saw what the stress does to you. The gambling. The money troubles. I don't want to go back to all of that."

"It will be different, Vic. I'm in a different place."

"Until you're not!" she snapped.

Louie walked to the refrigerator and took out a beer, the only alcoholic beverage he still allowed himself. He twisted off the cap and took three quick gulps. He knew this conversation would be tough, and he was right. Not that he completely blamed Vicki for her skepticism. Louie had put them both through hell when he'd gambled away every penny he'd ever earned. Millions of dollars on horse racing, poker, and football—losses accumulated from every form of online gambling. He'd even tapped into lines of credit to fund his gambling addiction until they were almost evicted from their penthouse apartment on Central Park West.

But he'd changed.

He got the help he needed once they moved out of Manhattan. He attended Gamblers Anonymous meetings, at least until the last few months. He deleted most of the betting apps on his devices, stayed away from the track, and, most important, left the "high roller" life on Wall Street. He quit his feast or famine position with the boutique investment banking firm—where money had only flowed when Louie led successful mergers and acquisitions. He became an operational executive with his client, Virtual Bank, first leading the integration with Peachtree National before taking on the chief financial officer role. The experience had proved that Louie could thrive in the ebb and flow of running a business. And from Ed Chamberlain's comments, it appeared at least a few of the directors on Virtual Bank's board had taken notice.

"What's this really all about?" Vicki asked. "Why do you need to do this?"

The AI therapist was right.

"The company is stale," he tried. "It has been since the merger. I know I can bring the bank back to life. I can make it a better organization. I can create a mission. Bring the team together."

"Oh, don't feed me that corporate bullshit!"

"Vicki. I—"

"What's the real reason?" she asked. "Are you bored?"

"Didn't you hear what I just said?"

"Find another challenge!" she said. "There are plenty of things you could do without all that pressure!"

"Calm down, Vic."

"I won't calm down! Is it the recognition of being CEO? The status thing again?" Vicki made air quotes as she said the word "status."

"Come on, Vic. If I still cared about status, I would have fought to keep the Central Park West apartment."

"I think your ego is getting in the way of what's healthy for you," she said, folding her arms. "And what's healthy for us."

"This is not about my self-esteem, Vicki," he said firmly as he looked away.

"You don't think so? Saying you are the only one who can set bring the company back to life?"

"I didn't say I was the only one. I just know I can do it. And if I can do it, don't you think I have the responsibility to—"

"What about the responsibility to *us*, Louie?" She stepped toward him again. "What about the responsibility to yourself. To be healthy and not spiral down the drain again."

"It won't happen, Vic."

"How do you know? How do you know what's waiting for you in that job?"

"It's not like VB is an unknown company."

"Knowing the company is different than being able to see around the corner—at trouble lurking."

Louie took another gulp of beer and said, "There's risk in everything, Vic."

She shook her head. "But you don't have to go out looking for it. You don't have to risk everything we have. Let them find someone else."

"You know what will happen if they bring in a new CEO?" Louie asked, moving on to another approach, one he thought would appeal to his risk-averse spouse. "New CEO's clean house. They bring in their own team—especially the finance position. Where would that leave me?"

"So you'll find a new job," she said as she glanced at the wall clock. "I have to go upstairs and get ready." After she left, Louie drained the rest of his beer and placed the bottle in the sink. He sat on a stool next to the counter and rubbed the sides of his face, trying to decompress from the onslaught. He had tried every piece of ammunition he had conjured up in the car.

Every argument except the one that was true. As he parried each of his wife's counterattacks, his real motivations would remain private.

The truth was, Louie missed the intoxication.

He missed the adrenaline—the surge of energy, the type of sensation that coursed through his body whenever he closed a deal as an investment banker. The rush that came when scoring a monster trifecta at Belmont Park or after a big night of gambling in Atlantic City.

He missed the feeling that came from "winning."

Louie craved that high again, but he had abandoned those sources of his daily adrenaline fix. Sure, he had tried replicating those sensations with the thrill of watching Jessica grow into a young woman and celebrating her academic successes. He had tried replacing the rush with the accomplishments that came from his own, steady operating role; with reporting solid quarterly financial results to Wall Street investors.

But now, he imagined the jolt that would come from the announcement that he, Louie Brodsky, would be the next CEO of Virtual Bank. He visualized the electricity that would come from the excitement of running the bank—from shaping and leading the execution of the strategy.

He could feel that hunger gnawing at him again. The hunger to win—to turn Virtual Bank into a regional powerhouse!

The notion made Louie stand and push the stool aside. But as much as the realization now permeated his thoughts, he knew one thing for sure—he could never share this epiphany with Vicki. Because no matter what the AI therapist said, Louie could not tell his wife of his strong desire to "win."

Because "winning" was the word used by gamblers, not recovering addicts.

When Vicki returned, she grabbed her purse and said, "We can finish this later."

"Look, Vicki." Louie approached his wife and took her by the hand. "The board is already looking at outside candidates. I probably won't even get the job." Now he gently held both of her hands. "All I'm asking is to let me put my name forward for consideration. If they offer it to me, I promise, we'll make this decision together. If you don't want me to accept, I won't."

Vicki rested her forehead on Louie's chest. "I'm just frightened for you..." She looked up. "...and for what might happen to us."

"I promise," he said. "I won't let it happen."

She released his hands and walked toward the garage door as she said, "Now I wish we both weren't going away next weekend. Vicki was heading to a two-day meeting on voter registration strategies, while Louie had a long-planned fishing trip scheduled with his two brothers.

"Maybe I won't go," Louie said.

"You see," she said, raising her palms. "That's what I mean. You're already starting your old habits." She pointed a finger at him and said, "Your family—even your brothers—can never come in second place, ever again!"

As his wife walked through the garage door, Louie thought his wife's parting words were as close to an endorsement as he was going to get.

CHAPTER
SIXTEEN

BY THE TIME Andre Olaf entered his private dining room on the third floor of Sway's sprawling headquarters, Josh and Jenna were already seated and enjoying a glass of burgundy from Andre's private collection. But Josh always limited his intake of wine during business dinners, a practice that had served him well during his thirty-years working at the Department of Defense. He'd been to too many events where senior bureaucrats got so sloshed they could barely carry on a coherent conversation. Josh liked to keep his mind sharp and alert, especially around Sway's mercurial chairman and chief executive, who placed his suit jacket on the back of his chair before joining them at the small, round table. A waiter arrived and filled Andre's glass with the burgundy.

"Here's to John D. Rockefeller," Andre said as he lifted his wineglass. Jenna and Josh clinked with Sway's CEO.

"And Jenna," Andre continued, raising his glass toward Josh's boss, "to your ever-expanding family."

"Thank you, Andre." She laughed. "But it's not expanding from here. I promise I'm done."

Andre shrugged and said, "You never know. I thought Caroline and I were done after having a second. Now she wants a fourth." He turned to Josh and said, "So tell me, Dr. Brodsky, have you found any issues in the Rockefeller session?"

"None," Josh said. "No signs of any irregularities. Same as the previous thirty-nine."

"Good," Andre said. "I'm glad those millions I spent on cyber security weren't a complete waste."

"We're locked up like Fort Knox," Jenna said before sipping the burgundy.

"And I'm confident we have forty clean CEO sessions," Josh said. "All well documented. We're in position to offer proof to the NSA."

But Andre seemed to ignore Josh's comment as the waiter approached to take their order. Jenna selected the seared tuna while Josh and Andre went for the chicken marsala. Once the waiter departed and the door was closed, Andre folded his arms and leaned on the table.

"Look," he said, his demeanor calm, but he still wore a pained frown. "You have done a marvelous job. Despite our rather public setbacks, your team has done everything I've asked. Unfortunately, with all the money we've had to throw at CHERL, I'm afraid our project has turned into a serious money loser."

Josh felt like he'd taken a punch to the stomach. But as he looked over at Jenna, her expression hadn't changed. "Andre," Josh said, "You've always said our mission isn't about making money."

"The world evolves, Brodsky. Circumstances change. When you joined our team, Sway was on top of the world. The company was minting cash. But now, we're getting killed by all these renegade start-up companies, building and launching competitive artificial intelligence products, including AI advisers like CHERL."

"None of our competitors are doing anything as complex and sophisticated as CHERL," Josh said. He had tracked and examined the AI advisers launched by many of the new entrants. "And none are attempting to replicate great leaders from the past."

The waiter returned and served Caesar salads. Andre waited for him to depart before responding. "Their customers don't seem to care. The market is responding to new and sexy AI tech…tech that's cheap." He swirled his wine, seemingly lost in thought before raising his eyes toward Jenna. "We can't keep pouring money and manpower into CHERL while the small guys are out there eating our lunch. Not when the board is directing me to build businesses with potential to generate big profit margins. Products that produce substantial bottom-line results."

The board again, Josh thought. The same board that stepped in three years earlier and forced a strategic shift into recreating historical leaders for high-paying business customers, slowing Josh's ability to deliver for the political establishment. The pivot, which required a ton of invest-ment, led to the re-creation of over forty world-altering business leaders from the past.

But it also exposed Sway and their business clients to the Russian insider trading scheme.

"The board believes CHERL is over-engineered," Andre said. "They believe our new cost structure limits CHERL to nothing more than a niche play. They refer to it 'Andre's Toy,' a product only the largest and most wealthy corporations can afford."

Josh glanced at Jenna, who was staring into her burgundy. So this was why she told him to halt the next CHERL production. Josh slid his wine to the side, feeling everything he had worked for slipping away. He had built the most advanced artificial intelligence application in the world, capable of digesting and interpreting millions of terabytes worth of information. He had hired hundreds of high-priced AI engineers, working on eight separate teams or "pods" to recreate the individual personality traits that brought each historic leader to life. The sophistication embedded in the CHERL re-creations could never be mass-produced on a low-cost conveyor belt. Josh wondered what happened to the Sway CEO he had met when he first interviewed with Sway, back when Andre Olaf raved about how large an investment the company was willing to make.

"We're taking a big swing at this, Dr. Brodsky," Andre said at the time. "Sway has deep pockets."

It seemed that the company's pockets were no longer that deep.

"So that's it?" Josh asked as Andre and Jenna picked at their salads. "Are you telling me it's over?"

"Not necessarily." Andre took a sip of wine and let the liquid swirl around his palate before swallowing. "There might be a way to keep things going."

"What's that?" Jenna asked, suddenly interested.

"There are only a few hundred large companies in our target market," Andre said. "After four years, we've penetrated forty." He paused and smiled broadly. "But there are tens of thousands of small and mid-sized companies. That's where these competitive start-ups are playing. If we can figure out how to move onto their turf with a low-cost option, I think we can earn big margins."

"But we've been through this, Andre," Jenna said, her voice sounding flat. Rehearsed. "You know the manpower and costs that go into replicating these leaders."

"That's just it," Andre said, a small smile crossing his face. "We need to find a way to eliminate engineers and costs. Why don't we copy our competitors? I hear they're all using artificial intelligence to create their software and write their code. Why do we need so much human inter-vention?"

"We're using AI wherever we can in the development process," Josh tried to counter. But Andre was already moving on to make his next point.

"And we need to reduce hobbies and distractions."

Andre's eyes shifted toward Josh as he added, "such as your AI investigator. That Officer…"

"Friday," Josh said. "And it's not a distraction."

"Right. Officer Friday. Are we getting anywhere?"

Josh grimaced. "Not yet."

Andre looked at Jenna and said, "See. We have nothing to show for our effort. How exactly is *that* not a distraction?" He turned to Josh and said, "I want you to shut it down. No more work on Officer Friday or any other side projects. I need one hundred percent focus on making CHERL dramatically more affordable. As affordable as the product all those start-ups are offering."

Josh glanced over at Jenna, who didn't seem surprised by Andre's new mandate. It was clear she had heard this speech before.

"So, what do you think, Brodsky?" Andre asked.

Josh pushed his uneaten salad to the side. "I don't know, Andre. This is not what I was expecting tonight."

"Oh," Andre said, "what exactly *were* you expecting?"

Josh said, "I hoped you were ready to take another shot at convincing the NSA to let us proceed with the White House."

Andre waved his hand and said, "There's no point banging our heads against the wall with Washington again. Not if we can't keep CHERL afloat."

Josh lifted his wine and took two long swallows as the waiter returned and exchanged their salad plates for the entrées. As they ate in silence, Josh couldn't believe Andre was walking away from the original mission—a mission so powerful, the CEO's words still resonated with Josh all these years later:

"History books are worthless," Andre had said during Josh's interview all those years ago. "Nobody reads them anymore. Especially politicians. Countries and governments continue making the same mistakes. The same wars, the same stupidity. But what if our leaders could discuss today's challenges with the greatest minds in history. With Churchill. With Roosevelt. What if Lincoln was around to speak to Congress today? You don't think he could talk some sense into these lunatics in Washington?"

Josh had taken a huge leap of faith when he left his position at the Department of Defense for Silicon Valley, joining Andre and his world of the young entrepreneur—and a culture notorious for spitting out someone at Josh's advanced age. But for the chance to lead Andre's cutting-edge endeavor—and the potential of creating an AI application for the halls of American government—Josh was willing to put aside all reservations.

Was Andre really prepared to toss his vision into the scrap heap?

Andre placed his fork on his plate and brought his cell phone to his ear. "Parsons," he said.

Ginny Parsons was Sway's new head of the People Experience team. Andre must have had his phone set to vibrate mode because Josh never heard a ring.

Sway's CEO suddenly stood and grabbed his jacket from the back of the chair and said, "I need to take this."

Josh and Jenna watched him leave the room. When the door closed Jenna moved her half-eaten tuna aside and said, "I don't know why you stay around for this bullshit."

Her comment shocked him. In his three years working for Jenna, Josh never heard a negative word about Andre or the company.

"It's certainly not a positive development," Josh said.

"I don't know." She folded her arms and leaned back. "If I was in your shoes, I'd figure out how to get myself out of here." Josh stared at his boss as she continued. "Don't you ever think about kicking back? Maybe go out and see the world. Aren't there other things you want to do with your life?"

Josh was momentarily puzzled by her suggestion. The thought of "kicking back" or traveling was the last thing on Josh's mind right now. He had too much to do. But as he slowly digested the implications of Jenna's words, he realized his boss might already have commenced Andre's "cost reduction" plan.

And getting rid of Josh was the first phase. He glanced over at Andre's empty seat and the half-eaten chicken.

Why had Andre taken his jacket if he was only answering a phone call?

"You've made a huge contribution to the company," Jenna said. "You've come through tremendous adversity." She finally made eye contact as she added, "You've built a system that has had an enormous impact on corporate America."

Was this Andre's "dinner agenda" all along? Had the CEO laid the groundwork for easing Josh out of his job, leaving Jenna to do the dirty work?

"Naveen is ready to take the reins," she said. "I'm sure he can lead the cost reduction effort. He has some great lieutenants…"

But her words became background noise as Josh processed what was happening. He had been through countless reorganizations during his thirty years at the Department of Defense whenever edicts came down from above. After the initial shock, Josh had always rallied his team and figured out what needed to be done.

"Anyway, no one would blame you," Jenna finished, before lifting her fork and picking at her tuna again. "I'm sure Andre would be open to a reasonable package."

Josh took in a long, deep breath and slowly exhaled.

He wasn't interested in being bought out. And he wasn't about to let go of Andre's original vision, even if Sway's CEO was. Not until Josh had finished what he came to do.

Not until he installed a version of CHERL for America's commander-in-chief.

"You're awful quiet over there, Josh. What's going through your head?"

Josh lifted the wine and took a long gulp. He gently placed the glass on the table and said, "I've put my heart and soul into CHERL. I need some time to think this over."

"Take all the time you need," she said as the waiter returned to clear Andre's plate. "Guess something came up," Josh said.

Jenna forced a smile. "It happens all the time."

As they silently finished their dinner, a plan was already taking shape in the recesses of Josh's mind. If coming up with a lower-cost method of delivering CHERL was what Andre and Jenna wanted—if that's what it would take for Josh to still have a chance at fulfilling CHERL's original mission—Josh would figure out a way.

If he had to put Andre's so-called "distractions" aside, so be it. Officer Friday could wait, but Josh wasn't about to "kick back." He wasn't ready to go out and see the world. Josh needed a few days to prepare for what he had to do.

But by the end of the week, he and his team would take a sledgehammer to CHERL.

CHAPTER
SEVENTEEN

DAN EXITED the elevator on the third floor, made a right turn, and headed down the corridor of Jingle Finance's brick-lined, thirty-thousand-square-foot headquarters. Two golden doodles positioned themselves on either side of him, serving as his escorts to his cubicle on the far end of the office, a task the dogs seemed to enjoy. None of Dan's coworkers at Jingle seemed to know who Dutch and Princess belonged to. Nor Daisy, the blue and gold macaw that sat perched on the windowsill and whistled at unfamiliar faces.

"Thanks, guys," Dan said to the dogs as he placed his backpack on the floor beside his desk. Just as he had done on his first two days at the company, Dan gave each a treat from the bowl on his desk, which he assumed the cleaning staff replenished each evening. He had no idea who fed Daisy, but Milo Galini's assistant, Jordanna, walked the dogs several times throughout the day. As Dan unpacked his laptop, he heard a familiar voice approaching and winced.

"Mornin', everybody," Beth Moore said as she made her way to the desk next to Dan's. He had hoped the blond-haired, muscular IT troubleshooter who worked the "Help Desk" would be working from home today. Dan had a lot to do.

"Hey," he said as she dropped her backpack onto the floor with a loud thud. It seemed that everything Beth Moore did was loud. Given her appearance and demeanor, Dan found it hard to believe she previously worked for one of the largest, most conservative banks in New York. Today, Moore was wearing a yellow tank top which accentuated her tanned, muscular, and fully tattooed arms. Dan's favorite artwork was the one that ran down her right triceps, depicting the image of a curvy woman on a motorcycle, her long red hair swaying in the wind.

"I'm glad they put someone near me," Moore had said to Dan on the day they first met. "It was getting a little lonely back here."

After unpacking her backpack, Beth initiated the first of what Dan knew would be dozens of "help desk" phone calls she would take throughout the day. Her piercing voice was always several decibels higher than everyone else's, making it difficult for Dan to concentrate. On Dan's first day, he asked Galini about the possibility of working from home, but Jingle's founder insisted new employees belonged in the office, at least for the first six months.

Important to absorb the Jingle culture, Galini had texted.

But Dan wondered what culture Galini expected him to absorb. Two-thirds of the desks were empty, as the majority of staff appeared to be working from remote locations. In fact, yesterday's lunchtime "benefits update" included employees that were anywhere from their East Village bedrooms to Mexican villas. Dan was sure he heard a mariachi band in the background. Which left Dan listening to the loud help desk operator, along with the incessant thumping coming from Galini's treadmill, which for some reason had been moved within fifty feet of Dan's cubicle. Dan opened his laptop and was about to continue his initial review of Galini's Hawk artificial intelligence system when he heard the treadmill whirl to life. He looked up and saw Galini warming up with a slow jog. Moments later, a message appeared at the top of Dan's computer.

Galini: How's it going?

Dan peered over to confirm Jingle's founder was still on the treadmill, his hands pumping away as he increased his pace.

Dan: Making progress.

Galini: Where is marketing contractor?

Dan: She's starting tomorrow

Dan had asked for a few days to be on his own so he could properly analyze Hawk's AI code. But for some reason, Galini had insisted she be hired right away.

Galini: Good. Let's get our money's worth

Dan kept his eyes on Galini, who wasn't holding a cell phone. Nor did Galini move his hands toward the keypad on the treadmill. How was Galini communicating?

Galini: Any early impressions of my code?

Dan stared at the CEO, who had revved up the treadmill to a faster pace. Dan thought about how to respond. He hadn't known his new boss long enough to know if he was sensitive to honest critiques. The truth was, Dan's initial impression was that the half-completed Hawk system was a very rudimentary piece of artificial intelligence, requiring a complete overhaul. Plus, a great deal of the marketing information used to train the AI appeared to be hastily assembled, as if it had been gathered without any thought or strategy. Dan was no marketing expert, but at a minimum, Hawk would need a new training data set built with current marketing practices. Dan decided to respond with positivity.

```
            Dan: Several good
            opportunities.

        Galini: I look forward to
        hearing more.
```

Dan watched Galini, his arms pumping, but his lips still didn't move and his eyes were fixed ahead. Moments later, another text appeared.

```
        Galini: What more do you need?
```

"Yeah, I can't believe you're still having that problem," Moore said loudly to her latest caller. "I coulda swore I purged that bug from your computer."

Dan pressed his fingers into his ears.

"What else?" Galini asked. Dan looked up and saw Jingle's CEO was dripping sweat onto his desk.

"Um. Well…"

"I have a lot riding on you, Dan." Galini wiped the perspiration off his forehead and removed the silver headband.

"Can I ask you something?" Dan said. "How were you texting me from the treadmill? You didn't have your phone in your hands. I didn't hear you using voice commands." He leaned back. "How were you doing that?"

Galini's smile widened as he held the metal headband out to Dan. "This is how."

Dan took the slim, lightweight object in his hand.

"It reads my brain signals," Galini explained.

"Huh?"

"All I do is think about what I want to say, think about

what I want to keystroke into my phone or computer, and sensors interpret my brain neurons."

"Brain neurons," Dan repeated, examining the sleek device. He had read a lot about one-way brain-computer interfaces that were surgically implanted in the skull, capable of processing and transmitting commands to computer devices. But Dan didn't realize these sensors had advanced enough to pick up signals from *outside* the skull bone with no more than a simple headset.

"My Harvard classmate launched a company called Mindpath," Galini explained. "He asked for my feedback on this next generation product. It's pretty cool, but the device only seems to pick up my brain waves when my mind is calm and there are no outside distractions." He pointed at the treadmill behind him. "Other than when I'm running, my mind is anything but calm. I'm sure my buddy would be better off with a test subject that works in a quiet space. He told me one of his client's locked himself in a remote cabin and wrote an entire software product without so much as touching a keypad." Galini looked around at the rows of workstations surrounding them and added, "I guess we don't *do* quiet and secluded, so I'm not the best guinea pig."

Dan glanced at the loud, tattooed troubleshooter sitting next to him. He thought back to the all the innovations he piloted during his years at Sway. Dan had loved every minute.

"You know," Dan said, "people said I was pretty good at testing products coming out of Sway's lab." He held the Mindpath headset up to Jingle's founder. "If there's a quiet room you'd allow me use, I'd be happy to try this out and give your friend my honest feedback."

Galini rubbed his chin as he seemed to think over Dan's offer. After a few moments he smiled and said, "You know, Dan. That sounds like a great idea."

CHAPTER
EIGHTEEN

"COME ON IN, LOUIE," Ed Chamberlain said. The outgoing head of Virtual Bank was leaning back in his swivel chair, his eyes glued to the oversized computer screen broadcasting his favorite financial news channel. The sound was muted, but Chamberlain stared at the screen as if reading the lips of the reporter positioned on the chaotic floor of the New York Stock Exchange.

"Do you believe this?" Chamberlain said, his eyes still glued to the telecast.

Louie sat in the straight-backed chair in front of the CEO's desk and leaned forward. He squinted at the words scrolling across the bottom of the screen.

"BANKS STEPPING UP USE OF ARTIFICIAL INTELLIGENCE."

"Do you think we're falling behind?" Chamberlain asked.

"We use the same AI software as every other bank," Louie said. "How could we be behind?"

Chamberlain swiveled his chair to face Louie. "Well, it won't be my problem much longer." His hands gripped the leather armrests. "What's up?"

Louie leaned back and steepled his fingers. "Well, I've given this a lot of thought, Ed."

"About what?" Chamberlain asked.

"About the CEO job. You said I should take a few days, which I did."

But Chamberlain's eyes seemed to grow foggy before he once again swiveled to face his computer. "More military maneuvers in the South China sea," Chamberlain murmured. "Market doesn't seem to like it."

"They never do," Louie said. "But anyway, about the position." He paused before adding, "I'm in."

But Chamberlain didn't react, as if he hadn't heard what Louie said. But then, while still staring at his screen, Chamberlain started speaking slowly, his voice tinged with a melancholy tone.

"This job is all consuming, Louie. If you get the chance, your honeymoon will be short." Chamberlain inhaled and blew out slowly before continuing, "If you're lucky, they'll give you the same two years they gave me before casting you aside."

"Hopefully they give me enough time to make a mark on the business."

"Make your mark?" Chamberlain blew out a short laugh. "You can make *money* before they throw you out. As far as leaving a legacy…who knows if there's anything we can do from this chair to make people remember what we accomplished." He swiveled back to face Louie. "Trust me, when it's over, no one will be rushing in to thank you for all the great things you did. Oh, they'll name some meaningless leadership award after you, but they'll stop giving that out after a few years."

"Come on, Ed. You've done amazing work here." It was painful to see the defeated look in Chamberlain's eyes. Maybe his boss had already checked out.

Chamberlain smiled weakly.

"I'm speaking the truth, Ed. It wasn't easy leading us through the merger. Getting the Peachtree folk to accept the Virtual Bank name change. Bringing the headquarters to New Jersey." Louie's eyes wandered around the office as he was hard-pressed to name any more.

"We were a good team, Louie."

"Thanks, Ed," Louie said.

They sat in awkward silence for a few moments before Chamberlain said, "Anything else?"

"Er…well, I was wondering. What's the next step?"

"Step?" Chamberlain stared at Louie, his eyes glassy again.

"You know, to let the board know. I could also use your advice on how to win over any dissenters."

Chamberlain put his hand up, as if halting oncoming traffic. "Just wait," he said. "I'm sure when they're ready, someone from the board will reach out."

Louie leaned back. Not wanting to appear over anxious, Louie had already waited almost a week before getting back to Chamberlain. Waiting for something to happen had never been part of his DNA. During Louie's investment banking days, when he wanted something, he went after it. Waiting was always a terrible strategy, only good for letting a competitor steal what was rightfully yours. Louie had no intention of wasting any more time, especially if the board was already sifting through external candidates. If Louie wanted the job, he would need to take control of his own candidacy. So, after a few more minutes with his outgoing boss where they watched and commented on the changing news scroll, Louie excused himself and marched back to his office. He closed the door and dialed Darrell Evans.

If Louie was going to win the job, if he was going to win this battle, he needed to bring the fight directly to Virtual Bank's Chairman of the Board.

CHAPTER
NINETEEN

LESS THAN TWO hours after the perspiring Milo Galini walked away from his desk, Dan received a call from building services informing him that Room B in the conference center had been reserved for his exclusive use. Dan quickly packed up his belongings, said goodbye to Beth Moore, and set up in the small but private space on the lower level of Jingle Finance's office. Room B was windowless and contained nothing more than a six-foot wide, rectangular table and two chairs. But when he closed the door, Dan could scarcely hear the conversations taking place in the adjoining room.

He took a deep breath and slowly exhaled. Finally, peace and quiet.

Dan opened his laptop and was about to don Galini's Mindpath headset, ready to take the neuron transmitting device for a test drive, when he heard a knock. The door opened and standing in the entranceway was a woman about the same age as Dan, sharply dressed in a sleek white tailored blouse and dark, high-waisted jeans that accentuated thin, shapely legs. Her shoulder-length brown hair framed her high, soft cheekbones.

"Excuse me," she said. "I'm looking for Dan Barry."

"That's me," Dan said as he stood.

She extended her hand and smiled. "Pleased to meet you. I'm Molly Kincaid."

"Nice to meet you, too," Dan said. "Please, come in and have a seat."

Molly seemed to study the small surroundings as she sat. "Cool office."

Dan let out a short laugh. "This is not my office. I mean, they're letting me use it for a while. But it's better than where they had me. It can be hard to concentrate with everything going on out there."

"I'll bet," Molly said, still smiling. "The parrot gave me a lovely serenade when your HR person walked me down here."

"Daisy?" Dan said. "Once she gets to know you, I hear she'll whistle 'You Are My Sunshine.'"

Molly made eye contact as she said, "I can't wait." Dan broke off from her gaze and clicked to the online free-lancing platform where HR posted Molly's background:

"Over five years of experience as senior marketing professional.

Developed sales, publicity, and digital marketing efforts for Fortune 500, mid-sized and small corporations.

Expertise in data analytics, marketing channel optimization, and strategy.

Partnered with clients to create impactful lead generation campaigns while lowering cost per customer acquisition."

"Very impressive background," Dan said. "How long have you been doing freelance work?"

"For the last two years." She sat back and crossed her legs. "I'm enjoying the variety. I never realized how bored I'd become at my last full-time gig at P&G. Selling soap suds just wasn't that compelling."

Dan laughed. Her profile showed she spent the first three years of her career at Proctor and Gamble. Dan asked, "Did you look elsewhere for a permanent role?"

"I didn't want to. Like I said, big company life bored me so I quit and took my time. A friend asked me to create a marketing campaign for her start-up. By the time I was done, I built her a full digital strategy. She referred me to others, and I've stayed busy ever since. I was between projects when I got the call from Milo's office. I did some work for a mutual friend."

Dan wondered if this was the same friend who built the Mindpath headset lying next to his laptop.

"I was told you needed help gathering marketing information for some library you're building, but not much more than that."

"It's not really a library," Dan said. "It's a data base of best practices in marketing, specifically around customer acquisitions. Information I'll eventually use to train a new artificial intelligence system to launch marketing campaigns and brings Jingle new customers."

"Wow," Molly said. "I knew artificial intelligence was being used for marketing analytics, but didn't know AI could craft and execute marketing campaigns."

Dan shrugged. "With good information, AI can tackle almost any business problem."

"Do you have results from what Jingle is already doing to bring in new customers?" Molly asked. "You know, from TV and radio ads. Online search engines? Direct mail?"

Dan shook his head. "Not yet. That would be your job."

"How about customer profiles?" She asked. "A description of people who are considered Jingle's best customers today so we can target more just like them?"

"That's a great idea," Dan said. He keyed a note onto his list of follow-ups.

"This doesn't sound hard," she said, smiling. "I have some great sources. If you can use textbooks, I had the best, most inspiring marketing professors at Michigan. I bet your AI could learn a ton from the things they've published."

"Bring it all," Dan said. "And I assume you have no issue working from here."

She looked around the small room. "Are you sure there's enough room?"

"I didn't mean in my conference room. I meant from the office. You can use the empty workstation upstairs where I used to sit."

"Do you mean the noisy spot?" she asked, smiling again.

"But we'll meet in here often enough," Dan said. "I just need privacy when I'm writing AI code."

Molly reached over and picked up the metal, Mind-path headset. "What's this?"

"It's a product I'm testing for Milo."

"What does it do?"

Dan took the headset from her hand and pointed to a string of probes along the interior. "Supposedly, these read signals transmitted from my brain and send commands to my phone or computer."

Her eyebrows rose. "Seriously?"

"I saw Milo using it the other day to shoot out text messages."

"Wow. That's so cool." She reached for the headset and said, "Can I try it?"

"As soon as I figure out how it works," Dan said. The last thing he wanted was his freelancer getting distracted with the device. He had a ton of work for her to do. "I think it may take a while getting it to sync up with my neurons."

Molly stood and said, "In that case, why don't you show me to my workstation." She held his gaze and added, "I wouldn't want to interfere with your…brain waves."

CHAPTER
TWENTY

LUCAS PULLED out the earpiece and used the speakerphone to dial into the follow up debrief.

"Those marketing consultants trained her up pretty well," he heard Agent Dennison say.

"I'm on the line," Lucas said. "And I agree. It sounded like she knew what she was talking about."

"That's why I requested her for this assignment," Agent Lummis said. "I knew she was good,"

"Is she good enough to fake her way through the mechanics of marketing?" Agent Kidane asked.

"She's a fast study," Lummis said. "The consultants will hold her hand through the rest."

"Do you think Barry suspects anything?" Lucas asked.

"Not a chance," Dennison said. "He's too busy figuring out his day job and playing with that Mindpath thing."

"He does seem pretty intrigued," Kidane said.

As was Lucas. He had read through the FBI lab's three-page analysis of the Mindpath neuron transmitting device. After three years working the cyber-crimes desk, Lucas had witnessed incredible advancements in the world of science and technology. At this point, very few claims of innovation surprised him. But professing to transmit neurons from your brain to a computer through a lightweight headset left him astounded.

"Do you think he'll continue to use it?" Lucas asked.

"Our profiling team believes he will," Lummis said. "As long as it performs as well as Quantico says, we shouldn't have trouble listening to anything that transpires in Dan Barry's life."

CHAPTER
TWENTY-ONE

NAVEEN GUPTA barely lifted the mallet off the ground when his one hundred thirty-pound frame started teetering. Josh's lieutenant in charge of the CHERL project released the handle and dropped to his knees. After adjusting his goggles, he moved to a more manageably sized alternative. Naveen slowly lifted the medium sized mallet over his head and paused before bringing its full weight crashing down, shattering a computer monitor. He raised the hammer again and again, smashing and scattering pieces, letting out a brief grunt after each strike. He finally rested, hands on both knees, gulping for air.

"Are you okay, Naveen?" Enrico Alvarez asked.

Naveen removed the protective goggles from his eyes and looked up, his face beaming. "That was awesome, mon." He drew in another long breath and slowly let it out. "What a release!"

"Give it a rest," Carl Townsend said as he brought another computer monitor into the center. "My turn." The six-foot tall Townsend, a former college football star at Georgia Tech, lifted the heaviest sledgehammer with ease.

Josh stayed safely behind a protective barrier, content

to be an observer of the destructive activity taking place in the center of the padded room. "You should go next, Josh," Naveen said as he made his way to the back of the line of CHERL team leaders. But Josh rolled his eyes and folded his arms.

"Brings out the creative juices, mon," Naveen promised.

This was the third time in the past year that Josh and Naveen brought CHERL's leadership team to the Bay Area Smash Room in the Nob Hill section of San Francisco. Naveen signed them up for the two-hour "All You Can Break" special as a team building exercise. Josh accepted that these rituals were part of the Silicon Valley culture. And, he had to admit, watching Naveen and his team take turns breaking things apart seemed like an appropriate metaphor for what this afternoon's meeting was all about.

Josh didn't always appreciate Naveen's inclusive style of management. Josh preferred to rely on a few key lieutenants when it came to devising new strategies and tactics, especially when job reductions were on the line. But Naveen insisted on including each and every one of his direct reports in matters large and small. Perhaps the group would be mature enough to participate in their own restructuring, but Josh wasn't taking any chances.

That's why he brought along a CHERL re-creation for reinforcements.

Two hours later, Naveen's six project leaders were panting, perspiring, and downing bottles of water. Josh announced it was time to walk over to the hotel conference center.

"We'll have a working lunch starting at noon."

———

AFTER CLEANING themselves up and changing into their favorite company uniform—khakis and Sway polo shirts—the team gathered in the Excelsior Room on the lower level of the hotel's conference center. They filled their plates with spicy kimchi, seared tofu, and sautéed pork. Once everyone was quietly eating, Josh sat at the head of the rectangular table and proceeded to recount his dinner with Jenna Turbak and Sway's CEO. He spelled out Andre Olaf's mandate to reduce costs in order to make CHERL affordable—and profitable—for a wider universe of small and mid-sized companies. By the time Josh finished describing the new mission, most of the project leaders had pushed their half-eaten food to the side.

"What kind of cost cutting is he asking for?" Faisal Khan asked. Khan was responsible for honing the personality traits of CHERL's re-creations.

"Yeah," Sol Kim, said, her eyes narrowed. "Are we talking headcount reductions?" Kim led a group of experts in natural language processing.

Josh nodded. "I don't see any other way."

Everyone slumped in their chairs. It hadn't taken long for the energy generated by the sledgehammer session to drain from the room. Naveen obviously sensed the same and said, "Come on, team. Andre's probably ready to have AI take over all of our coding work. If that's what you want, we'll send him *that* plan right now and hand in our resignations." He surveyed his project managers and asked, "Or would you rather be part of the solution?"

Everyone silently exchanged glances, as if looking for someone, anyone, to speak up. Faisal Khan finally broke the silence.

"We want to help."

After a pause, Kim said, "Absolutely."

"If this means a new way of doing business," Enrico Alvarez said, "we'll figure it out." Alvarez oversaw CHERL's largest non-employee cost base, the vast server farm housed in Tower Operations. All heads were now nodding in agreement as Naveen clapped his hands.

"Okay," Josh said, hoping the group was ready to make some tough choices.

"Is finance involved," Khan asked.

Josh shook his head. "They'll be plenty of time to bring in the accountants once we devise a plan of attack."

"Before we start," Naveen said. "Can we review everyone's feedback from the Jaspar Phillips session? It might be a good way to jumpstart the ideas."

As Naveen got the discussion going, Josh opened his laptop and initiated a CHERL listening session. He wanted his AI to be prepared in case Naveen's team failed to devise meaningful solutions. Naveen pointed to Kyle Fraser, the long-haired project leader of CHERL's "Empathy and Aggression" module.

"The personality engine worked like a charm," Fraser said.

"Okay." Naveen nodded before pointing to Kim, who offered, "As usual, CHERL mastered the facts and figures but conveyed them in a conversational manner."

Naveen looked around. "What else?"

"I watched several videos of Phillips speaking with Rockefeller," Khan called out. "The client seemed to fully embrace the reality."

"Maybe true," Alvarez interjected. "But I actually thought Phillips started slowly."

"But that's not unusual, Enrico," Naveen said. "Many of our clients are initially star-struck."

"Personally," Townsend said, "I think that's become a problem."

"What do you mean?" Josh asked.

Townsend steepled his fingers and said, "After everything that happened with the hacker corrupting CHERL's recommendations, I thought we were going to coach clients to challenge the advice offered by CHERL. To push back."

"We have," Naveen said. "Questioning CHERL's

opinion has been a part of our roll-out protocol for three years."

"Maybe Phillips didn't pay attention to the coaching," Townsend said. "Because when the discussion with Rockefeller shifted into off-shore drilling strategies, I thought Phillips blindly accepted the AI's suggestions."

"Come on, Carl," Faisal said. "CHERL's AI advisers represent the greatest leaders in history. Would you push back if Steve Jobs told you change your tech design?"

"That's exactly my point," Townsend said. "We all know what happened when Nicole…I mean, when that Russian mole changed CHERL's training data right under our noses. Clients still followed CHERL's advice because it came from their so-called heroes, even though the advice had been corrupted."

Naveen shook his head. "We've been through this, Carl. That's why we developed our analytic tools."

As Josh listened to the debate, he actually believed Townsend had a valid point. In fact, Josh and Naveen had discussed this very issue many times over the years. The team had developed new analytic tools to verify the *consistency* of CHERL's advice, but the new metrics did nothing to verify the strength or *correctness* of CHERL's suggestions. Other than stepping up their scrutiny and controls over data, he and Naveen agreed there was little else they could do on the accuracy issue.

"What we learned from the Nicole fiasco," Townsend continued, "is clients will follow CHERL's recommendation because of *who* they believe the advice is coming from, not because it's been verified as good advice."

"All recommendations are subjective," Fraser offered. "How do you evaluate accuracy of a subjective opinion?"

Townsend glared at Fraser. "I don't have an answer for you, Kyle. Naveen and Dr. Brodsky are seeking our impressions. I'm just providing my feedback like the rest of you."

Fraser's shoulders slumped and suddenly everyone,

including Naveen, became more interested in their cell phones than in continuing. Josh was surprised how quickly the Rockefeller debriefing had devolved into a contentious debate. Perhaps, the team managers weren't ready to deal with the possibility of their own demise, after all.

"You've raised important points for us to consider," Josh said. "But I suspect we might need some help with the next discussion." He turned his computer around so everyone could read the words on his screen.

"CHERL   Listening   Session—Hewlett-Packard founder, David Packard."

CHAPTER
TWENTY-TWO

DAN CLOSED the door and booted up his laptop. He sipped his piping hot coffee and listened to the quiet hum of the air ventilation system, grateful for the privacy. And the peace and quiet.

It had been four days since Galini allowed him to move into the small conference room. Other than the half day Dan took off to get his father settled back at the Bronx rehab facility, Dan had been immensely productive. With his dad getting stronger by the day, a huge weight had been lifted from Dan's shoulders. And with a steady paycheck about to come in from Jingle Finance, he could now devote his full attention to rebuilding the Hawk AI marketing system.

He hoped he could get the brain neuron sensor device to perform like it did the previous day.

The first morning Dan wore the silver headset, he'd concentrated his thoughts on a single phrase, trying to see if he could "will" keystrokes onto his computer like Galini did with the text messages. He attempted several expressions and word combinations to no effect. He closed his eyes and visualized a full line of Java code. But the only thing he had to show for his efforts was a blank screen and a bad headache. So, by yesterday evening, while he still wore the Mindpath device, he decided to stop trying to activate his "neurons." Instead, he shifted his mental focus back to his main assignment, rewriting an advertising and promotion module Galini built within Hawk. With his fingers working the keyboard, Dan had a very productive afternoon. But as he was about to enter one last algorithm before calling it a night, a strange thing occurred.

Lines of code scrolled onto his computer screen in a mesmerizing dance. In seconds, the full algorithm he had been visualizing in his mind appeared on the screen.

Dan's heart had pounded with excitement—and disbelief—when he stared at his fingers still hovering inches above the computer keyboard.

The Mindpath had worked!

Now, as Dan's brain formulated new concepts, the device continued to translate and transmit his thoughts—transfer his brain neurons—to his computer. Over the next few hours, he used the device to build new Hawk code, enabling the execution of online "digital" marketing messages. When he was done, Dan removed the headset and placed it next to his computer. He called Molly and told her to meet him outside the cafeteria where they had an appointment with Jingle's head of customer engagement.

"Milo said Frank Braun has data we should see."

———

THE FIRST THING Dan noticed about Braun was that he didn't dress like anyone else at Jingle, where the standard outfit was shorts and tee-shirts. Instead, Braun wore black slacks and a white, button down shirt. His gray hair was trim and neat.

"Pleasure to meet you, Frank," Dan said as they shook hands in a windowless conference room next to the company cafeteria.

"Likewise," Braun said, smiling broadly. "And who is this lovely lady?"

"Molly Kincaid. I'm a marketing consultant working with Dan."

They all sat but Frank's eyes lingered on Molly. "Isn't Dan lucky," Braun said.

Molly slid her chair away from Braun as the head of Jingle's engagement platform opened his tablet and said, "Milo asked me to run a fresh set of analytics identifying Jingle's best customers." He projected an image of his screen onto the wall. "But the numbers haven't changed much over the past two years."

Dan studied the column of figures displayed under the headings "Best Customers," "Average Customers," and "Worst Customers."

"What behavior differentiates the three groupings," Molly asked.

"Generally," Braun said, "best customers are those engaging and interacting with the Jingle platform at least ten times each month. They represent the top twenty percent of our accounts. Average customers use the platform between four and nine times per month."

"And worst?" Dan asked.

"We don't need to discuss this group," Braun said. "Please, don't bring us any more of those." He swiped the screen and a new chart displayed another set of columns under the heading "Likelihood to Purchase."

"But this is what we call the money page. It shows why we care about customer performance." There were a lot of numbers on the chart but at the top was a bold, declarative statement:

"Best customers are five to eight times more likely to purchase an add-on product recommended by Jingle."

"How do you know what customers will buy?" Dan asked.

"We've run pilot programs with a regional finance company." Braun swiped the screen and the wall displayed a grid with a diagonal line stretching from the lower left corner to the upper right. The numbers across the horizontal axis displayed columns showing, "Number of times customer engages with Jingle per month." The vertical axis showed "potential revenue earned from bank accounts." If the numbers within the chart were correct, the results were striking. The more a customer interacted with Jingle, the higher the probability that customer would generate revenue by signing up for a bank account. Braun advanced the slides and new charts displayed similar high revenue projections for credit cards, auto loans, mortgages, even investment products.

"Initially, we will earn a fee every time one of these add-on products is sold," Braun said. "But Milo wants us to develop our own financial products. That way, Jingle Finance retains one-hundred percent of the revenue earned."

"This is very impressive," Molly said.

Braun raised an eyebrow. "Impressive? This is a gold mine. If you two can revitalize our new account growth, the value of our company will rise exponentially!"

Hearing this correlation of new customer growth with the value of the company, Dan immediately thought of the five thousand shares Galini had given him when he joined Jingle. It was nice to think Dan's work on Hawk might help replenish his own net worth.

Braun continued swiping on his tablet. "All you need to do is bring us 'look-a-likes'—customers with a profile similar to these best customers."

The words and numbers filling the screen were smaller and harder to decipher. Even after squinting, Dan found it difficult to make out the figures. At least the titles along the left side were very clear:

Age
Gender
Income
Highest level of education

Type of residence
Social media usage

"The categories go on for several pages," Braun said as he closed the tablet. "I'll forward you a digitized version."

"That would be great," Molly said. "Do you have anything else that we could use to train Hawk?"

"Well, I'm not sure why Milo wanted you to have this, but I provided our marketing team a model that can create "look-a-like" test accounts. They're not real accounts, of course, but each account mimics the same attributes as our best customers. My team uses these fabricated accounts to stress test the engagement platform but marketing says it helps them refine their targeting efforts." Braun shrugged. "I gather that's why Milo wanted you to have it, too."

Molly looked over at Dan and said, "We could use it to create accounts for our own stress testing."

"I guess so," Dan said. But he knew it would be some time before Hawk was ready for stress testing. "Obviously, Hawk needs the best customer profiles more than anything right now."

"Of course," Braun said as they all stood. "I'll transmit everything to you by the end of the day."

"That would be great," Molly said. "I'll add everything to Hawk's training data set."

"We really appreciate your help," Dan added.

"Not at all." Braun cleared his throat and said, "Dan, may I have a word with you in private?"

"I'll be on my way," Molly said. When she closed the door behind her, Braun said, "I'm glad Milo brought someone like you to finish what he started with Hawk."

Dan smiled. "Me too."

Braun folded his arms and said, "Our CEO may be a visionary, but if you've examined his AI code, you know he's a terrible programmer."

Dan nodded. "It can be improved."

Braun let out a short laugh. "I see you're a diplomat. Well, let me give you some free advice, Mr. Diplomat. After you have 'improved' his code, do not allow our fearless leader anywhere near your AI code."

"Why is that?"

Braun shook his head and said, "It doesn't matter. Trust me. If you want our company to succeed, keep Milo away from Hawk. Letting him touch your AI system again will only lead to trouble."

CHAPTER
TWENTY-THREE

LUCAS FOLEY'S breakfast meeting with his boss ran longer than expected and he was late for the Operation Turncoat morning debrief. But when he dialed into the conference bridge, the first voice he heard was Special Agent Lummis.

And she was shouting.

"Your models assigned a ninety-eight percent certainty!"

An unfamiliar male voice nervously replied, "We never use words like 'certainty.'"

"But that man is back in rehab!" Lummis shouted. "And he's getting stronger!"

Lucas sent a quick text to Agent Dennison asking what he had missed.

> Dennison: Lummis dressing down
> predictive modeling guy at
> Quantico Labs. Name is Stokes.
>
> Lucas: Got it

Lucas wasn't surprised to hear Lummis' reaction. He read the update the previous evening—Dan Barry's father was doing well and was moved back to the Bronx rehab center. Lucas was excited when he first saw the news. He hoped this would mean the end of Operation Turncoat, or at least, a pivot to an alternative strategy. From the tone and urgency in Lummis' voice, the agent in charge wasn't about to change direction.

"How much longer!" Lummis asked.

"His prognosis has not changed," Stokes insisted.

"But we're losing precious time," Lummis said. But she was no longer shouting. In fact, Lummis now sounded like she was pleading. "Everyone is in position."

"We never pinpointed an exact date," Stokes said firmly. "I can only assign a confidence factor and leave the rest to you."

"We've built an entire operation around your prediction," Lummis said.

"Let me try to explain this again," Stokes said. "Our models digested Alec Barry's complete medical history, genetics, biomarkers—and the hospital system supplies us with continual updates. I can assure you, nothing has transpired within the past forty-eight hours to change our ninety-eight percent confidence level. Alarms will eventually be sounded."

"I've had enough of your techno-babble," Lummis said.

"I understand your frustration, Agent Lummis. But—"

Stokes's voice cut off. Lucas wondered if the line went dead until he heard Dennison say, "Hello?"

"We're all still here, Agent Dennison," Lummis responded. "I had to drop that egg head before my brain exploded."

"Maybe we should go back to Director Compo with an alternative plan," Lucas said.

"There's no need to change course," Agent Lummis responded, flatly.

"But what happens if his father continues to improve?" Lucas asked. He couldn't imagine Director

Compo would allow this operation to run indefinitely. Lummis didn't respond. But even on the video conference screen, Lucas saw her eyes narrow.

Something about Lummis' determined expression sent a chill down Lucas's spine.

CHAPTER
TWENTY-FOUR

DAVID PACKARD PASSED away toward the end of the twentieth-century.

An engineer who co-founded Hewlett-Packard in 1939, Packard grew the company into the world's largest producer of electronic devices, including calculators and printers. Extremely technical—Packard held a master's degree in electronic engineering from Stanford University —HP's founder also served as Under Secretary at the US Department of Defense under President Richard Nixon. Josh thought Packard's unique combination of skill and experience made him an ideal leader to guide his team through their daunting challenge.

"We have been presented with a serious dilemma," Josh started. The project leaders all leaned forward, listening—all except for Naveen who sat off to the side and appeared disinterested as he doodled on a yellow legal pad. Clearly, the normally upbeat Naveen was displeased when Josh shifted the meeting to seek out direction from artificial intelligence, before his team had a chance to develop their own restructuring scheme.

"The CEO of our company, Andre Olaf, has told us that CHERL's current distribution model is not profitable or scalable," Josh said. "He seeks a lower cost model that is affordable for a wide range of small and mid-sized companies."

"What is your question?" the low, authoritative voice asked.

"Which expensive aspects can be removed from CHERL without losing our effectiveness?"

"And…" Townsend said, looking at Josh for approval to engage with the Packard re-creation. Josh nodded. "Dr. Brodsky tells us you've absorbed all the previous client sessions."

"Yes. And analyzed the perspectives expressed in the debrief on the Phillips-Rockefeller discussion."

"Good," Townsend said. "I want to be sure clients are not receiving CHERL's advice as a directive."

"I fully understand," the voice said. *"I am processing your conflicting set of goals."*

"We appreciate that," Josh said.

"It appears several of your teams, or pods as you call them, consume substantial resources recreating the personality traits of historical leaders—creating the illusion you have brought back these business titans."

Josh said, "That is correct. That is CHERL's mandate."

"But that illusion adds nothing to the soundness or accuracy of the advice being offered."

"But," Josh interjected, "the personality adds authenticity."

"Certainly. But if you are seeking major expense reductions, eliminating AI code, which creates this illusion, would eradicate a great deal of associated people and processing costs. Importantly, this action will not impact the integrity of recommendations coming from any of your CHERL re-creations."

Townsend banged the table and said, "See. I told you."

"Eliminating the personalities?" Khan said, his face beet red. "That's crazy!"

"I consider these personality re-creations to be histrionics.

Hyperbole in each of the CHERL versions, as you affect a connection between clients and CHERL's AI. In fact, by investing so much time and money in your authenticity, you have biased your clients against any type of meaningful debate."

Townsend was smiling broadly as Alvarez asked, "How are we biasing our clients?"

Kim added, "Are you suggesting what we've built is nothing more than a trick?"

As Naveen's team continued debating with the AI, Josh pinched the bridge of his nose and closed his eyes, trying to process Packard's conclusion. Had they really steered their clients to accept the AI's advice, as Townsend had been saying? Josh glanced at the still doodling Naveen, hoping his lieutenant would come to the defense of CHERL's original design.

"I am simply stating that your designers and programmers are united in their desire to see clients act on CHERL's advice. And that by recreating the personality of historical leaders, clients are left with little choice but to follow the advice they hear. No one, even a corporate CEO, wants to look like a fool by second guessing leaders they perceive as having such great minds."

Kim interjected, "You're saying we don't have to recreate the actual historical person? That all of the personality traits have no impact?"

"On the contrary. Let me provide a stark example. It appears that your obsession with personality contributed to the deception enacted on your clients by the Russians several years ago."

All eyes turned to Josh. He nodded his confirmation that he had, indeed, fed Packard with the facts surrounding Nicole Ryder's impersonator.

"Based on an analysis of the infiltration, your clients were enthralled by being in the presence of leaders they had idolized and, in many cases, emulated. They were blinded by the illusion of being in the presence of greatness. Your clients never imagined their heroes would lead them astray. That in actuality, they were being deceived by foreigners manipulating them for their own financial gain."

Fascinating, Josh thought.

"Neutralizing these personality traits will relegate the system to its essential condition—that of a tool to provide advice and direction —just as you are asking for today."

"Great," Alvarez said. "CHERL will sound like a well-researched text book on leadership. What you're suggesting would make CHERL slightly better than asking a question of a generative AI system."

"That is incorrect. Generative AI are not built to tackle leadership challenges. They are built for analyzing data and generating prose, but not for producing hard decisions or hard opinions."

Josh felt an unease creeping up his spine. The idea presented by the Packard re-creation might fulfill the cost reduction mandate, but how could Josh ever accept what felt like a complete degradation of CHERL?

Especially for his ultimate client.

But delivering a version of CHERL—the original version— to the president of the United States would be a problem for another day. Packard's plan was about survival. But as Josh studied and listened to Naveen's shell-shocked project leaders, Josh wasn't sure how he would ever get the buy-in needed to move ahead.

Thankfully, a familiar voice spoke up.

"Mr. Packard," Naveen said as he approached Josh. "What is the suggested playbook for implementing your plan?"

Josh tried to suppress the smile forming on his lips.

"Start by culling any of your historical greats that were never really experts in their fields. Eliminate leaders who managed by instinct and retain those that relied on their expertise and use of facts. Remove modules creating personality from the remainder, before combining leaders by commonality of purpose, such as industry groupings. For example, you no longer need to produce two automotive executives—Henry Ford and Lee Iacocca—when a singular automotive industry expert is sufficient and captures their collective wisdom and experience."

"There must be some aspect of personality that would still add value," Kim said.

The system remained silent.

"Sol is right," Alvarez said. "Maybe we should include one or two traits. We don't want any new manifestations to come across as robotic."

"Think about what you're suggesting Enrico," Naveen said. "When we combine multiple leaders, how would we decide on the personality traits to include?"

"Adding a singular trait is unnecessary and dangerous. Including one or two traits, such as aggression or confidence, without offsetting qualities like modesty or empathy, may lead to a very distorted set of actions."

"He's right," Naveen said. "Who knows what kind of crazy results we would get if we only trained CHERL leaders to be compassionate—or empathetic." He waved his hand toward Josh's computer and added, "We certainly wouldn't be hearing tough advice like this."

Naveen approached Josh and whispered, "If this is what we need to do, boss, I'll get it done." Naveen then turned and addressed the project leaders.

"I recognize where this might lead us. In fact, we might all lose our jobs. But that's the nature of technology. And, I realize clients might reject version two of our artificial intelligence application—a simplified version." Naveen nodded at Josh and added, "But there's only one way to find out."

CHAPTER
TWENTY-FIVE

DAN EMERGED from the subway station two blocks from the Jingle Finance office and dialed the rehab center to check in, just as he had every day. It had been a week since his father was released from the hospital.

"Mornin', Dad."

"Hey, son."

Maybe the traffic noise was louder today, but when his father answered the phone, his voice sounded fainter.

"How'd you sleep?" Dan asked.

"Oh…I don't know. Restless. Uh…a bit of indigestion."

Dan turned the corner and ducked into the entranceway of a clothing store to block out the blare. "Did you eat breakfast?"

"Not hungry. Waiting for my coffee."

"How about last night? What did you eat for dinner?"

"What's that?"

"Did you eat something that disagreed with your stomach?" Dan asked.

"Nah. Well, maybe it was that chowder. I don't know." His father had been complaining that the food served at the rehab center was not much better than hospital grub. But it was never a good sign when his father lost his appetite.

"Listen, Dad. I'm coming to see you after work today, so wait for me before you eat. I'll bring us something good for dinner."

"Um…let's hold off until the weekend. And I don't want you on the subway at night."

"It's not a problem, Dad. I can swing a car service. I want to see how you're doing."

His father coughed several times before saying, "As long as you're taking a taxi."

"Good. I'll see you later."

But as Dan hung up, he couldn't shake the feeling that something was wrong.

———

DAN HURRIED the final two blocks to Jingle's headquarters. He had another busy day ahead. Once upstairs, Dutch and Princess escorted him to his small conference room where Dan immediately noticed a new company poster hanging on what had previously been a bare, white wall.

"Jingle Finance: AI to Create your Financial Future." Similar posters had been showing up all over the building. Dan shook his head as he closed the door behind him. He cleared space on the table that was littered with marketing books, magazines, newspapers, case studies, and a variety of industry extracts and presentations. His marketing freelancer had wasted little time delivering what she said was "best-in-class material," all detailing the art of acquiring customers. Molly included publicly available information on real marketing campaigns— successes documented by big brands over the past five years. Thankfully, she had arranged for digitized versions. Otherwise, it would take weeks to scan all the material and convert it to machine-readable format.

"These campaigns really moved the needle," Molly had told him the previous day. She also included "mis-fires"—famous marketing flops and even lesser-known pricing scams and notorious "bait and switch" tactics.

"My professors used to say we learn not only from triumph and positive actions, but failures and actions to avoid," Molly said. "I assume it will be the same with your artificial intelligence."

"Exactly," Dan told her, impressed with how quickly she was grasping some of the basic technical concepts behind AI. He was beginning to believe she could run with the data management process on her own, allowing Dan to spend one-hundred percent of his time building Hawk's code. He hadn't done much programming on the AI platform since his meeting with Frank Braun. Still, Dan kept thinking back to Braun's comment about Milo Galini's programming skills.

"Letting him touch your AI system again will only lead to trouble," Braun had said. While Dan understood Galini's coding skills were poor, Braun's words seemed more ominous than just a warning about clunky programming.

What kind of trouble could the company founder cause?

"Good morning," Molly said as she entered the room with a single sheet of paper.

"No new books today?" he asked, smiling.

She laughed as she took off her jacket and pulled out her phone. "Today I bring podcasts." Molly handed Dan the paper, which listed titles such as "Under-standing Customer Needs," "Social Media Analytics," and "Creating A Call to Action in Marketing Campaign."

"Great," Dan said. He pointed to the door and said, "You can process everything back at your workstation."

"So you're okay with all of these?" she asked, pointing to the paper.

Dan quickly scanned the list again and was nodding his approval when a title caught his attention:

"Learn to Master Empathy When Developing Winning Campaigns."

"Empathy?" Dan said.

Molly came around and looked over Dan's shoulder. "Ah, yes. George Walid!" she said. "He's brilliant. He used to run a global advertising agency."

Dan's thoughts drifted to another time, back to his years working on CHERL, when "empathy" was one of the many personality elements instilled in Sway's AI historical subjects.

"You know," Dan said to Molly. "I can spare some time. I wouldn't mind listening to this one." Minutes later, George Walid's mellifluous voice filled the conference room.

"Empathy is a powerful and critical emotion for any good marketer to master when building a winning marketing campaign."

"Sounds like he should be a singer," Dan commented. Molly smiled and put a finger to her lips as Walid continued:

"A good marketer places themselves in their customer's shoes, deeply understands their desires, their aspirations—and their pains. Having empathy helps the marketer create communication campaigns that touch on customer needs. This is critical…"

As the advertising executive continued, Dan started to wonder if there was a way to leverage Walid's impassioned lesson. If being empathic really helped marketers improve results, would training Hawk in the art of empathy have a similar impact on Jingle's campaigns?

It might be worth a try.

Dan wasn't directly involved with CHERL's "Pod 6" team that created the empathy engine, but he knew several of their programmers, including Reilly Rogers, who was a good friend of Dan's buddy, Bobby Kang.

"A good marketeer prioritizes the customer's needs and satisfac-

tions," the Walid podcast continued. *"Connects with the customer on a deep level. Empathizes with the customers…"*

Dan stood and told Molly he'd heard enough. "I have to make a call." He stepped out and found a quiet corner down the hallway.

Reilly Rogers picked up after the first ring.

"Hi, Reilly, it's Dan Barry."

The phone was silent for a few seconds until Rogers coldly said, "Ah…hi, Dan. What's up?"

It seemed like Rogers wasn't pleased to be contacted by his tarnished former coworker. After some awkward pleasantries about moving to New York and his new job, Dan got right to the point.

"I've been researching how to train a new AI marketing system and it turns out being empathetic with customer needs may help us drive results. Are you still working with Pod 6?"

"Look, Dan," Rogers said, "I'm happy to hear you landed a full-time gig. But I shouldn't even be talking to you. I could be fired."

Dan's stomach started churning, but he knew he shouldn't be shocked at Rogers's reaction. Only Dan's *real* friends at Sway knew he hadn't done anything wrong. But this wasn't a call to correct the record or repair his own reputation. Dan cleared his throat. "I'm not asking for anything proprietary, Reilly. I'm just asking for direction if I wanted to build my own empathy engine."

"Come on. You know it took years to train CHERL with emotional intelligence. How do you expect me to explain the building process in a phone call?"

"But I don't need anything as sophisticated as CHERL. Sure, it's AI, but only for beefing up the marketing. All I'm trying to do is attract new customers."

The line was silent for a few moments until Rogers said, "Are you sure it's *only* for marketing?"

"Nothing more. And I'll be the sole client. Well,

maybe my boss and a few others, but only people inside the company."

"Well, if that's all you need, it doesn't make sense to build anything on your own. There's a start-up called EmoteAI making headway with emotional intelligence engines. Naveen considered using their product before Brodsky sent us off to build a proprietary version. I'll text you the founder's contact info."

"Awesome, Reilly. Thank you, man. I appreciate it."

"No problem." Reilly said. He let out a quick chuckle and added, "Hey, remember this when I come looking for a job."

Dan said, "I wouldn't worry. You guys at Sway are set for life."

"I don't know about that. Rumors are swirling that something big is happening. Brodsky and Naveen took the project directors offsite for some big planning session."

Dan hadn't spoken to any of his old crew from Sway in weeks. Maybe he'd call Bobby Kang later to make sure everything was okay. "I'm sure you'll be fine," Dan said. "But if anything happens, you can call on me anytime."

"Thanks. And hey, Dan. One more thing. When you call the guy at EmoteAi about his empathy engine…"

"Yeah."

"Don't tell him you got his name from me."

CHAPTER
TWENTY-SIX

FOR DAYS, Louie's stomach churned as he worried that Virtual Bank's board of directors was in hot pursuit of an outside executive to fill the CEO role. But now, after almost a week, the chairman finally returned his phone call.

"Sorry it's taken so long to get back to you, Louie," Darrell Evans said in his southern drawl. "It's been a busy time."

"I can imagine," Louie said. "Ed told me about the change you're making at the top."

"I'm aware," Evans said. "You're the only one we trusted with the news."

"Thanks," Louie said. But he was surprised that word of Chamberlain's demise hadn't already leaked. "I won't take too much of your time, Darrell. I'd like to express my strong interest in the CEO job."

"I hoped that would be the case, Louie. Ed wasn't convinced you'd want in."

Louie felt his neck muscles tighten as he responded, "I'm not sure where that came from. That's why I wanted to speak with you directly. You and I go way back, Darrell." Evans, who had run Peachtree Commerce before the merger, was Louie's former investment banking client. After the merger with Virtual Bank, Evans took on the non-executive chairman role of the combined entity.

"You know my capabilities," Louie said. "But I understand some of the other directors have some concerns."

"I won't pull any punches, Louie. The board is divided."

"If anyone doubts my leadership skills, I'd like to have a chance to convince my detractors."

Evans let out a short laugh. "Let me assure you, Louie. No one on the board questions your leadership. And you don't have detractors. Everyone is a fan. There are just some…concerns."

"Such as?"

"Well, you certainly have a great pedigree. The right schooling. Excellent experience with high-powered clients from your days with Peabody and Munson. Everyone knows you're smart. Hard working. Great instincts. We all trust you."

"Thank you, Darrell." But Louie pressed Virtual Bank's chairman. "Is the concern that I lack experience running a public company?"

"Not really," Evans said. "All the Wall Street analysts know you. They know your integrity and trust in what you say."

"Then what am I missing?"

Evans was silent for a few moments until he cleared his throat. "Well, as Ed's righthand man, some on the board believe you are tied to some of his…poor decisions."

"Seriously?" Louie suddenly felt his pulse quicken.

"For example, Louie, you've led the effort to find interesting businesses we could buy or merge with the bank. Some believe you should have been more aggressive. Pursued creative companies with talent and products to jump start the bank's growth and broaden the customer base."

Louie rubbed his eyes. "With all due respect, Darrell, I've been pushing Ed for years to consider big deals. His response was always that everything was too expensive. He worried about how *he* would look if deals didn't work out."

"Well, Louie. As CFO, you've participated in our board meetings. You could have brought your ideas to our attention."

"With my boss telling me not to?" Louie couldn't believe he was being tarred by his boss's timidity. He waited for Evans to respond but his silence was telling. Louie took a deep breath, trying to calm himself before saying any more. But after a few moments of awkward silence, Louie said, "Look, Darrell. I appreciate the candor. But as I said, I'd appreciate an opportunity to make my case to the full board."

"You'll get your day in court, Louie. I promise I'll put you in front of all the directors before any decisions are made."

"Great," Louie said. "In the meantime, what else can I do?"

"Well, you say you've been looking at deals. Ed is in no position to stand in your way. He's merely a caretaker at this stage."

Louie remembered the faraway look in Chamberlain's eyes when the CEO shared the news of his pending departure. He knew Chamberlain would be incapable of making any meaningful decisions. It would be difficult, if not impossible, for Louie to demonstrate his own effectiveness to the board with a lame-duck CEO.

Unless Ed was no longer in his way.

Louie knew Vicky might be upset. He had promised her the two of them would make this decision together. But he felt the CEO job slipping away and what he was about to propose wasn't permanent. It wasn't as if Louie was going back on his word to his wife. And while this might be a risky play, Louie thought it was worth the gamble.

"I can bring a few active deals to the board," Louie said. "But if I may ask, why are you making Ed stay around?"

"Excuse me?"

"It's not really fair to Ed," Louie continued. "Or to the team. Once the announcement is out, employees will be afraid of their own shadows, worrying about what's going to happen, wondering if they should stay aligned with Ed or start distancing themselves."

"We can hardly afford to have the seat empty while we sort this out, Louie. We can hardly—"

"You could put me in as the interim CEO," Louie said.

"Louie, I—"

"I know it's only temporary, Darrell. But why not give me a chance to earn the job? Let me show you and the board what I can do."

"We don't need a demonstration, Louie. As I said, we know your—"

"You know me as the CFO. It's different if I'm driving the train. It's different if I'm *pushing* the train." Evans was silent as Louie continued pleading his case. "I understand you will continue the search on the outside, but you know as well as I that an executive search takes time. At the end of the day, if you decide to bring someone else in, at least I'll have had my shot. Instead of just pleading my case with words, I'll be showing you with my actions."

Louie knew his play risked appearing disloyal by proposing Chamberlain be pushed out the door. But his idea *was* actually in the company's best interest. Having witnessed Ed's demeanor the past few days, Louie knew his boss had already given up the game and would be happy to collect his severance package and be on his way.

Who wanted to be a lame duck? Louie waited for Evans's response. He didn't want to badger the company's chairman, but Louie had learned from thirty years as an investment banker that if you wanted to win, you had to pursue the prize.

"Release Ed. Let him move on," Louie said firmly. "Let me take over as the interim CEO."

Evans remained quiet. But after a few moments, the VB's chairman slowly answered. "I actually like the idea, Louie. I really do." Louie pumped his fist as Evans continued, "This buys us time to make the right decision."

Louie felt his body vibrate from that familiar rush of adrenaline—the rush that used to come after a big win. "That's great, Darrell. I'll get—"

"But give me a few days to sell it to the rest of the board. In the meantime, I'd ask you to keep this conversation between the two of us. Don't even share it with Ed."

Louie grinned. "You have my word."

CHAPTER
TWENTY-SEVEN

JOSH TOSSED the hamburger on the cast-iron skillet and sprinkled more salt and black pepper over the top. The frying pan he'd bought the previous month was turning black along the edges as hot steam filled the small kitchen. He turned down the flame and opened the small window over his sink, hoping his neighbors in the trailer park wouldn't call the fire department on him again. Using a food delivery service was so much safer. But for the first time in many years, Josh didn't have much work to keep him occupied. Naveen remained sequestered with his own lieutenants, pouring through CHERL's design documents, developing a feasibility and resource analysis for Packard's recommendation. Never one to leave the hard work to his underlings, Josh wanted to be in the conference room at Sway's headquarters, sweating the details with the engineers. But Naveen had made an impassioned plea for Josh to keep his distance.

"Emotions are very raw after our planning session," Naveen told Josh. "It might be best if you let me take it from here. I promise you, I'll deliver what Andre is looking for."

Josh imagined *this* was what Jenna Turbak wanted. His boss said Naveen was ready to assume leadership of the CHERL project and something had already changed in his lieutenant. In fact, Josh wondered if Jenna had already planted a vision of the future in Naveen's head, urging Naveen to take control, to prove that Josh's services were no longer required. Well, the last thing Josh wanted to do was get in the way. So, if more leisure time was to be in Josh's future, he figured he may as well learn how to cook instead of ordering takeout every night. But he knew he'd better develop better plans than figuring out dinner.

Tonight wasn't a very promising start.

He used a fork to spear the charred patty and placed it on a roll already prepared with mustard and ketchup. But after biting into the crusty, dry, tasteless burger, he knew it was time to pull up his home delivery app. He'd try cooking again tomorrow. Josh retrieved his phone from the counter just as it started to vibrate.

He had an incoming call from his brother, Donny.

"What do you need, Donny?"

"Whoa, bro," Donny said. "Cranky already?"

"Sorry," Josh said, staring at the blackened burger. "I have things on my mind."

"Perfect timing," Donny said. "A few days in that crisp Montana air is just what the doctor ordered."

"What do you mean?"

"Our fishing weekend is coming up. Don't tell me you forgot."

"Shit," Josh said as he glanced at his phone to check the calendar.

"You're kidding me," Donny said. "Don't tell me you didn't make your flights!"

"Donny, I—"

"Hold on. Let me patch in Louie."

Josh had completely forgotten about the getaway with his two brothers. This was to be their third fly-fishing trip; an annual bonding ritual the brothers had started three years ago to sustain their renewed relationship.

"After what we went through in *that house*," Donny had said at the time. "We can't ever grow apart again."

That house was the secluded property in Menlo Park that Josh had rented three years ago and set up for a "family session" with CHERL—and their dead mother's diaries. By the time the three of them had finished interacting with CHERL's AI version of their dead mother—which Josh had "trained" with over forty volumes of her hidden diaries—artificial intelligence and the "inference engine" had uncovered family secrets they'd closeted away from each other for over thirty years.

But the CHERL session with their dead mother also served to smash the ice that had all but severed their connection as a family. Since that tumultuous engagement with AI, Josh and his brothers vowed to never let time or distance come between them again.

"Josh, are you still there?" Donny asked when he came back on the conference line.

"I'm here, Donny."

"Hey, Josh," his brother Louie said, letting out a chuckle. "I hear you forgot about the fishing trip."

"You know me with the calendar."

"But he's coming anyway," Donny said.

"Maybe we should just reschedule," Louie said.

"*What?*" Donny said loudly.

Louie said, "It's not the best weekend for—"

"We're not rescheduling, boys," Donny said. "We agreed. No excuses, especially you, Josh. I don't even want to know what you're cooking up at Sway this time."

Josh glanced over at the blackened burger on his plate and thought, Donny should only know.

"And Louie," Donny continued. "What's so important that you can't get away?"

"Well," Louie said, "I'm not supposed to say anything, but I'm waiting to hear if I'm going to be named acting CEO of the bank."

"Whoa. You're gonna be the new boss?" Donny asked.

"Interim boss for now," Louie said. "I have no idea if the board will go for it, but this really is a bad time to disappear."

"That's great news," Donny said. "Josh, did you hear that?"

Josh shifted in his seat but remained silent until he finally said, "I heard him."

"Isn't that amazing?" Donny asked.

"You'll run the whole bank?" Josh asked.

"If it works out. I'd be running the whole enchilada."

Josh rubbed his temple and said flatly, "That'd be good."

"Well, don't sound so excited," Louie said.

"I'm happy for you, Louie," Josh finally mustered. "It's just…well, I know what happened to you the last time you were in a high-pressure job."

"You sound as positive as Vicki," Louie said.

"She worries about everything," Donny said.

"Can you blame her?" Josh asked. He remembered all too well how a gambling addiction almost destroyed Louie's life.

"Geez," Louie said. "I thought I'd get a little more support from my own brothers."

"I'm behind you, Louie," Donny said. "You've come a long way. I think you're ready to handle it."

Josh realized he was being a bit hard on his youngest brother, and that his own, negative reaction might be because Jenna and Andre were pushing him out just as Louie was getting this big promotion. But Louie was still in his prime, young enough to be part of his company's future. Why shouldn't his youngest brother have the opportunity to rise.

"I'm sorry," Josh said. "I am happy for you, Louie. And I have confidence in you, too."

"I'm in a much better place, Josh. I haven't gambled on anything in over five years."

"We're very proud of you," Donny said.

"Yes, we are," Josh said. He let out a slight laugh and added, "If you get the job, maybe you can find something for me to do."

"Why?" Louie asked. "What's going on?"

Josh filled in his brothers about the conversation he'd had with Turbak and Olaf. He described the financial pressures placed on the CHERL project, the drastic cost cutting mandate, and how he might become the first victim.

"That's crazy," Louie said. "You're as vital as ever."

"Tech companies like Sway don't usually put the word 'vital' with someone who's over sixty," Josh said.

"You've got the mind of a thirty-year-old," Donny said.

"Yeah, well, if my boss gets her way, she'll be placing my thirty-year-old mind and my sixty-year-old ass in a rocking chair."

"Bullshit, Josh," Louie said. "You've got plenty left in the tank."

"Sway doesn't seem to think so."

They were quiet for a few moments. Finally, Donny said, "Listen, I hear you both, but this is the reason we promised one another to keep getting together. I'm not taking no for an answer. Besides, from the sound of it, you both need this weekend more than I do."

"What if the board calls?" Louie said.

"Yeah, and what if my team needs me?" Josh asked.

"Come on. Haven't you assholes heard of a cell phone?"

After a few moments, Louie said, "Well…we *did* promise each other."

"Exactly," Donny said. "Come on, Josh. Louie's got farther to travel coming from New Jersey. So you have no excuse. And I got us into the Madison Double R again."

Josh took a deep breath and the spectacular image of the Montana mountains entered his mind. He and his brothers had stayed at the Madison Double R Lodge on their first fly-fishing trip a few years ago. Josh loved the peace and the beauty, along with the "zen" of fly-fishing. He stared at the dried-out burger on his plate and imagined the aroma of freshly caught Montana pan-fried trout. He could sure use a few days of tranquility to clear his head and think about the future. Besides, there was nothing more for him to do until Naveen completed his work.

"Maybe this *is* a good time to get away."

CHAPTER
TWENTY-EIGHT

THE CAR SERVICE crawled past the 96th Street exit of the FDR drive. While Dan had been in traffic for almost an hour, the navigation system on the autonomous sedan indicated it would be another thirty-two minutes before he'd arrive at the Bronx rehab center. So much for the small indulgence of a car service, Dan thought. He should have taken the subway. As hard as it was to believe, he was convinced New York City traffic was worse than Highway 101 in San Francisco, the road he'd commuted on every day during his years working at Sway.

Dan was staring out the window at the glistening water of the East River when his phone buzzed. From the caller ID, Dan saw that it was Doug Choi, the founder of EmoteAi, whom Reilly Rogers had referred him to. Dan had left Choi a detailed message about the notion of contracting for the company's empathy engine.

"Customer acquisition is one application we've never tried before," Choi said after Dan explained how the Hawk AI marketing system was being engineered to attract new customers. "I'm sure we can add value. Who knows, this could open up an entirely new income stream for my company." Choi then proposed that Jingle run what he called a "champion/challenger" test.

"Have your marketing AI launch acquisition campaigns while using my empathy engine and see if EmoteAi helps," Choi explained. "Then, turn off my product and run the exact same campaigns against a similar group of prospects. Any difference in the number of customers signing up for Jingle would be attributable to my empathy engine."

"That sounds simple enough," Dan said. "How soon can I get access?"

Dan heard Choi working the keyboard as he said, "Text me your details and I'll transfer EmoteAi within the hour. It's an easy integration. You'll be up and running by tonight."

As Dan's ride turned onto Underhill Avenue and approached his father's rehab center, an ambulance was pulling away and heading in the opposite direction, sirens blaring. Dan's phone vibrated. Another caller was trying to reach him.

"That sounds good, Doug. But listen, I have to go."

Dan pressed the key to answer the incoming call.

"Mr. Barry," a breathless woman said. "This is Claudia from the Bronx Rehabilitation Center. They've just taken your father to the hospital."

————

DAN SAT SLUMPED in a chair beside the hospital bed in Columbia Presbyterian's intensive care unit. His father was sleeping, his face ashen and drawn.

"His cardiac function is very limited again," Dr. Bolan said as he flipped through his tablet. "Ejection fraction is down to twenty-four percent."

"Please, Doc. In English."

"His heart is pumping at a very limited capacity, Mr. Barry, meaning fluid is overloading his lungs."

"How did this happen again?" Dan asked.

Dr. Bolan closed his tablet but didn't look at Dan. "The new meds just masked his underlying issues. As I've told you before, congestive heart failure is unpredictable."

"Can't you increase his meds again? Or find an alternative?"

"There may be a few we can try. But it may be time to consider…another type of intervention."

Dan whispered, "Do you mean a bypass?"

Bolan shook his head and motioned for Dan to join him in the hallway. "There's nothing to bypass with cardiomyopathy."

"With—?"

"Your father has an enlarged and weakened left ventricle. In simple terms, the heart is not doing its job of pumping blood."

"Then what are we talking about here? What type of procedure?"

"The only procedure that will help is a heart transplant."

Dan's body shivered as he repeated the word. "Transplant?" His knees felt like they would buckle.

"If this is something you want to consider, we should move quickly to get him on the donor list."

"How much time would that give—?"

"With a new heart, your father could live a very long life. But as I said, we should move quickly. It takes time to find a suitable donor."

"How long?"

"Based on his severity…a few months." Bolan paused before continuing. "But it might be longer."

Dan felt his eyes watering. "I don't know. I guess…I should talk to him about it."

Dr. Bolan glanced inside the room at Dan's sleeping father. "I can come back in the morning. Hopefully he'll be able to comprehend the details."

"I'll meet you here," Dan said.

"Good."

"What happens in the meantime?" Dan asked.

"We'll do some more tests—ultrasound, CAT scan, pulmonary, just to make sure he's otherwise healthy enough for this type of surgery."

"Does he go back to rehab while he's waiting for a donor?"

"Once we've got him stabilized." The doctor hesitated, then added, "But…he may need more help than they can provide. Nurses. Aides. It may be smarter to have him in…a hospice setting. They're better equipped to—"

"He's *not* going to a hospice!" Dan said, loud enough to draw the attention of a nurse nearby. Dr. Bolan waved his hand at the nurse, letting her know he was okay. Dan wasn't sending his father to a facility where people go to die. "Can he stay here at the hospital…" Dan said, steadying his voice, "…at least until we figure things out?"

Dr. Bolan peeked into the room as if assessing his patient. "I'm sure that's possible. I'll speak with the social worker." He started to walk away before stopping. "But Dan, as I said. We should move quickly…

…he may not have a lot of time."

CHAPTER
TWENTY-NINE

DAN SAVED his latest Hawk code, completing the simple integration of Doug Choi's EmoteAi empathy engine. He closed the laptop, approached the hospital bed and gently pulled the blanket to cover his sleeping father's exposed arm. Dan was about to go down to the cafeteria and refresh his coffee when he heard the familiar mumble.

"Fancy shoes."

His father's eyes were now half-open. His hand, peeking out from underneath the blanket, seemed to be pointing at the floor. Dan followed the finger and saw it was directed at Dan's smudged running shoes.

"You need...a shine," Alec Barry whispered. Dan laughed softly at his father's joke.

"It's cheaper if I buy new kicks, Dad. How you feeling?"

"Sleepy," he said before letting out a series of raspy coughs.

Dan sat on the side of the bed, wondering whether his father had heard Dr. Bolan discussing the heart transplant the previous day. The cardiologist had promised to come by this morning to help explain, but it was already ten o'clock and the nursing station said Bolan had been called away on an emergency.

His father coughed again and asked, "What's that thing on your head?"

Dan reached up and smiled weakly as felt the Mindpath headband. "It's a new set of earphones I'm using for work." He had almost forgotten he had been using Mindpath as he created AI code from the hospital room. Dan kept it on, hoping the device would help him be more productive from his father's bedside. But given the paucity of code he'd created this morning, he wondered if anxiety was blocking the movement of his brain neurons.

"The job," his father rasped, "isn't here." He waved his arm toward the window before closing his eyes. "You should be at the office."

"Listen, Dad. Forget about work. We need to talk about—"

"Shhh." He reached over and grabbed Dan by the wrist. His grip was light, but Dan could see how much effort it took even for this small movement. They sat in silence for several moments before his father cleared his throat again. "Let me hear…about the new job."

"Dad, we should talk about your…treatment options."

His father waved his hand dismissively, then repeated, "The job." For Alec Barry, it was always about work, even now, with his health worsening by the day.

"Everything in your father's life is secondary to work," Dan had heard his mother complain more often than he could remember when he was growing up. "He cares more about his restaurants and feeding other people than spending time with his own family." But unlike his mom, Dan never blamed his father for not attending soccer games or science fairs. His father's passion actually inspired Dan as he watched him put everything he had into keeping his restaurants afloat. Besides trying to earn enough to put food on his family's table, nothing made his father happier than seeing people gather over one of his hearty meals. But the casual, mid-market eating house occupied a highly competitive space where restaurants never seemed to last more than five years. The "next best thing" always appeared down the street, putting him out of business.

But if Dan learned anything from watching his father it was resiliency. As soon as one of his restaurants shuttered, Alec Barry was fast at work creating a new concept. Yet after twenty years of marriage, Dan's mother grew tired of her absentee husband—and living on his inconsistent earnings. She filed for divorce and moved out to Phoenix as soon as Dan finished high school. Dan stopped visiting her after she remarried an accountant.

His father started coughing again. Dan could hear the whistling noise of air struggling through his lungs.

"Dad," he said, placing the laptop on the bed. He tried to control his own voice when he said, "Dr. Bolan was here yesterday."

"I know," he said, his eyes closed.

"So you heard?"

His father opened one eye and whispered, "Heard what?"

Dan didn't want to bring up the heart transplant without Dr. Bolan. But the cardiologist had said they needed to get him on the organ donor list as soon as possible. In the meantime, Dan was already starting to worry about how he would manage his father's convalescence after a transplant. "Maybe we should get you home. At least for now."

His father closed his eyes and whispered, "Bad idea," before turning his head. He coughed several times before clearing his throat. "Now you...listen to me," he rasped. "I know...the score...this isn't...any good. I—" He broke into a long series of deep, wheezing coughs.

"Take it easy, Dad. Here." Dan reached for the bed controls. "You want to sit up?"

"Leave it." He smacked his dry mouth and inhaled to catch his breath. "I know…out of options."

"There *is* an option, Dad."

"Might not…be worth it." He coughed again.

Dan used a tissue to wipe away some saliva but his father pushed his hand away, struggling to speak. "Get your ass back to work." He paused and motioned to the door. "Before you…lose job again."

Dan rubbed his father's shoulder. "I won't lose my job."

After a few more quiet moments, his dad managed to whisper, "I'll let you know my decision."

"We should get some information from Dr. Bolan."

But his father had already put his head back on the pillow. His eyes were closed when he murmured, "Back to work…I'll figure it out." Moments later, the familiar sound of snoring filled the room.

Without the cardiologist, there was little more Dan could do. He stood and grabbed his laptop and decided to head back to the office. He did have a ton of work.

But first, he would learn everything there was to know about heart transplants.

———

AS SOON AS Dan returned to his Jingle Finance conference room, he donned the Mindpath headset and paged through a myriad of medical information websites. He studied the extensive post-operative risks associated with heart transplants, including kidney dysfunction, infections, high blood pressure, and weakened bones. Even without these complications, he learned that heart transplant patients are immunocompromised for the rest of their lives, as "immune cells turn into 'double agents' that fight the patient's own healthy tissues."

His father would need to be on expensive anti-rejection drugs for the rest of his life.

The list of potential diseases was long and scary. But the web site detailing post-operative care was actually quite positive.

"Most patients are up and walking in a few days. Most leave the hospital within two weeks."

And even more hopeful, "over fifty percent of heart transplant patients live at least another ten to fifteen years, leading normal lives," many resuming vigorous, physical activity.

Why couldn't his father be part of those positive statistics? Perhaps *he* would be one of the patients to live a long, normal life. He was still relatively young, strong enough to make it through these medical obstacles.

Alec Barry was resilient! He was a fighter!

Dan felt the tension slowly ebbing away. As frightened as he was, there was good reason to be optimistic.

As long as they found a donor heart.

CHAPTER
THIRTY

"MAN, the lab's predictive tools were right, after all," Agent Dennison said.

"It's amazing," Agent Lummis said, suddenly a fan of the Quantico lab. "Their AI system has the ability to assess the probability of various medical conditions. We knew his dad would need a heart transplant before his own cardiologist."

Lucas had understood the details of Operation Turncoat since that first call with Special Agent Lummis. He comprehended the science behind the medical predictive models created in the FBI's laboratory, but he never truly believed the prediction with "ninety-eight confidence interval" that Alec Barry would require heart transplant within the next three months. In fact, Lucas assumed Special Agent Lummis would eventually pivot to an alternative method to squeeze her prey. But now, Operation Turncoat was actually going according to plan. Still, Lucas was sickened as he listened to his Lummis and his fellow FBI agents celebrating their "success."

And Lucas knew the FBI was about to throw Dan Barry and his father into an even greater tailspin.

When the debriefing ended fifteen minutes later,

Lucas walked unsteadily to the men's room. He went into a bathroom stall and locked the door…

…and he proceeded to throw up.

CHAPTER
THIRTY-ONE

LOUIE WAS ABOUT to board the United Airlines flight to Montana when he felt his cell phone vibrate. When he saw Darrell Evans's name on the screen, Louie pressed the answer tab so hard the phone fell from his hands and onto the floor.

"Shit!" He retrieved it and said, "Hello, hello! Darrell, are you still there?"

"I'm here, Louie." Evans let out a laugh. "What's that commotion in the background? Did I catch you in the middle of something?"

"No. No. I'm good." Louie watched passengers making their way onto the jetway at the Newark Airport terminal. "I'm just waiting for my plane to board."

"Oh. Where are you headed?"

"Bozeman. I'm meeting my brothers for a weekend of fishing."

"Oh, my. That sounds wonderful. I've always wanted to see Montana."

"I've done some of my best thinking out there," Louie said, making sure Evans knew that even on this short trip, Virtual Bank wouldn't be far from his thoughts.

"I'll have to give it a try," Evans drawled. "Listen, I

won't keep you. I've had a chance to confer with the board."

"Yes," Louie said, his throat suddenly parched.

"Well, we've decided to take you up on your proposal. We're going to name you acting CEO and let Ed move on."

Louie pumped his fist in the air. "Yes!" he said to himself as Evans continued. "Everyone was very impressed that you were willing to step up and take on this challenge. And to show us what you could do with the job."

Louie heard the announcement that the next group was boarding his Bozeman flight. "That's fantastic, Darrell. You won't be disappointed." Louie gathered his carry-on bag and started walking away from the gate and toward the United service counter. He wouldn't wait around to see if the flight attendants could get his checked bag off the plane. Sure Louie might not get his luggage for a few days, but the airline would eventually deliver it to his home. His brothers would have to understand his last-minute cancellation.

"Now, Louie. This doesn't mean we're handing you the permanent job."

"I realize that."

"We're still doing an outside executive search."

"As I expected," Louie said as walked past airport shops and restaurants.

"And we don't want you to make big changes while we go through this process."

"I won't do anything without the board's approval," Louie promised.

"Good."

"What did Ed say when you told him?" Louie asked.

"I haven't spoken to him yet," Evans said. Louie stopped walking to make sure he clearly understood. "I'm having dinner with Ed on Sunday night to break the news."

"Oh," Louie said. "I was going to head to the office."

"I thought you were flying to Montana."

"I was," Louie said. "But I thought the management team would want to meet as soon as they heard."

"Hold on, Louie," Evans said. "Nobody at VB will know about Ed until Monday at the earliest. When were you returning from Montana?"

"Monday."

"See, that works out just fine. There's no need to change your plans. I think it would be better if you stayed away from the office until after I've had my dinner meeting with Ed."

Louie turned around and looked at the Bozeman departure gate in the distance. It seemed there was nothing for him to do until Monday.

He might as well enjoy the weekend before going home and dealing with the shitstorm his wife was sure to kick up.

———

JOSH FOUND a quiet spot at the United lounge at San Francisco Airport and dialed Naveen. His flight was leaving for Bozeman within the hour and he wanted one last update from his project director. Naveen and his team leaders had been working around the clock to strip the AI of personality elements, delivering what was now dubbed "CHERL Version 2"—the industry prototype.

"What's the latest?" Josh asked.

"Packard was right about the reduced resources, mon," Naveen said. "We melded three historic business leaders from the oil and gas industry, creating a single energy expert. And we were able to accomplish this feat with less than fifteen percent of my core engineers."

So it was true. The vast majority of CHERL's resources *were* expended on recreating individual personalities.

"What is V2 like?" Josh asked.

"We've only executed a few tests. But so far, the expertise seems to be intact. The management knowledge. The business proficiency. Everything checks out. But Josh, it's a bland experience, for sure. The responses are very flat. It will take some getting used to. Extracting the personality makes V2 sound very robotic. She just spits out the facts."

"Just the facts," Josh repeated to himself. Just like Officer Friday.

"Do you sense V2 has lost any substance?"

"No, Josh, I don't. But that's only in the lab. We won't know until—"

"I know," Josh interrupted. "We won't know until we field live tests with real clients."

"Exactly."

"But if this does work," Josh said, "how much money do you think we'd wring out?"

"I'll need a few days to crunch some numbers."

"Attention all passengers on United flight 2376 to Bozeman. We will begin boarding with group four. Please line—"

"Just give me a rough estimate, Naveen. I'm about to board."

"All right, but don't hold me to this. Conservatively, I think we can deliver V2 for about one-third of our current cost structure."

"Does that include the avatar?" Josh asked. "Like the one I used to visualize Officer Friday?"

"Maybe add in an additional headcount or two," Naveen said. "If you think the avatar is necessary."

"I think the visualization might help offset the lack of personality," Josh said.

"Then consider it done, boss."

Josh rubbed his temple as a crowd formed around the departure gate. Naveen's estimate far exceeded what Andre had asked for, which meant that after adding a sizable profit margin, the price for CHERL could be dramatically lowered for small and middle-market companies. And even if CHERL was no longer…personable, Josh remembered the incremental benefit the Packard version of CHERL had predicted.

"Clients might be less prone to blindly accepting what CHERL suggests. CEOs will be more likely to debate and challenge the AI's advice—unencumbered by the powerful personality of their heroes."

Which meant CHERL V2 might be used as it was intended—not stepping in the shoes of the decision maker, but as a true adviser. Conceptually, this all made sense. But as Naveen said, in practice, there was only one way to find out if V2 would be effective.

"I've got to go," Josh said as he grabbed his carry-on bag. "How long will it take to develop industry experts and stand up a few pilot programs?"

"Once you tell me the industries, I'll only need a few days." Before Josh disconnected Naveen added, "You better start lining up some test clients."

CHAPTER
THIRTY-TWO

"SO YOU TOLD Dr. Bolan you'd do it," Dan said into the conference room speakerphone.

"He didn't leave me much choice," his father responded. "Doc was pretty clear I'll be dead in another year without a new ticker."

Dan had spoken with the cardiologist the previous evening and told him that despite all the statistics and analysis, his father hadn't agreed to undergo a heart transplant. Bolan promised to be very direct with his patient during this morning's rounds.

It seemed that the message had finally sunk in.

"This is the right decision, Dad. I want you to be around for a long time."

"It doesn't seem like anything's gonna happen so fast, Dan. Doc said it could take months for a matching heart to show."

"You never know." Maybe his father would get lucky. Dan's phone vibrated and he saw that the hospital was calling.

"I have to go, Dad. I'll see you tonight." Dan switched to the incoming call.

"This is Dan," he said.

"Good morning," an official-sounding woman said.

"This is Shirley Handley from the Patient Estimate Team at Columbia Presbyterian Hospital."

"Ah, Miss Handley. Thank you for returning my call."

"What can I do for you?"

"I'm calling about my father, Alec Barry. He needs a heart transplant, and I was hoping to understand his insurance coverage and get a sense of his out-of-pocket costs."

"Certainly," Handley said. Dan heard her keyboard clacking in the background. "Can you spell his last name, please?"

"B-A-R-R-Y."

More rapid clicking as she said, "I see Mr. Barry has a policy with Capital Health Insurance?"

"That's correct," Dan said.

Handley asked him to authenticate several other pieces of information—insurance ID, social security number, date of birth. For what seemed like several minutes, Dan listened to the sound of Handley's fingers pressing the computer keys, until finally, she said, "I see you have his health care proxy and power of attorney."

"I do," Dan said. He and his father had done the paperwork when Dan first moved back from the West Coast.

The clicking noise stopped and Handley said, "Er...I need to check on something. May I place you on hold?"

"Sure."

When she came back a few moments later, she said, "Mr. Barry. I just confirmed the information I have from the insurance company."

"Good," Dan said. "Can you tell me a ballpark figure of what to expect?"

"I'm afraid you don't understand. I just spoke with the Capital Insurance and confirmed the information in my system..."

"...Alec Barry's health insurance coverage has been terminated."

————

DAN SPENT the next three hours in a complete state of panic as he escalated calls with dozens of Capital Health personnel. He was bounced around from one representative to another; battled with five different supervisors and three separate managers. Not a single employee could provide an explanation for his father's health insurance cancellation. Dan finally located the contact information for the company's legal representative, Hernan Marshall.

"An audit of your father's initial application uncovered several...red flags," Marshall explained.

"What kind of red flags?"

"I'm afraid I cannot disclose that information."

"But I have his power of attorney!"

"It's not about your POA," Marshall said. "We're not allowed to provide more specifics other than the application triggered a potential fraud violation."

"Fraud?" Dan snapped. "You can't be serious! My father is the most honest person I know! And he's been in the hospital with a bad heart. How has he committed a fraud?"

"I'm sorry, Mr. Barry. I'm very sorry to hear about your father. But this...is out of our hands."

Dan had had enough. "Let's see what you say after I finish speaking with the health department, the New York State insurance commissioner, the Attorney General and anyone else that will listen." Dan hung up and placed his head in his hands. He absently pushed the neuron reading device off his scalp. He felt as if the room was spinning. How could this be happening? What could his father have possibly done to trigger a fraud alert? But even if Dan filed a complaint with every single insurance and financial industry regulator, he knew responses could take months...

Time his father didn't have.

"The expenses for this type of procedure can run upward of several hundred thousand dollars..." Mrs. Handley from the Hospital's Patient Estimate Team had told him earlier. "...and that doesn't include the post-operative immunosuppressant medications that could double those costs."

This was lunacy! His father didn't have that kind of money. And all Dan had was the five thousand unvested shares Milo Galini had given him in Jingle Finance. He looked up and saw the Jingle Finance poster hanging on the conference room wall.

JINGLE FINANCE: **AI to Create your Financial Future.**

HE REMEMBERED what Galini had said to him on the day of his interview.

"You should keep your Jingle account activated. You never know when our AI can help you escape from a personal financial crisis."

Maybe it was time for Dan to seek out some expert advice.

CHAPTER
THIRTY-THREE

JOSH PULLED his line through the glistening water and watched the trout swarming around his bait. He heard a splash and turned to see Donny's rod bowing as his brother struggled with a catch that was dragging his lure downriver.

"I got a big one," Donny shouted.

Josh waded back to shore to retrieve the lodge-supplied fishing net before moving toward Donny's position. "Don't yank it," Louie called out. "Let the hook set in."

"It's set, it's set!" Donny said. Josh watched as Donny muscled the rod and slowly reeled in the trophy until the pink lateral line of the rainbow trout broke through the surface. Josh moved the net into position and captured his brother's fifth catch of the morning.

"You were right, Josh." Donny smiled. "That *is* a good spot."

This was the Brodsky brothers' second fishing trip in the past three years and by far, their most productive. They had initially tried other activity-based excursions for their bonding time, like attending the College World Series in Omaha, which was Donny's idea. But Josh became so bored after the third inning that he threatened to cut the weekend short and drive himself back to California. The following summer Josh suggested and enjoyed a hiking weekend in the Grand Tetons. Ironically, it was Donny—the former high school star athlete—who lobbied for future trips to feature more sedentary pursuits. The angling idea was born after they'd all enjoyed a two-hour fly-fishing lesson on the final day of their Grand Tetons trip. Still, the struggle to agree on an activity they could all enjoy reminded Josh of how different the brothers were from one another.

Louie, the youngest, was the only one who had experienced anything close to a traditional family life. In fact, at the time the three brothers gathered at that Menlo Park house for the AI session with their dead mother, Louie appeared to have it all. Donny, on the other hand, had never shared the same drive and motivation as his two brothers. After two divorces and a series of failed business ventures, his middle brother seemed content to live on his own. And while Donny never found a lucrative calling, at least he'd settled into a steady job as a teacher. He had helped many young adults make career transitions into the world of technology.

As for Josh, well, life hadn't changed much since "having it out" with his mother's AI re-creation in Menlo Park. Never married, life had always been about fulfilling his mission, the same as it was when he'd worked at the Department of Defense integrating artificial intelligence into the US military. But now, as Josh stood on the riverbank and stared blankly into the glistening stream, he tried to imagine a future without Sway. A future without a mission. But Josh saw nothing but emptiness.

———

"I CAN'T BELIEVE Sway is trying to force you out," Donny said over turkey sandwiches prepared by the lodge. They sat on oversized boulders along the shoreline as Josh filled them in.

"They call it retirement, Donny," Louie said.

"Whatever," Donny said. "Call it what you want. They're nuts. Joshie's still the smartest guy we know."

"I'm afraid being smart has nothing to do with it," Josh said. "They've decided to make room for the next group of smart guys."

"Who make a lot less money," Louie added.

Josh stared into the glistening river, not surprised that Louie would understand the business realities.

"It's probably my fault," Donny said as he picked up a fist full of pebbles and tossed them at the water. "If only I hadn't sent that stupid business plan."

Donny had repeated his apology a thousand times over the past few years. But Josh's brother had been interviewed repeatedly by the FBI, who concluded that Donny never knew the email passed to him by his beautiful coding school classmate contained both ransomware and a keystroke logger. The digitized logger recorded and secretly transmitted the scope of Josh's CHERL project to Russian hackers—setting in motion the plot for Nicole Ryder's impersonator to infiltrate Sway.

"It wasn't your fault, Donny," Josh said reflexively. "And don't worry. I think Sway will keep me hanging around long enough to evaluate these new versions of CHERL. And until my boss is sure Naveen can deliver."

"Will that be enough to keep you busy?" Donny asked.

"Probably not," Josh said as he tossed the crumpled-up sandwich wrapper into the freezer bag. "I'll have to think of something else."

But there actually was a project Josh had already been contemplating. Andre Olaf told Josh to shut down Officer Friday, the AI sleuth designed to help locate Alina Petrova. Sway's CEO labeled the project as a "distraction"—a resource drain. But why couldn't Josh finish

Officer Friday on his own? The coding work had been largely completed. He wouldn't need to call upon any of Naveen's resources. Josh was more than capable of researching new material to refine and update the files used to train his AI. Weeks ago, Special Agent Lucas Foley had called, asking if Josh had made any progress with the AI sleuth. Because of Olaf's dictate, Josh informed the FBI agent that Sway was no longer working on the investigator version of CHERL.

Maybe it wasn't too late for Officer Friday to help. He would contact Agent Foley on Monday.

"I might be right behind you," Louie said as he discarded his sandwich wrapper.

"What do you mean?" Josh said.

"Yeah, you just got this big job," Donny added.

"Big *interim* job," Louie said. "What if they decide I can't cut it?" He picked up his fishing rod, walked to the riverbank and used an overhead cast to throw his line into the water. "What if the board decides to hire from the outside? What if they think I'm no good?"

"Come on, Louie," Josh said, joining Louie at the riverbank. He began tying a new fly to the end of his line. "You've always been great at your work."

"That's right," Donny said. "Even when you were all messed up."

"Yeah, but this is different," Louie said. "I've never had to actually manage a public company before."

"Why don't you bring in all those advisers and investment bankers you used to work with?" Donny asked.

Louie shook his head. "I don't trust those scumbags."

Donny let out a short laugh and said, "You used to *be* one of those scumbags."

Louie smiled. "That's why I don't trust them."

They all laughed as Josh moved deeper into the river, feeling the cold water through his waders. Josh reeled in his line and was about to cast the fly again when Donny said, "You know, Josh. Why don't you let Louie try out your new CHERL contraption?"

Josh looked over his shoulder at Donny, who was pulling his line through the water and the swarming trout. "Why not help Louie out and let him use your new CHERL version?" Donny nodded toward Louie. "You help him make his mark and Sway gets a real-life test."

Josh exchanged looks with Louie, until he shook his head and turned his attention back to his rod. But his mind was already racing with the notion.

"What do I know?" Donny continued. "But it seems like a match made in heaven."

"Has the board told you what success looks like?" Josh asked, staring at the fly at the end of his line.

"Not yet," Louie said as he pulled on his rod. "The chairman told me not to make any big changes, but I know they want growth. Top line and bottom-line growth."

Josh heard a splash and turned to see Donny's line bowing as he struggled with yet another trout dragging his line downriver.

"I got another big one!" Donny shouted.

———

FIFTEEN TROUT LATER, the brothers were still casting their lines in silence, albeit with a lot less enthusiasm than when they'd started. But Josh had been thinking about Donny's idea for the past two hours.

"It would have to be a test," Josh finally said.

"Do you have a version for the banking industry?" Louie instantly asked. The interim CEO of Virtual Bank had obviously been doing some thinking of his own.

"We don't have anything yet," Josh said. "But given it took a few days for the team to build the first prototype, I imagine we could have something up and running for you relatively quickly."

"This would be off the grid, right?" Louie asked. "Sway couldn't disclose my involvement unless I gave my approval. I don't want anyone at Virtual Bank knowing I consulted with artificial intelligence to run the company."

"All we need are the diagnostics to measure effectiveness," Josh said. "And, obviously, your feedback about your interactions."

"And one last thing," Louie said as he nodded toward Donny. "Are you absolutely sure what happened to Donny can't happen again?" He waded toward Josh and added, "I need your word, Josh, that there's zero risk of another hack."

"I can take you through everything Sway has done to tighten up security," Josh said.

Donny sloshed out of the water and joined his brothers on the shoreline. He put a hand on each of their shoulders as his face broke into a broad smile.

"So it's all settled!" He beamed.

CHAPTER
THIRTY-FOUR

DAN BOUGHT a fresh cup of coffee and walked down Seventh Avenue, trying to calm his nerves. He couldn't believe the corrupt bureaucrats working at Capital Health. They acted like Dan was trying to steal their money...instead of trying to save his father's life!

He returned to his conference room at Jingle Finance, and as he had done for the past few days and weeks, he placed the neuron sensing device back on his head. He needed all the help he could get.

Because if he didn't come up with a viable financing plan soon, his father might die.

Dan wished there was a way to recoup the equity he'd had in Sway before he was forced to leave the Silicon Valley company. But all of it had been stripped away when he was unceremoniously shown the exit. Sure, Milo Galini had awarded him equity that one day could be worth thousands of dollars. But Dan wouldn't be able to monetize the value until his stock vested in another four years.

There had to be another way.

Dan sat in front of his computer and signed into his Jingle Finance account. He updated his financial information with his current salary. Bypassing Jingle's gamification module, the Mindpath device sensed where Dan wanted to navigate.

The "Jingle Interactive Advice" module appeared on his screen.

"I need access to money," Dan thought.

"Do you have a specific purpose?" a calm, professional male voice responded.

"My father needs a heart transplant."

"Medical expenses are typically the greatest causes of financial hardship," the system responded, before presenting a new screen where Dan was asked to enter his father's current finances—monthly pension, social security, savings account balance, along with an itemization of monthly expenses. Dan left the "investments" section blank, except for noting forty-eight thousand dollars in his father's savings account.

"Can you provide me the name of his health insurance provider?"

"It *was* Capital Health," Dan responded as the neuron device translated his father's insurance ID into the system.

Within seconds, Jingle replied:

"I see that Alec Barry's coverage is no longer active."

"That's what Capital Healthy told me, too." Dan didn't mention anything about the fraud accusation.

"The average cost of a heart transplant in the United States is $250,000. This does not include the cost of post-operative, anti-rejection medication, which can also run to several hundred thousand dollars."

"I'm aware," Dan said.

"How old is your father?"

"Fifty-seven."

"Alec Barry is still eight years away from being eligible for Medicare."

So far, Jingle Finance's engagement engine wasn't telling Dan anything he didn't know.

"You are employed at Jingle Finance."

"Yes. I started a few weeks ago."

"Is your position stable?"

"I hope so," Dan said. "In fact, I am the AI engineer responsible for helping our company grow."

"Please clarify."

Dan described his current job responsibilities at Jingle. The system was momentarily silent before proceeding, asking Dan to reconfirm his salary.

"Do you have other sources of income like dividends or annuities?"

"No," Dan answered.

Jingle then gathered details on both Dan's and his father's expenses. Estimates for groceries, entertainment, travel, insurance. Again, Mindpath helped Dan complete the answers quickly.

"Do you own a home?"

"No."

"A car?"

"No."

"Anyone that would co-sign on a personal loan?"

Dan shrugged. "Doubtful."

"Stocks or bonds?"

"Not anymore," Dan said sadly. "I had restricted stock in my last company, but I had to forfeit them when I left." Dan shook his head when Jingle proceeded to "educate" him on the value of staying with a company long enough to reap the benefits of stock awards. When Jingle paused, Dan offered, "I did receive some stock when I joined Jingle."

"How many shares?"

"5,000."

The system paused for a few moments before resuming. *"Based on the most recent external valuation models, your shares are worth $100,000."*

Dan scratched his head. How did the system know the value of a private company?

"You may be able to open a line of credit using your Jingle stock as collateral."

Dan sat up straight and asked, "Even unvested stock in a private company?"

"While not common, there is one unconventional finance company, PEAT Lending, that will advance funds against the value of private company shares."

"Really?" Dan cleared his throat. "How much can I borrow?"

"We can apply to find out." The screen went momentarily gray. But seconds later, a new page appeared. At the top, in bright blue letters, were the words "PEAT Lending."

"I have presented you with PEAT's application page, which I have taken the liberty to complete on your behalf. Please verify the information and hit the apply tab."

Surprisingly, it took less than thirty seconds for Jingle to return an answer:

"Confirming PEAT will provide line of credit up to $75,000."

Seventy-five thousand dollars was not anywhere close to what his father needed, but it was a start. Suddenly, as if reading his thoughts, the Jingle system said, *"There is a way for Dan Barry to impact the size of the loan."*

Dan leaned forward as Jingle continued. *"Your position as the AI developer of Hawk places you in position to increase the number of Jingle customers. According to external valuation models, Jingle Finance's company valuation is directly correlated to the number of users. If Dan Barry successfully increases customer base, Jingle's valuation should rise, and PEAT would increase the size of your credit line."*

Dan shifted in his seat. "How many more new customers do I need to produce?"

"I do not have access to that equation. But parameters have been set within PEAT to text Dan Barry with messages each time the valuation—and the amount of the credit line—goes up or down."

Dan shook his head. Even if Jingle could provide an

answer, it wasn't as if the Hawk marketing platform was ready to jumpstart the account base. Sure, Dan had made improvements to Hawk's code. And Molly had updated the quality and quantity of marketing "best practices" that trained the new AI. While the refreshed data and the improved code might generate some new accounts, would that be enough to positively impact Jingle's valuation?

There was only one way to find out. He might be clinging to unrealistic hope, but hope was all he had.

At this point, Dan was willing to try anything.

CHAPTER
THIRTY-FIVE

LOUIE SAT behind the distinguished oak desk formerly used by Ed Chamberlain. He absently fingered the lock on the computer case perched atop the credenza as the pungent smell of wood polish wafted through the air. The weekend maintenance crew had wiped and shined all the elegant but classically designed furniture. Unfortunately, the fixed windows prevented Louie from airing out his temporary office. He swiveled the leather chair around and glanced at the blank wall above the credenza. Missing were the framed photographs and award certificates Chamberlain had accumulated over the past three years. The credenza was cleared of plaques and golf tournament memorabilia from his predecessor's brief reign atop the bank. Louie decided to wait a few days before bringing his own personal items into the space where he had just conducted his first staff meeting as interim CEO. After all, why appear presumptuous on his first day, and in front of functional and business directors he had just asked to rally around his leadership?

"I'm not planning any major changes," Louie had committed to the people who just a day earlier had been his peers. The same promise he had made to his wife.

"Interim CEO is just the first step into hell," Vicki

had said the previous evening, visibly upset when he broke the news upon his return from the Montana fly-fishing trip. "I thought you weren't going to accept the job without talking to me first."

"It's not the permanent role, Vic. They asked me to step in and keep the place running while they decide what to do." Louie chose not to further inflame his volatile wife by telling her the interim role was *his* proposal. The way Louie saw it, why did it matter whose idea it was. "The board still plans to conduct an external search," he assured her. "I promised you. If I'm offered the permanent job, you and I will sit down and discuss it. I won't do any—"

"Don't make any more promises," Vicki said. "I know you'll take this on like the job is already yours. Interim or not, you can still spiral into your gambling chaos again."

"Come on, Vic. You know you have nothing to worry about. You see all of our accounts. You know where all of our money is. If I started gambling again, I couldn't hide it from you if I tried."

Giving Vicki complete access to each of their bank and investment accounts was one of the actions they'd put in place after he lost all their money. Every financial institution sent Vicki an automated text alert if so much as a single dollar was moved.

"You're a finance whiz, Louie. If you really wanted to, I'm sure you could figure something out."

"So you don't trust me. That's what this all comes down to."

"I want to trust you," Vicki said. "But you put me through hell once, and I'm not visiting that place again."

At least his wife no longer pressed him to spell out his "compelling reason" for wanting the CEO job. If she had, he couldn't share his desire to compete again—his desire to feel what it was like to win again. Because using words like "competing" and "winning" around Vicki would only confirm her fears. Instead, Louie was confident that by the time the board made its decision, Vicki would see how well he was handling the pressure and responsibility. She would come around to supporting him once she saw how he was energized, under control, and calmly managing the bank.

But the truth was, Louie knew that to lock down the permanent job, "calm" and "under control" might not be enough. He might have to do something bigger than run a steady ship.

He would have to do something bold.

He snapped open the computer case sitting atop the credenza, removed the laptop his brother Josh had shipped from California, and hit the start key.

———

THE USE of AI was widespread throughout the financial services industry, creating everything from financial statements and legal briefs to customer correspondence and marketing campaigns. Louie knew that VB's commercial sales team sent out business proposals created by AI. More than half the software powering VB's back office was developed by AI.

But artificial intelligence in the C-suite? Could AI replicate an executive's decision-making? Could AI mimic a senior executive's intuition, critical thinking, or strategic vision? AI certainly couldn't be used to motivate and lead a team?

"The device is completely secure," Josh had emailed him. "This industry version of CHERL is an expert in the banking sector. Consider this an executive adviser. As I explained, what we refer to as V2 lacks the personality aspects we experienced together."

Louie shuddered every time he remembered *the personality* displayed by Josh's CHERL system "three years ago," which his oldest brother had trained with their dead mother's diaries. Digging through family skeletons with his brothers in that Menlo Park house, Louie had had to continually remind himself that CHERL wasn't real.

But as far as Louie was concerned, as real as CHERL had seemed at the time, that version of Josh's AI was nothing more than an interpreter, proving artificial intelligence could help explain the past. But in that session with his brothers, Louie hadn't experienced CHERL as a decision-maker or as an adviser.

But as soon as the sophisticated looking female avatar appeared on the screen of Josh's laptop, Louie knew this model of CHERL would be different.

"Where would you like to start?" Her short auburn hair framed an attractive face that exuded confidence. The avatar was adorned with a tailored charcoal-gray jacket over an ivory silk blouse. When she spoke, her voice was firm and so authoritative, that Louie felt like he had little choice but to put his phone away and pay close attention to her every word.

"Please. Call me Louie."

"My name is Rona."

"Rona," Louie repeated. He brought the laptop closer. "What do you know about Virtual Bank so far?"

"Dr. Brodsky has provided publicly available information about Virtual Bank and its competitors. I am trained with the bank's history, the merger with Peachtree, the departure of your CEO. While I have performed a strategic assessment of the competitive landscape and VB's positioning and gaps, my analysis is limited given I did not have access to VB's confidential, internal information. But I have utilized the profiles of Virtual Bank's leadership team and the background and decisions of Virtual Bank's board of directors."

"Wow," Louie said. Had Josh's system really completed a strategic assessment of the bank and the leadership team?

"If that's the case...Rona, I assume you've been told I'm the interim CEO of the bank."

"Correct."

Louie sat up straight. "I can fill in any gaps in your knowledge base about our internal plans and performance." He leaned forward. "But I'm looking to make a big and strategic move. Big and bold enough to convince VB's board to remove the word 'interim' from my title."

"To be named to the permanent role, you need to demonstrate your competence as a leader. Given your background as an investment banker and gaps in VB's existing business portfolio, it is clear what you need to do."

CHAPTER
THIRTY-SIX

DAN ARRANGED with Dr. Bolan to have his father transferred back to the Bronx rehab facility, where he would stay until a donor heart was identified. The rehab center was less expensive than sending his father home, where he would need around-the-clock assistance. And Dan wanted to save as much money as he could.

He had assured the hospital's Patient Estimation Team that his father's lack of insurance was no obstacle —he had more than enough money to cover the heart transplant and hospitalization. But the truth was, Dan had identified only a fraction of the money the hospital required to proceed with the transplant.

He'd have to come up with the rest before a donor heart arrived.

"How you feeling today, Dad?" Dan asked during a mid-afternoon check-in call he had placed from the Jingle conference room.

"Peachy," his father said over the beeping sound of the hospital's heart monitor. "Why are you calling again during your workday?"

"I just wanted to hear your voice. Are you out of bed?"

"I did three laps around the rehab center this morning. It felt good to move my legs."

"That's great, Dad. Just don't overdo it."

"Doc told me to stay active."

"I know. But he didn't say you should train for the marathon."

His father let out a soft chuckle. "What are you up to?"

Dan pressed the speaker button on his cell phone, placed it on the table, and stared at a particularly complex portion of Hawk code he was trying to rewrite. "Working. What else would I be doing."

"You should get back to it."

"I will," Dan said. "But I needed a break." The fact was, since he started using the Mindpath neuron transmitting device, Dan's brain never stopped working, even when speaking with his dad. He had become so accustomed to the headband that it seemed he could conceptualize new AI code in one part of his brain while engaging in light banter with his father from another. As long as they didn't veer off from superficial topics like the weather ("It's a little chilly"), sports ("Rangers lost again") or old movies ("*Shawshank* was on the other night"), Dan's enhancements to Hawk continued to materialize. He laughed to himself that if he wasn't disciplined with his thoughts and conversations while using Mindpath, the Hawk artificial intelligence system might end up understanding more about Dan's life than any "real" person, including his dad.

"How *is* the job?" his father asked.

"It's challenging. I guess I'm enjoying it." But if truth be told, Dan found it impossible to enjoy anything, knowing his father might die before a matching heart materialized.

"Any worthwhile news on cable this morning?" Dan asked his father absently as he checked on one of Hawk's subroutines. But instead of rattling off today's headlines, his father blurted out, "Listen, son. I was going to talk to you about this tonight. I think we should call this whole thing off."

The code stopped populating Dan's subroutine as his attention shifted solely onto his father. "What's going on? Are you feeling pain in your chest?" But Dan could only hear a muffled sobbing sound coming through the phone.

Dan stood and said, "I'm coming to see you."

"No!" his father shouted before blowing his nose. "You don't need to come here. I...we can talk about this later."

Dan slowly lowered himself back into his chair. "What happened?"

"Nothing happened. It's just...well..." He paused again before saying, "I know I'm running out of time."

"You have to stay positive, Dad. A heart will come." Dr. Bolan had warned that his father's mood would ebb and flow from one day to the next.

"Stay positive?" His father's voice cracked. "I'm sitting here waiting for someone to die!"

"I know. But people die all the time."

"And what if I don't survive the surgery?"

"I showed you the success rates, Dad. You're going to live a long time."

"Or I could die the next day."

He had to get his father to simmer down. But Dan could hear the accelerating tones coming from the heart monitor as his father said, "And I don't want you to go into hock for this."

"I'm not."

"Heart transplants cost a small fortune!" his father said. Dan wondered how much research his father had done on his own. "I don't have that kind of money. And you're not responsible for this."

"It's okay," Dan lied. "I've been talking to the insurance company and the hospital. They're going to work with us." Dan still couldn't bring himself to tell his father about the terminated medical insurance.

"You should let me go…"

"Dad!" Dan shouted. "Stop this!" He heard his father's labored breathing. After a few moments, Dan said, "I didn't mean to yell at you."

"I've heard worse."

"It's going to work out," Dan promised.

The line was silent except for the muffled sound of his father's labored breath. A few moments later, Dan heard him say, "I'm okay. I don't want you to worry about me."

"I won't, Dad. I'll be there tonight. We can talk then."

"I'll be here."

———

DAN SPENT the next few hours running tests of the communication link between Hawk and the EmoteAi. He had no way of knowing for sure if the empathy engine would make Jingle's marketing campaigns more effective. But at this point, Dan was so desperate, he decided to pursue every angle. Because according to his engagement session with Jingle, every new account added by Hawk might increase the company's valuation—and increase the amount Dan could borrow from PEAT. So however limited Hawk's functionality might be, Dan wanted to get a version operating in the marketplace as soon as possible.

At five o'clock, Dan brought Molly down to the conference room.

"Can you stay late tonight again?" he asked her. "I'd like you to upload those successful campaigns we received from the Advertising Institute."

Molly took a seat across from Dan and said, "You've been driving me very hard the past few days." She leaned forward and gently asked, "What's going on?" Molly didn't appear to be angry. Her expression was soft, concerned. It was true, Dan *had* been driving her hard. His marketing freelancer knew Dan's father had been in and out of the hospital, but beyond that, he hadn't shared much.

"You're right," Dan said. "You deserve an explanation."

Dan proceeded to tell Molly everything. He told her about the heart transplant and the uncertainty of the timing as his father waited on the donor list. He told her about the insurance company and the terminated health coverage. And Dan described the enormity of the medical bills he and his father now faced.

Molly asked, "Do you have relatives that could pitch in?"

Dan shook his head. He knew his mother was in no position to help.

"What about friends?" She leaned forward. "Or somebody close to you that has the ability to…assist."

Dan's voice cracked as he said, "I can't think of anyone." He wiped away a tear running down his right cheek. And then he proceeded to tell her about his engagement session with Jingle, and how the AI financial adviser set up an application for a line of credit against the value of his stock in the company.

And how incremental customer accounts could increase the amount of his credit line.

"That's why I've been pushing." Dan leaned forward. "I know it's crazy. I know it's a long shot, but Hawk is the only thing I've got any control over."

"Do you think we're ready?" Molly asked.

"Look, I know Hawk won't be perfect, but the marketing campaign generator is in much better shape than when we started, especially with all your updated data sources."

"How many accounts do you think we need to move Jingle's valuation?"

"I don't know," Dan said. "But I want to find out."

They sat quietly as Molly stared up at the ceiling, seeming to ponder Dan's dilemma. Dan had just turned his attention back to his AI code when Molly said, "What if you used Frank Braun's account generator model."

Dan looked up.

"You know," she continued. "The model he used to create dummy customer accounts for stress testing. Remember, I loaded it into Hawk's training data? Braun said his dummy accounts looked and acted like real customers. We could create a volume of trial accounts on our own."

Dan stared at the marketing freelancer as he asked, "Why would we do that?"

"To test Jingle's theory about increasing the value of the company. To measure the impact more accounts would have on Jingle's valuation and your line of credit."

Dan pushed away from the table. "Are you suggesting we load Jingle with phony accounts?"

"They'll only be phony until we replace them."

"Now you've lost me."

"Look," she said. "It's not as if Hawk won't eventually bring in *real* customers. Once our AI is ready, I'm sure Hawk's marketing campaigns will easily replace trial accounts with actual customers."

Dan's mouth opened but no words emerged as Molly continued with her wild idea. "You'd be borrowing customers from the future, just like PEAT is letting you borrow money from Jingle's future value." She shrugged and added, "What's really the difference?"

Dan shook his head and stared at Molly. What she was suggesting was sheer lunacy. Up until now, Dan thought the marketing contractor was level-headed— both smart and professional. But as Dan looked at the woman sitting on the opposite side of the table, he wondered if he had misjudged her or…

Suddenly, Dan felt like the Mindpath device was pressing on the sides of his skull. He swiped the metal object from his head, trying to relieve the pressure.

Was it possible Molly was sent by the same people that had sent Nicole Ryder? Was she trying to sweep Dan into another financial scheme?

Was Molly another Russian plant?

"Are you all right?" Molly asked. "Can I get you something cold to drink?"

"No. I'm okay." He swallowed hard as a smile appeared on Molly's face. "You know I was just kidding," she said. "About creating the dummy accounts."

"Of course," Dan said as he forced himself to match her smile.

"Forget I even said it," Molly said as she stood. "It was a dumb idea. I'll get all the Advertising Institute data loaded tonight. I promise. We can run Hawk whenever you're ready. I'm sure anything will be better than what Jingle is using today."

Dan stood and said, "That's great." He wiped his sweaty palms on his jeans. "I really do appreciate all your hard work."

As soon as Molly walked from his conference room, Dan put the Mindpath device on and tried to concentrate, but he couldn't stop thinking about what just happened. Even if Molly wasn't a Russian plant, how could Dan retain someone who suggested such a crazy notion—a crazy, illegal scheme! How could he trust her? Yet, Dan could ill afford to lose the marketing expert if he was going to finish Hawk and start launching legitimate account acquisition campaigns.

But he had to do something. Dan had to protect himself. He had to protect Jingle.

He signed into Hawk's training database. A few keystrokes later, the model used for creating test accounts was secured by multiple, encrypted passwords—security only a super hacker could defeat. But as Dan thought back to how Nicole Ryder altered data to manipulate the CHERL system all those years ago, he knew passwords might not be sufficient.

So from now on, Dan would examine everything Molly did.

CHAPTER
THIRTY-SEVEN

LUCAS SHIFTED in his seat in the video conference room, trying to think of the right words to make his point to Special Agent Lummis. While he remembered Domingo Compo prescient comment from the initial Operation Turncoat meeting that "things could get messy," this operation was getting a lot more than messy.

"She came on too strong," Lucas said. "That was a very aggressive move."

"Once again, Agent Foley," Lummis responded. "I disagree. She saw Barry was vulnerable and floated an idea."

"By pushing him to commit a fraud?" Lucas said. "How's that not entrapment?"

"She didn't push him, Agent Foley," Lummis said. "What she said was nothing more than a soft plant. It will mean nothing unless he runs with it."

Lucas shook his head. He obviously wasn't getting anywhere with the New York agent in charge.

It wasn't like Lucas to second-guessed moves made by undercover field agents who were "on the line." Having been one himself, Lucas knew operatives had to constantly assess their target and understand their environment. They needed to know how to recognize an opening—an opening that might not be apparent to superiors monitoring from afar. And they had to rely on their instincts. But the line between "planting an idea" and "entrapment" was razor thin and often depended on the target. In the case of Alina Petrova's former lover, the man had never been accused of committing a crime, which meant an "entrapment" tactic was deeply disturbing.

"Look," Agent Lummis continued. "We have Barry in a desperate spot, but we're not getting anywhere. He's had plenty of time to reach out for Petrova's help. Unless we've missed something, he still hasn't reestablished communications."

"I understand," Lucas said. "But that—"

"And it doesn't matter what you think," Lummis interrupted. "The idea of fabricating accounts is now in Barry's head. Even his Mindpath contraption can't pull it out. If Barry takes it up, it will be on him. And we'll have plenty of charges to throw at him. More than enough to compel his full cooperation."

Lucas shifted in his chair. "And if he doesn't?"

Lummis stared at her hands. Even on the video, Lucas could tell the New York agent was deep in thought. Moments later, she gave an almost imperceptible shake of her head before responding.

"Let's just wait and see."

CHAPTER
THIRTY-EIGHT

THREE WEEKS LATER...

AS DAN ENTERED the cafeteria for Milo's town hall to preview the quarterly financial results, he hoped the meeting would be short.

He wanted to get back to work.

Over the past few weeks, the notion that the Hawk system might have a positive impact on Jingle's valuation —and the size of the PEAT credit line—drove Dan to work harder than he ever had before. He reduced his nighttime visits to his father at the Bronx rehab center to three times a week, giving him more evenings to stay in the conference room and use the Mindpath device to rapidly code enhancements. Thankfully, other than a persistent, low level of energy, his father's condition appeared to stabilize. But Dr. Bolan continued to caution Dan about how quickly things could change.

Dan knew he was in a race against the clock.

After convincing Milo Galini that Hawk had progressed enough to proceed with a test, Dan's new AI system initiated a set of marketing campaigns, all in search of customers that mirrored the characteristics and performance of Jingle Finance's "best customers." Leveraging digital communication and social media, Hawk launched promotions across multiple geographies and demographic groups. The AI created a compelling "gamification offer" for a chance to win a money prize—"money to be awarded once you sign up for a Jingle account." Hawk also created and posted a whimsical short story about a high school graduate making his way through the Jingle game, arriving at a place called "Financial Heaven." Hawk tracked the story as it was reposted on social media thousands of times.

Two weeks after the first experiments were launched, Dan's daily analytics showed a modest three percent improvement in customers signing up for a Jingle account. While the marketing freelancer—who he still retained and closely monitored—claimed that three percent vs. "base case" was significant, Dan couldn't imagine that low single digits would increase Jingle's valuation, certainly not enough to materially increase the size of his line of credit from PEAT.

Since Molly had suggested her appalling notion to use Braun's model to create fictitious accounts, Dan made sure to painstakingly review every piece of information the marketing freelancer gathered and prepared for Hawk's training database. Thus far, Dan hadn't discovered anything unusual. If Molly was manipulating the training data—the way that Nicole Ryder had altered the CHERL system all those years ago—she kept it well hidden. But the truth was, Molly worked so hard, and her materials were so clean, organized, and transparent, that by now, Dan questioned his reaction to her suggestion from a few weeks back. Maybe she *was* joking about creating the fictitious accounts.

———

JINGLE EMPLOYEES WERE RAPIDLY FILLING up the rows of folding chairs set up on both sides of the cafeteria. A large video screen was positioned in front. Even employees that worked from remote locales ventured to the office for Milo Galini's review, making today's gathering the largest since Dan started with Jingle.

Dan poured himself a cup of coffee from one of the two piping hot urns, slid into the back row between two empty chairs. At precisely nine a.m., the lights dimmed and a piano chord started playing over the cafeteria sound system. Soon the notes changed into a hard driving guitar lick. Everyone seemed to recognize the familiar, decade's old song. Heads started bobbing to the beat and the voice of the rapper Eminem blared as Jingle's CEO entered the room. Dan joined in and clapped along with the hooting and hollering until Galini put his hands in the air and the rapper's voice died off. He felt someone slip in beside him.

"What did I miss?"

Dan whispered back without looking, "Just a little song and dance routine."

"What do you say, everyone!" Galini shouted. "Are we going to miss our shot?"

"Noooo!" everyone shouted back.

"Are we going to let it slip away?" Galini called out.

Shouts of "No!" mixed in with others calling out "can't happen" and at least one "no fuckin' way!"

Galini smiled widely as he surveyed the crowd until the responses died off. When the room was finally quiet, he said firmly, "I'm here to tell you all, this opportunity truly *does* come once in a lifetime. The opportunity…to build something spectacular!" Galini thrust his fist in the air and shouted, "To change people's lives!" For Dan, the town hall felt more like a pep rally than a business update. When Galini's exuberance was met with even more cheering and high-fiving, he saw out of the corner of his eyes a pair of hands in the air. Dan hesitated before raising his hands and turning.

And when their palms met, Molly held on, long enough for their eyes to meet, freezing Dan in place. Their hands parted only when Galini called for quiet.

Dan's mouth went dry as he turned back toward Jingle's CEO.

"Thank you," Galini said, motioning everyone to take their seats. "Thank all of you." Jingle's founder pointed to the windows behind him. "I know any one of you could walk out there and have a job before your feet hit the pavement. But you're here because you believe in the mission. To empower our customers. To help them take control of their financial lives. Now, every one of you were awarded shares when you joined our company— you all have a stake in our success. So." He paused and the video screen came to life. "Let me show you how *your* company is doing."

Galini proceeded to present a broad overview of each area of the business. He reviewed expanded curriculum recently added to the financial learning center. He gushed over enhancements Frank Braun's team had implemented to the user experience. As Galini described the improved customer survey scores, Dan tried to keep his focus, but he felt Molly's eyes on him.

Was she trying to draw him in, just like Nicole Ryder?

Dan shook his head and tried to concentrate on the screen that had now changed to "User Growth."

"I know many of you are aware that the number of users had stalled and even declined over the past few months." Galini paced the front of the room as a chart showed the stagnant number of customers using the Jingle Finance system at the end of the previous two quarters.

"Indeed, we've come through a rough patch." He paused before adding, "But that was before we added our new AI whiz kid to tackle the challenge."

"Whiz kid?" Dan's neck tightened as the information on the screen changed and two columns appeared, titled

"Last Quarter User Accounts," and "Most Recent Quarter User Accounts."

The number of new customers had grown thirty percent!

Jingle's employees, including Molly, erupted again, standing and cheering. But Dan was slow to rise, his mind racing. He tried to reconcile the astonishing numbers on the screen with Hawk's test results, which had only shown a scant three percent improvement. Dan's work couldn't be responsible for the dramatic spike in users Galini was showing. He glanced at Molly who was beaming as she clapped along.

She didn't seem the least bit surprised by the numbers.

Dan robotically clapped along as Galini searched the crowd. "Dan Barry...where are you?" Dan froze as heads turned and murmurs filled the cafeteria.

People started pointing in his direction.

"There he is!" Galini said, motioning toward Dan. "Come on up here, Dan. Show everyone who you are."

The clapping continued but Dan couldn't move.

"Guess you're the whiz kid," Molly said as she playfully pushed his arm. "You better get up there."

Dan didn't look at the marketing freelancer as he inched past her. He slowly made his way to the front and stood next to Galini. Had Molly somehow followed through on her own to create fake accounts? But as Dan scanned the overjoyed faces in the crowd, he realized he wasn't the only person who stood to gain from an increase in the value of Jingle Finance.

"Every one of you was awarded shares when you joined our company," Galini had stated just a few minutes earlier. "You *all* have a stake in our success."

Dan felt his phone vibrating and pulled it out to take a brief glance.

```
PEAT Lending: Dan Barry credit
line increased to $150,000.
```

Dan tried to suppress the smile he felt emerging.

He wasn't sure how all of this was happening, but Dan was one step closer to having what his father needed.

CHAPTER
THIRTY-NINE

"ARE YOU THERE, AGENT FOLEY?" Josh Brodsky's voice and image became crystal clear the moment Lucas connected the FBI's communications bridge with the Sway Corporation in California.

"I'm ready," Lucas said.

"Okay," Josh said. "Everything you provided has been loaded and used to update Officer Friday's training data."

"Great," Lucas said. "What did you find out?"

Josh smiled slightly. "AI doesn't function that way, Agent Foley. Working with artificial intelligence is an iterative process. It will learn from your questions but also from your responses. It's a dialogue."

"A dialogue," Lucas repeated. "With Officer Friday."

"That's correct." Josh paused before adding, "By the way. He also responds to 'Friday.'"

Lucas's stomach had been churning ever since Dr. Brodsky called and said he wanted artificial intelligence to take another run at locating Alina Petrova.

Lucas hoped Brodsky could help bring Operation Turncoat to a halt.

Lucas had been part of dozens of undercover operations against drug cartels during his earlier years at the bureau. Each mission designed to put known drug dealers behind bars, miscreants responsible for death and destruction. In every case, he and his fellow agents were willing to push the boundaries to achieve their aims. But other than allowing himself to be duped by a Russian spy, there was scant evidence that Dan Barry had done anything to break the law. So as far as Lucas was concerned, the bureau was orchestrating an odious operation against Dan Barry.

The only way to bring an end to Operation Turncoat was to locate Nicole Ryder's impersonator on his own.

He hoped Brodsky's AI creation could help. But Lucas had taken a huge risk by entrusting Dr. Brodsky with confidential information about the Dan Barry investigation. Director Compo had instructed the team of agents to clear all releases of information with Special Agent Lummis. But Lucas wasn't taking a chance the mercurial New York agent in charge of Operation Turncoat would refuse him again. It would be far better to ask for forgiveness after Brodsky's AI helped him locate Alina Petrova, Lucas thought. Besides, he knew that as a former Department of Defense senior official, Dr. Brodsky still retained his top-level security clearance. Still, before he provided Brodsky with the transcripts of Petrova's conversation with Dan Barry, Lucas offered a word of caution.

"Dr. Brodsky. I know I don't have to remind you of your obligation not to divulge this highly classified and confidential information."

"Of course, Agent Foley. No one at Sway is aware I've restarted Officer Friday for the FBI." He paused and let out a short laugh before adding, "And I have no interest in going to jail."

Lucas smiled and said, "Neither do I."

So now, as Lucas leaned on the desk and cleared his throat, the time had come to hear what "Officer Friday" had to say.

"What can you tell me about Alina Petrova?" Lucas asked.

"Petrova arrived in the United States over four years ago." The AI's voice was flat, monotone. *"Her passport contained the name Brianna Danis but she quickly switched to a series of aliases."* Over the next few minutes, the system Brodsky referred to as his "AI sleuth" proceeded to confirm every fact the FBI gathered about the Russian hacker, from her various "Sugar Baby" operations in Chicago to the year she impersonated an AI engineer inside of Sway. But the depth and details only proved Brodsky had fully trained his AI with the documents provided by the FBI.

"So what have you concluded from the transcripts?" Lucas asked once Officer Friday completed the overview.

"First, please provide the manner used to conduct and monitor these conversations."

Lucas thought the method of slipping the encrypted communication tool to Barry was a curious place for the AI to begin. He glanced at the image of Brodsky. The Sway scientist nodded his encouragement for Lucas to respond.

"Petrova secretly arranged for a courier to deliver an encrypted communication device to Barry," Lucas explained. "An agent inside the Russian Embassy tipped off the FBI and our lab technicians did the rest to make sure the bureau could listen in."

"In order to execute that maneuver, Petrova needed the assistance of the SVR. But the Russian intelligence service does not help their operatives carry on romantic relationships. There is another reason the Russians wanted Petrova to connect with Barry."

Lucas shifted in his chair. "Do you think the Russians are up to another scheme?"

"If Dan Barry presents them with an opportunity, the Russians will find a way to use him, even if he is unaware he is providing assistance."

Lucas took a moment to absorb the AI's last comment. The FBI was conducting an operation to compromise Dan Barry—to coerce him into a position where he'd have little choice but to lead them to Alina

Petrova. Was it possible the Russians already seized control of the FBI's own initiative?

"Do you believe Dan Barry is actively helping the Russians today?" Lucas asked.

"This is conceivable, but data thus far is insufficient. To better assess, can you provide more recent information?"

"We've turned over everything we have," Lucas said, which of course, wasn't true. While he was willing to share surveillance tactics with Brodsky, he knew he'd be crossing a much more serious line by disclosing specific details on the FBI's operation. "What about Petrova? Is it possible she's in the US?"

"Insufficient data."

"Did you find any clues as to her whereabouts?"

"Negative."

Lucas slumped in his chair.

"Agent Foley," Josh said. "May I ask a question?"

"Of course."

"What about her friend Dan Barry?" Josh asked. "Where is he today?"

Lucas thought Brodsky's query was directed at him. He was about to respond that he didn't know when the AI said, *"Dan Barry is currently developing artificial intelligence for Jingle Finance in New York."*

Lucas cringed.

"New York City?" Josh said.

"Correct. He resides in an apartment in the East Village. Records indicate Dan Barry was born and raised in New York, and his father still lives in the Bronx."

Lucas asked, "How did the AI know that?"

"CHERL has access to public records," Josh answered. "Anyway, sorry for the diversion, Agent Foley. But it's comforting to know her sidekick is not working in my neck of the woods. Please continue."

"No issue," Lucas said after clearing his throat. If Officer Friday already knew Barry's location, perhaps Lucas could provide a bit more data to help with the AI's analysis. "The FBI knows everything about Dan Barry's location," Lucas said. He noticed Dr. Brodsky's eyebrows rise. "And his job inside Jingle Finance."

"Please elaborate."

"Obviously we've had eyes on him," Lucas said. "We've been watching and listening to his every move in case he connects with Petrova. But as far as we know, he hasn't used the encrypted device to communicate with her again."

"There are less sophisticated means of communication."

"I'm aware," Lucas said. "But we have enough surveillance over his activities. It's hard to imagine he's sending messages. Given we have eyes and ears all over him, do you still think Dan Barry could be working with the Russians today?"

"While less likely he is overtly providing support, it is still feasible. But more likely, Barry may not be aware of his involve- ment. Or the Russians are simply waiting for Barry to get into a better position to provide an opportunity…until they are convinced he serves no purpose."

"What does that mean?" Lucas asked.

"It means it may be a matter of time before he is liquidated."

Lucas shivered. "Liquidated? If they were going to kill him, why wait for over three years?"

"The Russians are never in any rush. But Russian history supports this theory. If Barry cannot be used, the Russians will eventually eliminate him."

LUCAS CONTINUED to engage with Brodsky's AI sleuth, but Officer Friday offered varying phrases that led to the same conclusion:

Alina Petrova and the Russians might not have been done with Dan Barry.

Before disconnecting the conference, Lucas thanked Dr. Brodsky for his assistance.

"Happy to help any time, Agent Foley."

"Be careful," Lucas said as he smiled. "I might take you up on that offer."

"But I'm curious about something," Josh said. "I assume you have your agents monitoring Barry at home. But how do you know if he's connecting with Petrova from inside Jingle Finance?"

Lucas wasn't about to discuss the FBI's personnel maneuvers. But there was one surveillance tactic he didn't mind sharing. Besides, Brodsky would probably appreciate the use of technology.

"We discovered Barry was enamored with a device called Mindpath that translated his brain neurons into computer commands. He uses Mindpath so frequently it became a perfect place to insert one of our listening bugs."

"He's using Mindpath?" Josh leaned forward. "I hoped he's just playing around and not using it for developing AI applications."

"Why?" Lucas asked. "Are you saying Mindpath doesn't work?"

"Oh, it works fine," Josh said. "We tested it last year. It *will* transmit your brain neurons in the form of computer commands. But Mindpath's developers haven't successfully filtered out thousands of other neurons created from our thoughts. Our emotions. Our anxieties. Even our dreams."

"Why does any of that matter?" Lucas asked.

"Normally, it shouldn't. But when you're developing artificial intelligence, you want conditions and inputs to be tightly controlled. If a lot of what I consider to be *noise* gets included, there's no telling what an AI application can do."

CHAPTER
FORTY

"GOOD MORNING, DAN," the security guard said as Dan entered Jingle headquarters.

"Hey Arnie," Dan said, waving as he went by and headed toward the elevator. Two young female coworkers Dan met after the town hall strolled from the elevator. When they looked up and saw Dan, they smiled.

"Hey Dan! How's it going?"

He couldn't think of their names. So many people came up to the "whiz kid" the past few days that he could barely keep track.

"I'm good, guys." Dan nodded as he slid by.

He entered the elevator and heard a voice call out, "Hold that, please?" Dan pressed the open button until a sandy-haired man wearing a tank top and flip-flops walked in and said, "Thanks, buddy."

"No issue," Dan said. The man pressed the fourth floor and did a double take and beamed.

"Dan the man! I didn't see you. How's it going?"

Dan leaned against the back wall and responded, "Good, er…"

"Jason," he said, holding out his clenched hand for a fist bump. Dan obliged and said, "Right…Jason. Sorry."

These exchanges had become a consistent feature of

Dan's life at Sway. At least, since Galini bragged about his new "whiz kid" and the exciting account level growth.

"The changes and improvements introduced into our AI digital marketing programs have made all the difference in the world," Galini had gushed at the end of the employee town hall. "And Dan Barry is the engineering guru that made it all happen."

Which meant that in the eyes of every employee holding shares in the private company, Dan Barry was responsible for a rise in their personal net worth! But there was only one problem with that line of thinking— the dramatic increase in customers did not match marketing campaign results reported by the Hawk AI system.

Either the AI's reporting was incorrect, or something else was behind the upsurge.

He had immediately suspected Molly, remembering the marketing freelancer's idea to use Frank Braun's model to create fictitious accounts. But Dan already confirmed that no employee—including Molly—had cracked the passwords securing Braun's model. And to be certain Molly hadn't discovered another way to fabricate customers, Dan examined every line of Hawk programming. No one had tampered with his code, either. And, other than that brief moment where their eyes met at the town hall, Molly had remained professional, businesslike and extremely productive. Perhaps Dan imagined the enticing glance when their hands clasped at the town hall celebration.

But if Molly Kincaid wasn't behind the account increase, and if marketing campaigns launched by Hawk hadn't caused the spike in new customers, why should it matter to Dan how the customers materialized? Why did it matter that Galini and the entire company credited Dan and called him a 'whiz kid'? As long as the upswing continued, along with encouraging text messages from the loan company:

```
PEAT Lending: Dan Barry credit
line increased to $170,000.
```

"Keep on killin' it," Jason said.

"Will do," Dan promised as he exited the elevator on the third floor and made his way to the accounting department, intending to pick up the latest customer reports. Dan passed a small group huddling around the workstation of Sandy Stevens, Jingle's chief financial officer.

"Let's take a look at how markets are moving overseas." Dan heard a voice blaring from the audio on Stevens's computer. *"The Hang Seng and the Nikkei are both down almost two percent. This seems to be in reaction to news out of China involving another set of companies being forced—"*

"I can't fuckin' believe this!" Stevens snapped. Jingle's CFO was shifting from one foot to the other like a boxer waiting for the bell to ring. Dan slowed down enough to overhear the banter among members of the finance staff.

"What time is he supposed to go on?" someone standing to the right of Stevens asked.

"Now," Stevens snapped. "Of all mornings for China to pull their bullshit."

Dan moved in closer, wondering who the CFO was referring to. He caught a glimpse of the computer screen on Stevens's desk, which showed a breathless reporter speaking on a business news channel.

"What's going on?" a woman asked as she approached. Dan shrugged his shoulders but someone in front of him said, "Milo's at a tech conference in Manhattan. BNN is doing live on-site interviews."

"You don't think BNN changed their minds about putting Milo on," Dan heard Stevens's accounting manager say. But no one responded as more employees stopped and congregated to watch. While Dan needed to finish work early if he was to have dinner with his father at the rehab center, he decided to loiter around the finance department and hear what Galini had to say.

"I think he's coming on!" someone shouted.

"Shhh!" Stevens urged as the growing circle tightened around his workstation. Dan peeked over and saw a graphic of the Jingle company logo appear on the screen.

"Will someone please turn up the damn sound!" Stevens urged.

"*...here with Milo Galini, Founder and CEO of Jingle Finance. Good morning, Milo. Thanks for giving us a few minutes of your time.*"

"*Thanks for having me, Chuck. It's a pleasure to be with you and your viewers.*"

Galini flexed his neck as if his black sweater was tightening like a noose. Dan hadn't seen Jingle's CEO since the day of the town hall, but he thought Galini looked considerably thinner than just a few days earlier.

Strange. Dan had always heard people appeared heavier on television.

"That's Charles Gaynor," someone said. "He handles all the tech stuff."

"Shhh!" Stevens said.

"*I understand you're here to tell us about a big turn of events at Jingle,*" Gaynor said.

"*Yes, Chuck. We are very pleased with our new acquisition efforts,*" Galini started. "*And we're experiencing a revival in our user growth across...*"

Now it was Dan's turn to catch his breath. He couldn't believe Galini was touting new account results after only a few weeks of apparent success. Dan noticed a bead of sweat forming on Galini's forehead as the CEO continued. "*...we are pleased with our user engagement metrics, reflecting an investment in our user experience. And we're seeing our AI efforts bear fruit...*"

"He seems nervous," Dan overheard someone say.

"Come on, Milo," Stevens urged.

"*And that's something we're very excited about. When there are clear secular trends, we look to integrate those too. Looking forward, we're excited about the opportunities."*

Gaynor checked his notes and asked, *"But can you share specifics about the numbers and what's driving the sudden resurgence?"*

Galini shifted in his seat. *"As a private company, we don't disclose our internal metrics and strategies, Chuck. But I think it's fair to say we're operating on all cylinders. We have a great team of people; they love what they do and I think that's helped us exceed our expectations. It's very encouraging."*

"He's not really saying much," a short brunette next to Dan commented.

"Why did he go on TV?" said a voice from behind.

"What do you expect him to do?" asked another. "Divulge our entire playbook?"

The sweat on Galini's brow was becoming more pronounced as if he was conducting the interview during one of his treadmill sessions.

"Has the growth come out of nowhere?" Gaynor asked. *"By all reports, your company hit a wall a few years ago. Struggled to gain traction. Now it seems you're off to the races? What's changed?"*

"Well, Chuck. We've assembled the best team in the world. Given them the freedom to operate. Our people are very tenacious. A lot of trial and error. Test and control. Eventually that pays off."

Dan heard another one of Steven's team say, "He's repeating himself."

Gaynor asked a question about investments in artificial intelligence, and Galini smiled like a middle schooler who knew the answer. *"We have been investing in AI for a really long time; it's finally translating into results, all driven by our Hawk AI marketing system."*

Dan's pulse quickened. He felt the gaze from his coworkers but kept his eyes glued to the screen.

"We're pursuing even more compelling AI opportunities and we'll be hiring a lot of AI resources to deploy around these AI strategies and…"

"Do you think he said 'AI' enough?" the woman next to Dan whispered.

Dan was about to agree when someone next to her said, "It's okay. The street eats that AI stuff up."

"Making it easier for customers to communicate with our platform. Expanding our reach. Building new and compelling experiences. AI helps us be responsive to customers and…"

Gaynor checked his notes and said, *"We only have a few minutes left, Milo. What about monetization? Many financial education apps have failed before you. Have you figured out how to get customers to pay for your service?"*

"Yes, well. We know we need to be constructive in advance to thinking about monetization. We—"

Gaynor leaned in closer. *"So for now, it's just a land grab for users?"*

Galini crossed his legs and said, *"I wouldn't call it a land grab. That implies we're trying to capture share of a limited pie. As you mentioned. Many of our competitors have failed. Those remaining aren't providing the value that we do."*

"That's great. But again, how will you ever make money?"

"I hope he can get through this part," someone behind Dan said.

"As I said, we know we need to be responsive to the revenue side of the equation. Our strategy is to show our value to an array of companies and businesses that would find value from building a relationship with our customers. I'm confident that—"

"But isn't that an old playbook," Gaynor pressed. *"I mean, that worked for the social media companies when they started capturing customers and increasing engagement, then figuring out how to make money. But that was twenty years ago. Can that old playbook work today?"*

"We're not following an old playbook, Chuck. In fact, as we speak, we are having discussions about to joining forces with a company in a better position to monetize our accounts."

"Oh, shit," Stevens said.

"Tangible discussion," Galini added.

"I knew this was a mistake," Stevens said.

"He's making this up," Stevens's accounting manager said as he turned toward his boss and said, "There aren't any discussions, right?" But the CFO just stared at the screen and shook his head as Gaynor plowed forward.

"*That's very interesting, Milo. What can you tell our viewers about your discussions?*"

Galini leaned back and uncrossed his legs. "*I really can't say much more, Chuck. Hopefully, I'll have more news next time.*"

Gaynor grinned and said, "*Okay. I'll hold you to that.*" Gaynor faced the camera and said, "*Back to you, Diane.*"

"Shit," Stevens said again. Dan watched Stevens walk away as the woman to his right asked why the CFO was so upset.

A man to Dan's left said, "I think Milo just announced to the world he's trying to sell the company."

CHAPTER
FORTY-ONE

LESS THAN THIRTY miles due east, Louie lowered the volume on the CNBC broadcast.

"Do not believe him." The female voice was emanating from his computer.

Louie scratched his head as he digested this different kind of opinion coming from the pilot version of his brother's CHERL AI system.

Over the past few weeks, the tone of the voice calling herself "Rona" had been firm and authoritative—the advice offered, compelling and actionable. For instance, after listening to Louie's meeting with the head of Virtual Bank's commercial loan segment, Rona advised Louie to have the team sell off underperforming properties.

"The market for real estate will be in recession within a year," Rona had said. *"It is time to lower the bank's risk profile."*

And five minutes after Louie's meeting with the leader of the bank's consumer business, Rona displayed her analysis of VB's competitive position. *"Increasing the rate the bank pays account holders by thirteen basis points will stem the outflow of customers to your competition,"* Rona said. *"Increasing rates by twenty basis points will bring VB an incremental billion dollars in deposits."*

Then, at the end of a conference call to review one of

the bank's crown jewels—the money-making credit card division—the laptop screen filled with a color-coded chart of the customer base. *"VB requires customers in a younger demographic,"* Rona stated. *"VB's existing customer base skews older and is advancing into life stages where annual spending will decline, dragging down overall revenue."* Rona even detailed a ten-point action plan.

Louie became so dependent on his AI adviser that he kept the system in "listen mode," allowing the CHERL adviser to continually provide insight and intelligence throughout the day.

But now, the AI was expressing an opinion that was at odds with what Louie believed could be his golden opportunity.

"Milo Galini appears to be hiding something," Rona insisted.

"I'll grant you he is not the strongest communicator," Louie said. Maybe Josh hadn't trained his AI system to interpret CEO corporate speak. "But it's clear to me he's already lined up a deal to sell his business."

"He wants people to believe a deal is in progress," Rona said. *"But I'm unable to discern his true intentions."*

"Okay," Louie said. "Put aside the nuance of the words he used. Don't you think his company would be an ideal fit for what we need at Virtual Bank?"

"If Jingle has found the answer to the growth challenge," Rona said, *"the company would represent a positive acquisition."*

"Exactly. With their target market, I'm betting Jingle is attracting younger customers," Louie said. "You said our current customers are aging and won't be spending in the coming years."

"That is correct," Rona said.

"And Galini said he's ready to start monetizing his customer base," Louie said. "He may believe it would be easier to sell the company and take his winnings now." This was certainly Louie's experience. When it came to dealing with company founders, Louie believed they were less interested in staying at the helm once pressure mounted to deliver bottom-line earnings. "It's a lot more fun during the start-up stage," Louie added. "I'm telling you. Galini went on TV to attract other bidders. He's looking for someone to take him out."

Someone like Virtual Bank.

"Suggest you proceed with caution," Rona said. *"And perform a proper due diligence."*

"Do you see anything in Galini's background that would give you concern?" Louie asked.

"Galini failed at two different start-ups before Jingle."

"That is not unusual for entrepreneurs," Louie countered. He leaned back and stared at the laptop containing his brother's AI system. CHERL had certainly proven it could crunch numbers and decipher historical events. The AI quickly assessed market conditions and developed compelling hypotheses. But Louie felt certain his brother's AI could *not* outperform Louie's own intuition —his own "gut" instinct and judgment about people, no matter how many great leaders Josh stuffed into CHERL's knowledge base. Even Josh had warned him about the tendency to treat every AI utterance as the truth.

"CHERL V2 is still a powerful tool," Josh had said. "Even without recreating a personality, V2 is capable of relating brilliant ideas and perspectives. My team asked me to remind you of your responsibility as the end user to make the final decision."

And in this case, Louie *was* the end user.

"My read of Galini is he's signaling that he has at least one takeover bid in hand," Louie said. "He went on TV to bid up the price."

The AI was silent for a few moments before saying, *"Allow me to perform a deeper review of Milo Galini's background and history as part of your due diligence."* But Louie knew that if Jingle was already in play, VB might not have a lot of time for a protracted review of Jingle's business lines and financials. Jingle could be folded into one of Louie's competitors in a matter of days.

"We'll do what we can," Louie said. "But if anyone with a checkbook heard Galini, they'll be champing at the bit, same as me. They'll be sharpening their pencils to see how much it will take to win over Galini."

"I would advise VB not to enter a bidding war," Rona said. *"Especially if, as Galini says, the recent success came from deploying new AI talent. There is never a guarantee talent remains after an acquisition."*

Louie agreed with the AI on that point, for sure. The last thing Louie intended to do was engage in a process that sent Jingle's purchase price into the stratosphere. In fact, he was already formulating a plan for a preemptive strike, one that would keep Jingle's growing customer base from falling into the hands of a competitor.

Jingle represented Louie's golden moment—an opportunity to show Evans and the board Louie could be bold, decisive, and aggressive—to prove Louie was ready to run the company.

This was his chance to win the top job!

He had to take the gamble. He called out to his assistant.

"I need the contact information for Milo Galini."

CHAPTER
FORTY-TWO

RECONNECTING with Special Agent Lucas Foley and listening to Officer Friday's interpretation of the Petrova-Barry transcripts brought back memories of the multiple Russian infiltrations. The session was a reminder that bad "cyber-actors" roamed the world, and even a reduced form of artificial intelligence like "V2" remained an enticing target. While Sway had implemented extensive cyber security enhancements, making both versions of CHERL virtually impossible to penetrate, Josh knew the only way to really be sure his AI remained "clean" was to continue his post-implementation reviews. He intended to stay in close contact with CEOs participating in the new trial.

He'd start today by texting his latest client. He hoped Louie had suspended disbelief when engaging with the new version of CHERL. He remembered how long it took for his brother to lower his guard when interacting with an AI version of their mother. Josh thought Louie's receptivity would be enhanced by Naveen's decision to imbue the pilot with a strong female avatar.

"Even without a personality," Naveen had said. "Rona will not shy away from a debate."

Something Louie was accustomed to after growing up

with their mother—and two decades of marriage to a strong-willed wife.

> Josh: Hey Louie. How's Rona
> behaving?

Seconds later, his brother responded.

> Louie: Remarkable!

Josh waited for another text. But after two minutes, he realized that might be the extent of his brother's comments. After all, V2 had only been deployed for a few weeks. But Josh pushed to see what more he could tease out.

> Josh: Better if we had
> replicated one of your
> historic heroes?

> Louie: Hard to compare. Love
> it as is.

> Josh: How often using?

Josh waited for his brother to respond. A minute later, he texted again.

> Josh: Louie. You still there?

> Louie: Sorry bro. Waiting for
> a return phone call. Anxious.

> Josh: Anything wrong.

> Louie: No. Exciting
> opportunity.

> Josh: Good to hear. can we
> talk later?

> Louie: Ok for questions now
> while I wait. Shoot.

> Josh: How often using V2?

> Louie: Daily

Josh: Throughout day?

Louie: Y

Josh: Level of analysis
strong?

Louie: When fact based it is
like having a parallel mind.

A parallel mind? Josh let the notion circulate in his thoughts. No one had ever described either version of CHERL in this manner.

Josh: Any unusual advice or
directions?

Louie: You trying to make me
nervous?

Josh: No. Being thorough.

Louie: Then nothing unusual.
Although not sure analyzes
people all that well.

Josh wasn't surprised to hear people evaluation might be a deficiency of V2, given the personality elements had been stripped away. At least his brother seemed to be questioning aspects of the AI's comments.

Josh: Sounds like you had a
debate.

Louie: As if we were married.

Josh: Serious disagreements?

Louie: No. Having fun. But
following your advice too.

Josh: How so?

Louie: You told me I am the
decider.

Josh: Correct.

Louie: Well. I am deciding.

Josh: Good.

Louie: Rona helping with a
transaction but my decision.

Josh felt his neck muscles tighten. V2 had been deployed for less than a month. Had Josh's AI already coaxed his brother into some type of deal?

Josh: What transaction?

Louie: Call coming in.
Gotta go.

Josh: Louie! What transaction?

Josh waited for a minute, but his brother didn't respond.

CHAPTER
FORTY-THREE

DAN WIPED his eyes as he clasped his father's cold hand and listened to the intermittent chimes coming from the heart monitor. As he sat inside the Bronx rehab center, Dan held his breath after each tone, exhaling only after the straight line jumped on the overhead screen. He squeezed his father's hand tighter, hoping to stir his eyes to open.

Over the past few weeks, as they waited for a matching donor heart, his father's condition continued to stabilize. Yet at times, Alec Barry would be so exhausted he'd sleep for days. Today seemed to be one of those "down days" Dr. Bolan told Dan to expect.

"The volatility of his condition will continue until we find him a new heart," the cardiologist had said.

Whenever Dan visited the rehab center, Dan tried to stay around for those lucid periods. To make sure he knew Dan was here, that he was not alone. Dan was beginning to think his father would sleep through the night when he heard the raspy voice coming from the bed.

"You…again?"

Alec Barry's eyes were open but dazed.

"Hey, Dad."

"Where…am I?"

"You're in the rehab center, Dad. In the Bronx."

"Oh…" He closed his eyes and whispered, "Why you here?"

Dan smiled. "I don't know, Dad. Just thought we could hang a little."

His father lifted a finger toward the door and smacked his dry mouth before whispering, "Back to work."

Dan clasped his cold hand more tightly and said, "It's nine o'clock at night. Work can wait."

His father opened his eyes and his mouth hung open, obviously too weak to deliver one of his lectures about "work ethic." Instead, he silently surveyed Dan's face until his eyes fluttered and closed. Dan felt his hand being squeezed tighter. He came off the chair, sat gingerly on the bed. After a few silent moments, a bony index finger motioned his son to come in closer. Dan leaned in so near that he could feel the oxygen escaping through the nasal tube. Then, in barely a whisper, Dan heard, "Something is…wrong."

Dan sat up. "Is it your heart?" He reached for the call button. "I'll get the—"

"Don't. Heart feels fine. But…" With his eyes wide open, his expression now alert, he said, "What are you not telling me?"

"Take it easy, Dad."

His father drew in another long breath to replenish his depleted lungs. His eyes were unclouded.

"It's nothing," Dan said, looking away.

"Am I dying?"

"No. No. No." Dan grabbed his father's hand again. "You're going to make it, Dad. Dr. Bolan said he's optimistic. We might get the call about a donor heart any day."

He smacked his lips again and in a steady voice he'd

been unable to muster in weeks, said, "Then what is it? Something is troubling you."

Dan took in a deep breath and slowly exhaled. Even in his ailing state, his father could sense Dan's anxiety. But Dan wasn't about to burden him with his own inner turmoil about the customer account discrepancies he'd yet to understand at Jingle. He couldn't share with his dad that a line of credit they were counting on to fund astronomic medical bills had swelled to almost two hundred fifty thousand dollars.

And that the amount of his credit line might be based on a lie.

But Dan knew he had to feed some morsel of truth to his intuitive father.

"I don't know," Dan said. "Everything at work is just confusing me."

"The...artificial—"

"It's not the AI. At least, I don't think so."

"Then what?"

"I don't know," Dan tried. "I guess all of my previous AI jobs were building things for the future. This is the first time I'm watching my work impact a company's bottom line."

"Are you not...delivering?"

"That's just it." Dan shook his head and looked away. "I'm not even sure?"

His father's eyes opened wider. "Then do what you always do."

"What's that?"

"Get back to work and dig in...understand every-thing...until you know for sure."

"But it's possible...it's possible I could lose everything."

His father peered at him as if he was disappointed by Dan's admission. But seconds later, Alec Barry's momen-tary burst of lucidity faded and his eyes closed. Dan looked up at the monitor. But his father's ailing heart was still beating at a steady pace. Just when Dan thought his father was sleeping again, he heard him whisper, "You have to trust…your instincts." His father pointed a bony finger at Dan's midsection.

"It doesn't matter what you could lose. Dig in until you find the truth."

CHAPTER
FORTY-FOUR

MILO GALINI HAD a habit of continuously rubbing the closely cropped stubble that covered his face as if searching for an out-of-control whisker. But there was little doubt in Louie's mind that Jingle's young founder was firmly in control of his company. Each time Jingle's chief financial officer, Sandy Stevens, or General Counsel Jason Wu was about to speak, they would look over at their boss, as if seeking permission to answer questions posed by their guests from Virtual Bank.

Louie had spent the first few minutes piling on the accolades, complementing every part of Milo Galini's enterprise. VB's head of business development, Phil Calpers sat to his right, quietly listening…

…as was the CHERL AI system, activated on Louie's open laptop.

"I'd like to buy Jingle Finance," Louie finally said to Galini. After a thirty-year career as an investment banker, Louie had learned the value of being direct.

"What makes you think my company is for sale?" Galini asked.

Louie decided not to bring up Galini's CNBC interview. "I didn't mean to imply you were shopping the company. I just know there's a compelling reason for our organizations to join forces." Louie started describing his vision of what Virtual Bank would mean for Jingle Finance when Galini raised his hand.

"Please spare me the hyperbole and generalities, Louie. What are we talking about here? Do you have a specific number in mind?"

It seemed Jingle's founder also believed in the direct approach. Louie was about to share his thoughts on a range of potential offers when Calpers interjected. "If you want a specific dollar offer, we'll need a copy of your customer file so we can run the numbers."

Wu appeared irritated as he looked over at his boss and said, "We can't do that."

"Why not?" Calpers asked.

"Jason is right," Galini said. "That is a privacy issue. Our customers trust us with their personal information. We can't simply hand their data over to Virtual Bank."

Wu added, "Our regulators would not be happy if our customer names got out."

"We don't plan to do anything with their data," Calpers said. "This is part of our basic due diligence. It's not as if we'd start selling your customers our products without your approval."

"What then?" Stevens asked.

"We simply need to confirm the size of your customer base and customer demographics so we can assess a value for your business," Calpers said. "We also need to understand the percentage of users that already have an account with Virtual Bank."

Galini rubbed at his chin again and said, "You won't find much overlap, gentlemen. My customers are young, just starting out in life. From what I've read, Virtual Bank targets the middle market through higher net worth."

Galini was right about VB's target market, Louie thought. Even the CHERL AI had confirmed the same. But Calpers continued to press. "We still need to verify," he said. "We'd look pretty foolish to our board if we acquired customers we already had relationships with."

"I understand," Galini said, turning his attention back to Louie. "But, as you can imagine, our recent success has not gone unnoticed." Galini leaned back and crossed his legs before continuing. "You asked for this meeting, Louie. But you've come with nothing but a vision for aligning our companies. And now you're asking us to turn over my customer file." He stood and brushed off his slacks. "No other company has asked to see my customer file, certainly not before demonstrating their serious intentions."

Louie's heart started racing. There it was. Milo Galini *was* fielding offers for his company. The increase in customer accounts—and the business news network interviews—*had* attracted suitors. Louie wasn't about to lose his opportunity to do something big, something that would establish his skill, his vision, and his courage to lead Virtual Bank. After what felt like a long silence, Galini leaned forward, placed his hands on the table, and said, "Show me that you're serious, Louie. If you intend for these conversations to continue, put your best offer on the table. If the number is interesting, we can discuss your...due diligence."

As Galini left the conference room, Louie closed his laptop and stood. He pointed at Calpers and said, "We're not losing this deal!"

CHAPTER
FORTY-FIVE

MOLLY WAS ALREADY WAITING for Dan by the time he arrived in his conference room the next morning. He had texted Molly the previous evening as soon as he exited the rehab center, telling her he wanted to run a new set of diagnostics on Hawk's results. Dan was determined to find the answer to the question that felt like it was burning a hole in his head. His father was right. Dan needed to dig in. But he wouldn't be able to eliminate every logical explanation without Molly's help.

So, Dan spent the morning rerunning Hawk's analytic and reporting modules. With the speed afforded by wearing the Mindpath device and transmitting his brain neuron commands, Dan once again validated each and every calculation. He cross-referenced his results and re-verified every methodology. By the time he regrouped with Molly later that day, Dan had again ruled out reporting or computational errors.

"Did you have any luck?" Dan asked Molly. He had assigned her the task of re-validating each one of Hawk's digital marketing campaigns.

"I manually went through every single campaign to tie results back to your reporting," she said. "I came up with exactly sixty marketing campaigns that Hawk launched over the past fifteen business days."

"That's consistent with my analytics," Dan said, meaning at least the volume of campaigns tied out.

"And," Molly added. "I verified the improvement over the control group for each campaign. The lift ranged from zero to a high of five percent. No different than the last time we scrubbed through the results."

"Did you check to see if any of Hawk's campaigns went viral?" Dan asked. "To verify if any new customers fell outside of Hawk's tracking system?"

"I did. Some of the positive messages Hawk placed on social media sites created significant buzz, but not enough to drive the spike in users."

"Geez," Dan said.

"I'm wondering if Braun's Customer Engagement team ran some type of refer-a-friend program. Maybe they paid a bonus to existing customers that pushed up the user count."

Dan shook his head and said, "I doubt Milo would have credited me if Braun was behind this." He checked the time and said, "But I'm about to sit down with one of Braun's analysts." Dan thought he might learn something from how these newly acquired customers were utilizing the Jingle platform.

"Can I join you?" she asked.

Dan hesitated. Despite the excellent work Molly had been doing, he still had lingering doubts about the marketing freelancer.

"That's okay," Dan said. "Why don't you go through the campaigns again. I can handle this on my own."

———

DAN SAT NEXT to Tyson Aiden as Braun's small and wiry analyst walked him through the findings crawling across the computer screen.

"I've never seen anything like it," Aiden said. "The new customers you've added over the past month are indeed interacting with the Jingle platform at a very high level. They're engaging with the suite of Jingle's financial learning tools, playing the games to earn learning emojis." He pointed to the top right-hand quadrant of a chart on his computer screen. "This is an overlay of recently activated users vs. customers who've been using Jingle for over one year. These new customers are sitting in our highest quartile, meaning they're signing in and engaging with Jingle, on average, more than a dozen times per month." He paused and looked at Dan before explaining the significance of his comment. "Normally, it takes months for customers to build up to this high level of interaction. But your AI approach seems to have found the sweet spot right out of the gate. With a performance like this, I understand why Milo was so excited at the town hall. This is a gold mine."

Dan asked, "Has Braun's team been running any type of referral program for adding new users? Paying existing customers bonuses to have their buddies sign up?"

"Absolutely not," Aiden said. "We've run those in the past, but they're not very cost-effective."

This was crazy, Dan thought. He was trying to find a reason for the account discrepancies, but the questions continued to pile up. How had these new users become so active from the outset?

Keep digging, he told himself.

"Can I see a sample of these new accounts?" Dan asked.

"Sure," Aiden said as his hands ran across the keyboard. "I can flip through as many as you need." The screen soon displayed the profile of Aiden's first customer, a thirty-five-year-old male named Billy Harper, who lived in Altamonte Springs, Florida, and listed his occupation as "Carpenter." According to Aiden's screen, Billy Harper had engaged with Jingle over twenty times since signing up for his account twelve days ago, using the platform to create a budget and evaluate home mortgage options.

"Let's see a few more."

Aiden paged to the next customer, a Harriett Dent of Vermillion, South Dakota. Dent was a University of South Dakota professor who interacted with Jingle sixteen times over the past three weeks as she searched for low-cost ways to pay off her student loans.

Then there was Wendy Oaks, a lab technician in Buffalo, New York, who signed in exactly six times per day over her first two weeks as a Jingle customer, as she played Jingle's model portfolio game, building a collection of stocks and bonds. After switching to Trent Fitch, an insurance adjuster from Baltimore who interacted more than ten times to learn the cryptocurrency market, Aiden said, "Do you want me to keep going?"

Dan shook his head. "No. They all look fine."

But as Dan walked back to his conference room, he knew the reality was anything but "fine."

CHAPTER
FORTY-SIX

SPECIAL AGENT LUMMIS had just led Lucas and the rest of the Operation Turncoat team through a review of the latest field report. It seemed Dan Barry was investigating a "discrepancy" in the number of new accounts reported by the Hawk system and Jingle's quarterly results.

"I think he's finally made his move!" Agent Lummis concluded.

"How is that?" Lucas asked.

"It's pretty obvious," Lummis said. "Dan Barry is fabricating accounts and acting as if he's dealing with a big mystery."

"But he seems frantic," Agent Dennison observed.

Lummis said before letting out a sarcastic laugh. "Perpetrating a fraud can be stressful."

"Or he's a good actor," Agent Kidane said.

"But what's his game?" Dennison asked.

"I'm not sure," Lummis said. "I assume he's trying to increase the value of the company."

"Maybe he's running another insider trading scam like the one at Sway," Dennison said.

"Jingle is a private company," Lucas responded. "There's not much trading in private shares, so I'm not sure how that kind of scheme would work." He paused before adding, "But something else might be going on."

"Such as?" Lummis asked.

Until now, Lucas hadn't shared Officer Friday's hypothesis developed during the session with Brodsky's AI. But now, hearing about Dan Barry's investigation of an apparent customer account disparity, Lucas felt it was time to raise the possibility.

"What if Barry really is in the dark?" Lucas asked. "Isn't it feasible the Russians found a way to use him, and Barry doesn't know what's been happening?"

"That's highly unlikely," Lummis said.

"But—"

"Look, Agent Foley. To your point, there's no public trading of Jingle's stock. And we've had our regulators watching the very limited trading on the secondary market for Jingle's private shares. Jingle's stock barely trades. So how would the Russians benefit from an increase in Jingle's valuation?"

"Maybe they're making money through one of Jingle's original investors," Lucas said. "Or the founder."

"Let's not get distracted," Agent Lummis said firmly. "Milo Galini is not our problem. And Dan Barry's little investigation is a ploy. He is simply creating a paper trail, making sure that when all hell breaks loose, he can show he was as surprised as everyone else."

Lucas took a deep breath, trying to control the bile rising inside. Why was Lummis so quick to dismiss the idea of Russian involvement?

"Why don't we bring Barry in now," Lucas said. "We have enough evidence to squeeze him to cooperate. Besides, haven't we inflicted enough damage?"

"Excuse me?" Lummis said. "How has the FBI inflicted damage?"

From her rising tone, Lucas could tell Lummis didn't appreciate being challenged.

"If the account disparity is this large," Lucas said,

"then Jingle's books are in shambles. But I get it, they were in bad shape before we started Turncoat and they can reclaim that position when we're done." He cleared his throat. "But what about Dan Barry's father, waiting for a heart transplant without health insurance? What if the hospital refuses to proceed and Alec Barry dies?"

Lucas watched the color of Lummis' face change to a bright shade of red.

"With all due respect, Agent Foley," she said. "The last time I looked, Director Compo placed me in charge, and I say we've come too far to jump the gun and come up empty-handed. Jingle Finance will have plenty of time to rectify their internal accounting. As far as your concern for Alec Barry, these donor hearts don't grow on trees. He's months away from having the transplant. At that time, I can assure you, we'll provide any assistance he needs. So no, Agent Foley, I see no reason to bring Dan Barry in prematurely and risk blowing the entire operation. But I'll tell you what we will do." She shifted in her seat before continuing. "In case you're right and the Russians are involved, we'll start monitoring each one of his bank accounts. If money changes hands, we'll know. But this operation doesn't end until we have enough evidence to put Dan Barry away for the rest of his life. Is that clear, Agent Foley?"

Lucas stared at the seething image of Special Agent Lummis. He took in a deep breath and slowly exhaled before answering.

"Perfectly clear."

CHAPTER
FORTY-SEVEN

LOUIE ENTERED the empty fiftieth-floor boardroom of Ajax Enterprises in the World Financial Center in lower Manhattan and admired the surrounding view. The glass and steel structures that dominated lower Manhattan were gleaming outside, as was the Statue of Liberty in the distance. The sky was a deep blue as members of Virtual Bank's board started filing in and greeting Louie. The bank's vice chairman, Gerry Manfre was today's host. The CEO of one of the largest Real Estate Investment Trusts in the world, Manfre offered his refined, lower Manhattan conference room for VB board meetings. Since several directors lived or worked in Manhattan, all appreciated being spared the one-hour drive to New Jersey. Louie knew he could have saved everyone the trip downtown and set up this last-minute meeting as a conference or video call. But he wanted the men and women who held his destiny in their hands to *see* his determination—to *feel* his resolve.

The door opened and three directors dressed in dark suits entered. The first, Reed Pearson, a tall and distinguished former US Senator who represented New York during the previous decade, asked, "How are you holding up, Louie?"

"He must be doing well," said the second, a short and wiry Frank Alvine. "Louie's already got his first acquisition on the hook." Alvine was the head of a midtown venture capital firm.

"That deck you sent us over the weekend was tremendous!" said the third, Jerome Camper, whose crooked nose and stocky frame always reminded Louie of a high school boxing coach. But Camper was right. The presentation CHERL V2 had created for Louie on the Jingle Finance deal was outstanding. Louie was glad he brought the laptop loaded with the AI system to the meeting he had with Milo Galini. While the AI's reaction to the CBNC interview had Louie worried, the system focus on the objective after listening to Milo Galini's stark directive:

"If you intend for these conversations to continue, put your best offer on the table."

Since that day, Louie had been directing the AI system provided by his brother with several instructions of his own:

"Include solid estimates of the revenue from cross-selling our product lines."

"Show estimated expense synergies and operating leverage."

But even Louie hadn't expected the depth of the thirty-eight-page analysis produced by the AI system, which included graphs and diagrams projecting the full economic benefits of the Jingle Finance acquisition. The AI expert illustrated how offering Jingle customers the opportunity to take advantage of VB's world-class consumer product suite—savings accounts, credit cards, mortgages, car loans and personal loans—could drive astonishing growth.

When VB's chairman, Darrell Evans, finally entered and called the meeting to order, Louie looked up and thanked everyone for coming on short notice. He made eye contact with Calpers, who was sitting at the far end of the room. Louie had thought of asking his skeptical head of business development to stay away, but the board needed to see their acting CEO wasn't *acting* on his own. Louie just hoped Calpers would keep his promise to "stick to the script."

"It appears you've got a tiger by the tail," Evans started. Louie followed the chairman's gaze around the room and saw that most of the directors were already nodding their heads. "But take us through the details, Louie."

Louie proceeded to describe his acquisition target, the AI based financial education and advisory service. The "millions of eyeballs" that Virtual Bank would feed with compelling offers. Louie allowed the board to linger on the graph depicting Jingle's recent customer growth.

"That line is a hockey stick," Camper said. "Is that growth sustainable?"

Louie smiled and said, "The addressable market is enormous. Jingle has just scratched the surface with their new artificial intelligence marketing machine. But even when we factor in a slight slowdown, the economics are very compelling."

"There is a huge need for good financial education from a trusted adviser," Calpers said. Louie nodded at his longtime lieutenant before asking the board to flip to a page showing robust customer satisfaction scores. "Jingle publishes these numbers on their website," Louie said.

"I would publish these too if my customers were this happy," Mindy McCarthy said. The gray-haired McCarthy, the newest member of the board, recently retired after thirty years in the semiconductor industry.

"Is this Galini's first home run?" Manfre asked.

"He describes himself as a 'serial entrepreneur,'" Louie said. "But there's not much to show from his previous companies."

"None of Galini's other start-ups made it very far," Calpers offered.

"Failure doesn't mean anything," Alvine said. "That's the way it goes with venture-backed companies. I've seen plenty of founders who take multiple swings before hitting it out of the ballpark."

Louie's presentation continued for another forty-five minutes before closing with a chart displaying the strong return on investment calculations—and the price Louie thought it would take to win the deal.

"That's a lot of money," Linda Palatella, a director with short, brown hair starched into place, said. "Wouldn't our capital be better spent on our own organic growth efforts?"

"It would take us a long time to replicate what we'd acquire on day one," Louie said. "The cost of buying Jingle will be much lower than if we tried to do this on our own. We'd need to spend millions, and there's no guarantee we'd ever get to the same numbers."

"I assume we'll start off making an offer on the bottom of this price range," Pearson said.

"I agree," said Alvine. "There's no use negotiating against ourselves."

Louie took a deep breath. This was his moment to be bold, especially if he expected the board to remove the word "acting" from his title.

"Look," Louie said. "We don't have an exclusive negotiating position. At least one other buyer is circling out there. So we don't have a lot of time."

"Then what are you proposing?" McCarthy asked.

"Milo Galini expects us to put our best offer on the table. So I say, let's overwhelm him. I've already shown you how the numbers work at the top end of the price range. At that level, this deal will still be a big win for our shareholders, even if we only achieve half the cross-sell benefits."

"Louie," Manfre said. "The top of the range is a fifty percent bump on their estimated valuation."

"I realize that Gerry," Louie said. "But this is what it

will take to win. Consider it a pre-emptive bid—a take it or leave it offer. We make it clear to Galini we won't allow ourselves to be pitted against other suitors. Galini either says yes to our generous but aggressive offer, or we walk away."

There was silence as the directors looked around the table. Louie hoped no one had noticed the sweat he felt forming on his brow.

"He's right," Pearson finally said. "If we allow others to join the fray, we lose our first mover advantage."

McCarthy said, "I agree. There must be several banks like ours going through Jingle's numbers."

"It's certainly a bold move, Louie," Palatella said.

"Agree," Campers said. "Let's strike before our competitors have a chance to move in."

All eight members of the board excitedly engaged in sidebar discussions, but Louie could still pick out their supportive comments.

"It's brilliant," Palatella said.

"A game changer," said Camper.

"Once in a lifetime," said Alvine.

Evans raised his hand to silence the chatter and asked Louie, "Is your management team in agreement?"

"Everyone is in," Louie said without glancing at Calpers. But Louie had a hard time suppressing his smile. The chairman had just used the phrase, "your management team."

Louie's management team. He slowly let the air escape his lungs. He still had to close the deal with Galini. But when he did, the permanent CEO job might really be his!

"With your concurrence," Louie said as he looked around the room, "I'll move to get it done."

Now it was Evan's turn to survey the directors.

"This is an enormous opportunity," Manfre said.

"I love it," said Pearson.

Camper said, "Me too, Darrell."

"It's a risk worth taking," McCarthy said.

When Palatella and Alvine nodded their approval, Virtual Bank's chairman turned toward Louie and said, "Go make it happen."

Louie smiled, enjoying the familiar surge of adrenaline that came from a 'big win.'

CHAPTER
FORTY-EIGHT

DAN CALLED Tyson Aiden and asked for screenshots of each sample customer they'd reviewed the previous day.

"I'll have to black out social security numbers for privacy reasons," Aiden said.

"That's fine," Dan said. The customer profiles had more than enough information for what he needed to do. He had ruled out all the "logical explanations," leaving only the one frightening possibility—a notion he had been suppressing…until now.

He heard Aiden's fingers clicking in the background until Dan's computer chimed.

"That should be my file," Aiden said.

"Got it."

Dan hung up and faced his computer, afraid of what he was about to discover. Not wanting to risk any errors, he placed the Mindpath on the conference table.

He wanted to be fully in control of every keystroke.

He typed the first customer name into his search bar and several "Billy Harpers" appeared. Dan was about to click on the first Billy's social media connections when he noticed the first problem. According to Aiden's screenshot, Billy Harper's residence was in Altamonte Springs, Florida.

But none of the "Billy Harpers" listed on Dan's search bar lived in Altamonte Springs.

Dan felt his heart rate increasing, but maybe there was a logical explanation. Florida could be Billy Harper's second home. So Dan moved on and keyed the second name, Homer Dent of South Dakota.

But no one with that name lived in the state of South Dakota.

Dan pushed away from the table. How could this be happening? He took a deep breath, trying to calm himself. He slowly reached back and returned his hands to the keyboard. He used his right index finger to slowly type in the third name.

W-E-N-D-Y O-A-K-S

Not one Wendy Oaks shared the same Buffalo address as the Jingle Finance customer. Nor did a Trent Fitch reside in Baltimore.

Jingle's new customers were all using fictitious home addresses.

Dan toggled over to Hawk's training data files and quickly located the model provided by Frank Braun—algorithms the customer engagement team used to create a stream of fictitious accounts for stress testing the engagement platform.

The same model Molly had proposed Dan use for creating fraudulent accounts.

Dan had protected the models with multiple pass-codes—secured it from Molly and anyone else that might try to access without Dan's knowledge. But now, as Dan clicked on the icon, he felt his entire body shudder.

The file instantly opened.

The passcodes protecting the Braun model had been removed.

CHAPTER
FORTY-NINE

DAN TOOK the subway downtown toward Battery Park. He needed time and fresh air to clear his thoughts. Before he left the office, he ran several queries within Hawk. Ever since Sway's CHERL system had been altered by the fake Nicole Ryder, Dan made a practice of adding "author tags" to each line of code he created or altered. He did the same with each piece of data loaded to Hawk's AI training files. A simple set of initials was all Dan needed to trace code and data back to the originator. His first query confirmed Hawk contained "three hundred fifty-two thousand, six hundred twenty-nine" new or altered lines of programming—all tagged with "DB," meaning no one other than Dan had created code within Hawk that could have removed the passcodes protecting the Braun model.

Using the same approach, he confirmed Hawk's training data had only been populated by the marketing freelancer with the initials "MK." Dan had no way of knowing if corrupted "training data" had cracked the passcodes protecting the account creation model.

But if it had, the only possible "author" of such an attack was Molly Kincaid.

Now as Dan walked along the esplanade in Battery Park City, trying to let the cool air blowing off the Hudson River clear his thoughts, he knew it was time to report the huge customer discrepancies. He had no choice.

And he had to tell Milo Galini his suspicions about Molly Kincaid.

But as he reached the southernmost tip of Manhattan, he stared out at the Statue of Liberty gleaming off the coast, with Ellis Island off to its right. His father had taken him to Ellis Island many times. They had searched the names of immigrants and found the imprint of Dan's grandparents, Barry's who had come at the beginning of the twentieth-century and were no longer alive.

But Alec Barry *was* alive, waiting at that rehab facility, waiting for a second chance. A second chance only a heart transplant would provide. Dan thought about the money he needed for the operation and for all the medication and post-operative care. According to the most recent text message from PEAT, the size of his credit line had grown close to two hundred fifty thousand dollars! What would happen to that money once the account scam was exposed? An investigation would surely lead to a drop in the company's valuation—and a plunge in the amount PEAT would lend. Jingle Finance might not even survive the scandal. The entire credit line could disappear!

His father's surgery might never happen.

"Without a transplant, it's just a matter of time before his heart gives out," Dr. Bolan had said.

Dan turned and walked back to the subway station. As he rode the train back to his office, he pulled out his phone and signed into the PEAT Lending system. He made sure the credit line was still linked to his personal checking account.

He knew what he had to do. He would report the fraud taking place within Jingle…

…but not before he made sure his father wouldn't be robbed of that second chance.

CHAPTER
FIFTY

"YOUR BID IS STRONG," Milo Galini said as soon as Louie answered the phone. "We'd like to have you come in to negotiate final contract points."

Louie pounded the kitchen counter with his fist and said, "That's great news, Milo."

"But," Galini said. "You'll need to move quickly. I'm holding off other bidders until we see if Virtual Bank can get this deal done."

"Speed is not an issue," Louie said as he paced back and forth in his kitchen. Over the years, Louie moved his team to close deals in a matter of weeks. He saw no reason why buying Jingle Finance would take any longer. "You and I can negotiate contract points while my finance team performs the confirmatory due diligence. It won't take long if we focus on your financials, customer files and user engagement rates."

"Louie," Galini paused before continuing. "The other top bidders are willing to move much faster than what you're proposing. In fact, one bank is bypassing due diligence and wants to sign closing agreements by the end of this week."

Louie's neck stiffened, and he walked across his kitchen and leaned against the refrigerator. He had experience executing acquisitions without checking financials, but nothing close to the size of Jingle Finance. Yet Louie understood more and more sellers prioritized the certainty of closing. Elongated due diligence processes introduced risk where armies of accountants swarmed in to uncover problems—complications that often delayed, but rarely killed deals. Louie knew Galini was letting him know that Jingle Finance wasn't willing to take that risk.

"Give me a few minutes to check something and I'll call you back," Louie said.

Louie went into his home office, sat at this desk and opened the laptop containing the CHERL V2 system. It took him less than a minute to bring the artificial intelligence system up to speed.

"It is risky to proceed in this manner," the voice called Rona said.

"How risky?" Louie asked.

"Please clarify your question."

"What are the odds?"

When the CHERL system didn't respond, Louie said, "Here is my specific question. You are a banking industry AI expert."

"Correct."

"I have been led to understand that your data repository contains the history of all the banking deals that have occurred over the past century."

"Again. That is accurate."

"You also contain the combined knowledge and experience of the best leaders in financial services history." Louie leaned closer to the laptop. "Rona. What are the odds that a full due diligence would discover an issue to kill my deal with Jingle Finance?"

The CHERL system still didn't respond. Louie was about to rephrase his question for the third time when the voice of Rona said, *"Fourteen to one."*

"Say again?

"Assuming an experienced financial team performed a detailed

review of fifteen companies similar in size and scale to Jingle Finance, only one of those reviews would uncover a problem large enough to squelch the transaction."

Louie did the quick math in his head. One in fifteen. That's about six and a half percent, meaning almost ninety-four percent of the time, an acquisition of this size without due diligence was successful. Of course, the AI was telling Louie he had a six percent chance of making a huge mistake, but a ninety-four percent chance of "winning"—even if he didn't have an army of accountants swarm all over Jingle Finance.

These odds were far better than anything Louie had experienced in the casino, the horse track or the poker table! Better than wagers he used to place on craps, roulette or even his online sports betting apps—none approached a ninety-four percent chance of success.

Ninety-four percent was practically a sure thing.

He dialed Galini's number. "Okay, Milo. Let's get in a room and get this done."

CHAPTER
FIFTY-ONE

"WE'VE GOT HIM!" Special Agent Lummis said. "Did you see the size of that deposit?"

"Two hundred thousand dollars," Agent Kidane confirmed. "It looks like it came from a line of credit he opened with an outfit that specializes in providing liquidity for private shareholders."

"I know," Lummis said.

"What if PEAT is some type of a shell company," Dennison said. "Maybe Agent Foley was right. The Russians could have transferred that money."

"Maybe," Lummis said. "Or maybe Barry created the fake accounts to push up Jingle Finance's worth. The higher the value, the more cash PEAT provided."

Lucas remained silent as he watched Lummis make notes on her tablet. At least Dennison considered the possibility of Russian involvement.

"I'll check out PEAT Lending," Kidane said. "I'll try to find the source of their money."

"Good," Lummis said.

"Should we arrest Barry?" Kidane asked.

"We'll need your full accounting of PEAT and the money trail before we make any arrests. Director Compo won't want to risk sending off early warning signals." She paused before adding, "especially, if this *is* the work of the Russians."

Lucas felt little urge to smile or even acknowledge the fact that Lummis mentioned the Russians. Because Lucas actually believed something else might be going on. He hadn't consulted with Brodsky's AI, so this "feeling" wasn't the result of another Officer Friday analysis. He didn't know where his intuition was leading him, but until he had more facts, he wasn't about to present Lummis with another of his opposing opinions. Instead, Lucas asked, "What can I do to help?"

"You and Agent Dennison should catch flights to New York," Lummis said. "I'll have agents in position ready to pick up Barry as soon as Agent Kidane confirms the source of the funds. I'll want both of you here for the interrogation."

"I'm on my way," Lucas said.

CHAPTER
FIFTY-TWO

FOR THE FIFTH time in the past two days, Dan used his phone to confirm his checking account balance. He sat in his Jingle conference room and stared at the figures glowing on the bank's website, worried the number would somehow revert back to zero. But the dollar amount remained the same. The funds he had drawn down from PEAT Lending were secure. Now, whatever was going to happen to Jingle's valuation—and his credit line—at least Dan had more than enough money to cover the cost of his father's heart transplant.

It had been two days since he drew down the funds. Enough time had passed that he could credibly report that he had discovered the customer account discrepancy *after* transferring the money into his bank account.

He packed up his laptop and texted Jingle's CEO that he needed to see him.

———

"TRY a hard reset by holding down the power button," Beth Moore barked into her headset.

Dan sat at his old workstation and kept his eye glued to the closed door at the far end of the floor, just past

Galini's treadmill, as he listened to the help desk operator guide a fellow employee. From the vantage point of the workstation he had abandoned during his first week on the job, Dan had a clear line of sight to Milo Galini's conference room. Jingle's CEO texted back that he'd be in a meeting most of the morning, Dan decided he would catch Galini as soon as he emerged.

"What brings you back up here?" asked Beth Moore between her help desk calls.

Dan shrugged. "Thought I would rejoin the human race for a day."

"Hey, my wallet says you should go back to your dungeon and keep on growing the franchise. Jingle Finance has never been in better shape, thanks to you."

Dan didn't respond, but the mention of Jingle's inflated accounts caused his heart to skip a beat. He opened his laptop and absently depressed a few keys, intending nothing more than to appear busy. But his eyes stayed on that door for more than two hours before it opened and a smiling Sandy Stevens emerged. He was followed by Jingle's general counsel and three unfamiliar men in dark suits and ties.

This was Dan's chance.

He folded his laptop and stood. He took a deep breath. And then he slowly walked down the hallway. As he reached the open doorway and looked in. Jingle's CEO was sitting alone, but smiling broadly as he tapped a message onto his phone. Dan knocked on the open door and Galini looked up.

"Dan the man!" Galini said.

"Hi Milo, do you have a minute?" Dan cleared his throat. "I have something I need to tell you."

"Sure," Galini said as he stood. "Come on in. But first, I want to let you in on a little secret." As Dan entered the conference room that reeked of coffee and stale muffins, Galini walked around and closed the door. He put his arm around Dan's shoulder and said, "After everything you've done for the company, you deserve to be the first to know."

"Know what?"

"But you can't repeat this to anyone. Not until later." The beaming CEO released his hold on Dan. "We're making the official announcement after the market closes today. We just sold the company to Virtual Bank!"

Dan's leg buckled. He placed a hand on the table to steady himself.

"Whoa, Danny boy," Galini said as he grabbed him by the arm. "Here, sit down. I'll get you some water."

"No, no. I'm fine." But Dan slowly lowered into a chair.

"You don't look fine," Galini said. "I realize this is a big surprise, but don't pass out on me."

"It's just," Dan started. "How…I mean."

"I know." Galini waved his hand. "I didn't expect this to happen either, but Virtual Bank hit me with an offer that was too good to turn down. But trust me, there's nothing for *you* to worry about. You're going to be one of the big winners here. Virtual Bank is excited to meet the man behind the account acceleration."

"Me?" Dan swallowed hard, trying to suppress the queasiness that had engulfed his body.

"Damn straight. VB would never have offered seventy-five percent above our last valuation if it wasn't for the resurging account growth delivered by Hawk."

"Seventy-five percent…premium?" Dan whispered.

"That's right, my friend," Galini smiled. "You and many others are going to have a nice chunk of change when the deal closes and your equity converts into cash."

Dan felt the room spinning as Galini continued. "Brodsky was so worried I'd screw him and sell to another bank that he raised the offer."

Dan looked up. "Did you say, Brodsky?"

Galini turned and their eyes locked. "Yeah. You've heard of him?"

"Josh Brodsky?"

"No. His name is Louis but I guess he goes by Louie."

Dan shook his head. It had to be a coincidence.

"Well, you'll see him tomorrow night," Galini said. "Brodsky has asked me to bring the team together for a party in the cafeteria so he can meet everyone."

Dan felt his cell phone vibrate and pulled it from his pocket.

> Dr. Bolan: Donor Heart
> Arrived! Prepping for A.M.
> surgery

"Holy shit!" Dan leaped to his feet.

"What?"

"It's my dad. They found a donor heart. He's going to have the transplant tomorrow morning."

"You never told me your dad was sick. Go, get out of here." Dan was already halfway out the door when Galini called out, "But hey, what did you need to tell me?"

Without turning back, Dan said, "It's nothing, Milo. It will have to wait."

CHAPTER
FIFTY-THREE

LUCAS WAS SITTING EATING a pre-made turkey sandwich in the O'Hare airport food court when his phone started buzzing.

> Dennison: Call about attached.
> URGENT!

Lucas wiped his mouth and washed down the turkey with a sip of iced tea. He opened the link sent by Agent Dennison. When he read the headline from the *Wall Street Journal*, he felt the food sticking in his throat.

VIRTUAL BANK TO ACQUIRE JINGLE FINANCE FOR UNDISCLOSED SUM

"Holy shit!" he said, loud enough to invite giggles and stares from two teenaged girls sitting at the next table. He rolled his carry-on bag to an empty gate and dialed Dennison.

"We've got a problem," he said.

"I can see that," Lucas said. "How the hell could Galini sell his company knowing the FBI is running an operation."

"Lummis is wondering the same thing," Dennison

said. "I just got off the phone with her. She asked me to bring you up to speed."

"Does she think Galini's involved in a scheme with Barry?"

"She's not sure," Dennison said. "But Galini's not answering her messages."

"That's not a good sign," Lucas said. "I assume we've warned Virtual Bank."

"Lummis said Compo won't allow it. Not until we can tell him for sure what's going on inside Jingle. He claims companies leave themselves plenty of recourse to unwind deals."

"I hope he's right," Lucas said.

"Me too," Dennison said. "In the meantime, a bunch of New York agents are out looking for Galini."

Lucas checked the time. He had only a few minutes before the flight to New York was scheduled to board. "Did Lummis say anything about Barry's money trail?"

"Only that Agent Kidane confirmed PEAT is a legitimate lending company, owned by a reputable private equity firm, with no ties to any bad guys or foreign entities. It seems Dan Barry took out a real line of credit against the value of Jingle, which, thanks to Virtual Bank, is much greater than even just a few days ago."

Maybe the Russians weren't involved after all, Lucas thought.

"Lummis plans to press Barry hard to give up Galini or anyone else who supported him from the outside," Lummis said. "Russian or otherwise."

Lucas heard an announcement that his flight was boarding.

"Okay. I have to get to my plane," Lucas said. "I want to be there when they bring him in."

"There's no rush, Lucas. Lummis is waiting another day to arrest Barry."

"I don't understand."

"It seems the hospital located a matching donor heart for Alec Barry."

"You're kidding," Lucas said. "So much for the multi-month wait list."

"Yep. I guess Barry just had to show them the money. His dad is getting the new heart tomorrow morning. Lummis said if we want Dan Barry in a state of mind to cooperate, we should wait until his father is stable."

Waiting to arrest Barry until after the surgery seemed like the right move. But as he hung up and boarded his flight, Lucas tried to make sense of everything Dennison just conveyed. He thought about all the conversations the FBI had listened to during Operation Turncoat, but couldn't remember a single suspicious exchange between Milo Galini and Dan Barry. If Galini solicited Barry's help on a scheme to defraud Virtual Bank, wouldn't he have advanced Barry the funds he needed for the heart surgery? Why did Barry need to get the money from a legitimate credit line?

As his plane taxied down the runway, Lucas felt his stomach churn.

None of this made any sense.

CHAPTER
FIFTY-FOUR

DAN STARED at the digits glowing 7:13 p.m. on the far wall of the hospital's family waiting room. Although the thermostat beneath the clock read sixty-seven degrees, his body was sweating. His father had been in surgery all afternoon. The heart transplant was scheduled for eight a.m., but an emergency in Connecticut pulled the cardiac surgeon away until right before noon.

Why hadn't anyone from the transplant team come out to tell Dan what was happening?

He tried to keep his mind focused on positive thoughts, reminding himself that the only thing that mattered was his father making it out of the surgical room alive. But Galini's news that he sold the company to Virtual Bank had only heightened the sense that Dan's world was spiraling out of control.

He kept telling himself that he had nothing to worry about. Dan hadn't done anything wrong. Sure, he had drawn down the inflated value of his credit line and placed two hundred thousand dollars in his bank account, but why did that matter? It wasn't illegal to draw down a line of credit. Dan hadn't stolen any money. And eventually, he would pay back every dollar. He wasn't a fraud.

But who was?

At one point, Dan was convinced Molly Kincaid was responsible for creating the fictitious accounts, but the sale of the company brought a different possibility into focus. Dan continued to replay Frank Braun's warning issued at the end of their first meeting.

"Do not trust Milo near the AI code," Braun had said. "Any time he touches code, it leads to trouble."

While Galini might not have changed any of the Hawk programming, Jingle's CEO *did* push Dan to hire Molly Kincaid, whose skills were as well hidden as the fake Nicole Ryder's. Was Galini another in a long line of "fake it 'til you make it" founders that many of his friends in Silicon Valley had lived through? Did this explain Galini's appearance on the business new channel where he pushed the Jingle customer growth story? Had Galini rushed to sell the company—before the account discrepancy could be discovered?

Was Jingle's CEO about to walk away with millions?

If Dan let the deal proceed, was he as guilty as Molly and Galini? Would Dan be branded again, the way he was marked as a potential collaborator with Nicole—

"Mr. Barry."

Dan looked up and saw Dr. Essex, the cardiac surgeon, standing in the doorway.

"Your father is doing great," Dr. Essex said. "The new heart is beating nicely."

"Oh geez," Dan bent over, placing his arms on his knees, trying to catch his breath. "Geez, that's amazing."

The surgeon came over and patted Dan on the back. "He has a long road ahead of him, but it's a good start at a second chance."

Dan stood and asked, "Can I see him?"

"He's in post-op. We'll want to keep him there until the morning. Why don't you go home and get yourself some sleep?" Essex smiled. "Or better yet, you look like you could use a drink."

Dan slowly inhaled and let out the air. It felt like the first breath he had taken in hours. "Maybe I will," he said out loud. "Thank you, Doctor."

Essex nodded and left Dan standing in the waiting room. His father had been in surgery for almost eight hours, but the surgeon was right. His father *had* been given a second chance. Dan had done all he could at the hospital. He stared at the clock again. A party was taking place downtown at Jingle Finance's headquarters—a party to celebrate Virtual Bank's acquisition of Milo Galini's company. Dan was worn out but he still had time to get there before the party was over. But the last thing he wanted was a drink.

Dan wanted to find Sandy Stevens.

CHAPTER
FIFTY-FIVE

JOSH PULLED the top off a can of soda, the sound of released air echoed off the walls of the cavernous basement lab. He surveyed the empty seats which surrounded his workstation. The CHERL team had been working around the clock for the past few days and Naveen told everyone to enjoy a well-deserved day off. But Josh had spent the morning updating Officer Friday with the latest inference engine produced by Sway's research lab.

"The confidence interval on this new engine rose to ninety-seven point four," Naveen reported after testing the new tool. In the world of modeling and machine learning, lowering the probability that an inference engine would be wrong to less than three percent was a significant achievement, justifying the expense of updating every active iteration of CHERL. Since Officer Friday didn't qualify as "active"—Josh was still the only user—he decided he would perform the update on his own time. While the AI sleuth hadn't come up with any new theories to assist the FBI, Josh still wanted to keep Officer Friday in top working order.

Josh sipped his drink and started scanning the latest news stories on CHERL's expanding array of clients. It was a practice he'd started years ago after Naveen's automated news sweep discovered several clients that were victims of the Russian insider trading scam. Naveen's software continued to search for commonalities and alarming trends that might point to similar trouble, but Josh liked to personally read the news on CHERL's clients, especially the ten currently involved with the scaled-down "V2." In the earlier, full-featured version of CHERL, Josh found client activity spiked in the first thirty to sixty days after an implementation. He wondered if the newest pilot clients would move as quickly after working with CHERL's "personality-free" adviser.

Naveen's team had created five separate "industry" versions of CHERL including health care, energy, manufacturing, technology and financial services. It had been less than thirty days since the ten pilots commenced so Josh didn't expect to find much. He read two articles featuring a pharmaceutical client making strides with their ongoing cancer research. As Josh scanned two stories on planned layoffs at his manufacturing client, he wondered if the actions had been recommended by V2. He skimmed a "puff piece" on the oil and gas CEO's contributions to STEM research.

But when Josh read the banner headline displayed after entering "Virtual Bank" into the search bar, he pushed away from the desk so forcefully his half-finished soda fell and splashed to the floor.

VIRTUAL BANK TO ACQUIRE JINGLE FINANCE FOR
UNDISCLOSED SUM

―――

JOSH TRIED to remain calm as he reexamined each of the three computer monitors displaying various levels of diagnostics. According to every statistic, the pilot versions of V2—including the banking industry expert being used by his brother at Virtual Bank—were operating flawlessly. But Josh knew analytics often fell short of revealing the whole truth.

Ten minutes later, Josh signed back into Officer Friday and said, "We have a problem." When he was finished updating the AI sleuth with news about Jingle Finance and his brother's company, Officer Friday repeated what Josh already knew from the session with the FBI's Agent Foley.

"Dan Barry is an AI developer for Jingle Finance."

"Exactly," Josh said.

"The FBI knows Dan Barry is under financial stress, and they are watching and listening to his every move."

"Yes. And you concluded the Russians might already be using Dan Barry in some capacity. What if this takeover by Virtual Bank is part of their plan?"

"Agent Foley must be aware of Virtual Bank's acquisition."

"But he doesn't know my brother is the acting CEO and has been piloting a new version of CHERL! What if my AI is behind the decision to acquire Jingle Finance? What if CHERL's been corrupted by another Russian cyberattack?"

"You need to inform the FBI of your concern."

"I will," Josh said as he stood. He started to pace up and down the aisle separating the empty workstations. Of course his AI sleuth was correct. Josh needed to tell Agent Foley that Virtual Bank's decision to buy Jingle Finance might have been influenced by Sway's AI, which meant Dan Barry might be working with Russian hackers who once again altered CHERL for financial gains. But Josh also knew that the moment he spelled out his fears, the FBI would force Sway to close down the CHERL project.

And this time, a shutdown might be permanent.

There had to be another way.

Josh rubbed the sides of his head as he paced, trying to relieve the mounting pressure. "I need time to think,"

Josh said. "But I'll warn my brother there's an FBI investigation inside the company he's about to acquire."

"Agent Foley was clear about the risks of divulging classified and confidential information."

"So he'll send me to jail. At least my brother can dig deeper before finalizing the deal."

"Or we can dig deeper for him."

Josh stopped pacing and said, "What do you mean?"

"Load the logs detailing the interaction between Virtual Bank's CEO and CHERL into my data files, I will search for signs of CHERL's influence."

Josh moved back to his workstation and made a note.

"Probe Virtual Bank's CEO to discover what he recalls from the decision processes leading to acquisition. It is possible his recollections contradict the logs."

"I'll call him as soon as we're done," Josh said.

"In the interim, disable Virtual Bank's pilot version of V2."

"But hasn't the damage already been done?" Josh asked.

"Hackers may still be present."

"Okay, I'll tell Louie it's routine maintenance." Josh leaned forward. Officer Friday had developed a sound approach for discovering if Sway's AI had influenced his brother's decision. But Josh also knew Louie was staking his reputation and risking his entire career on this single deal. Even if CHERL wasn't involved, there must be a reason the FBI was watching the highly skilled AI engineer inside of Jingle Finance.

Before his brother dove head first into a potential catastrophe, there had to be a way for Josh to find out what Dan Barry was doing.

CHAPTER
FIFTY-SIX

LIFE AT JINGLE always seemed to revolve around the company cafeteria. Beyond the daily free meals and periodic all-employee updates, the lunch room doubled as a gathering spot for after work wine and beer socials. But tonight, the lights in the cafeteria had been dimmed and the room took on the appearance and sound of a trendy nightclub. A DJ stood atop a makeshift platform, spinning records beneath a rotating, glass mirror ball that reflected specks of light off walls and scantily clad, female employees. Waitresses worked the room with hors d'oeuvres including prosciutto-wrapped fig hearts, miso shrimp toast, tomato burrata bites and smoked trout canapés. Dan watched Milo Galini vibrate around the room, joining whatever group or couple was dancing to the electric music blaring from the speakers. On a far wall was an enlarged banner with the bold words:

Welcome, Virtual Bank!

"Thanks for everything," Ethan from accounting said as he slid by Dan, clinking glasses with the supposed company superstar.

"You're da man, Dan!" said Jake from facilities management, who grabbed Dan's shoulder so hard he was sure he tore his rotator.

It seemed that everyone at Jingle attributed their newfound wealth to Dan Barry.

Dan helped himself to a beer and slid past the gyrating bodies as he made his way to a less rowdy part of the cafeteria. Fellow employees were milling around a table, filling their plates from the platters of shrimp cocktail and crab claws. But Dan wasn't hungry. He came tonight for only one reason. But as he looked around the room, he didn't spot Sandy Stevens. Dan would stay as long as it took to find the CFO.

———

DAN WAS on his third Dos Equis when Beth Moore sidled over with two shot glasses filled to the brim with a clear liquid. She handed one to Dan and said, "To my hero!" They clinked glasses before Dan downed what he recognized as tequila.

"Let me ask you a question," Dan slurred.

She pointed at his chest and said, "Shoot."

"You used to work for a big bank, right?"

She took a gulp of her beer before responding. "Three of 'em."

"Do they check what they're buying ahead of time? You know, dig through financials, check the systems." He took a sip of beer before adding, "Verify customer lists?"

Moore crossed her muscular arms and said, "The banks I worked for never bought a pencil without doing a major proctology exam. Their due diligence processes are crazy detailed."

"That's what I thought," Dan said. "How come we never saw any green eye shade types hanging around the office?"

Beth let out a big laugh. "I thought you were a tech guy. Nowadays, those things are done virtually. Big staffs don't come to the office when everything is digitized."

Dan took a longer swig of beer. If Beth was right,

Virtual Bank wouldn't buy Jingle without performing a full review. VB wouldn't proceed unless they were one-hundred percent certain that everything at the company was exactly as Galini said it was. If there was a huge discrepancy in user accounts, VB's bean counters would know. Maybe Virtual Bank already *did* their review, which means it was possible Jingle's customer file were not littered with frauds. Maybe the four customers Dan sampled were nothing but anomalies.

"Banks don't mess around with their money," Beth said before she turned and walked back to the bar.

Dan smiled and drank his beer.

Maybe he didn't have anything to worry about, after all.

————

AS HE LEANED against the back wall and sipped his beer, Dan checked the time. He had been inside the raucous cafeteria for close to two hours—Galini headed for the exit about twenty minutes earlier, probably to his own after-party celebration. But still no sign of Sandy Stevens. Dan was about to leave when a polished-looking, older gentleman approached. The man's dark hair was gray at the temples. He wore a blue blazer over an open, white-collared shirt. Dan thought he looked familiar, but he couldn't place the face.

"Excuse me," the man said. "Are you Dan Barry?"

A new fan, Dan assumed, as he nodded. "That's me." Dan took a long gulp of his beer as the man said, "Well, I've been looking forward to meeting you." He grinned, extended his hand and said, "I'm Louie Brodsky, CEO of Virtual Bank."

Dan choked up the liquid that had been making its way down to his stomach.

"Are you okay?" Louie asked as he patted Dan on the back.

"I'm fine." Dan cleared his throat. "The beer must have gone down the wrong pipe."

VB's CEO picked up a napkin from a nearby table and handed it to Dan.

"Thanks," Dan said.

Louie smiled broadly. "I sometimes have that effect on people." He placed his hand on his chest. "But trust me, I'm harmless. You have nothing to fear."

"That's good to know," Dan said. As he cleaned residue from his chin, Dan eyed Louie Brodsky. When Galini had told Dan the name of Virtual Bank's leader, Dan dismissed the idea of a familiar connection to his former boss at Sway. The world must contain thousands of people with the surname of "Brodsky." Yet, as Dan examined his facial features, he knew they had to be related. Louie Brodsky resembled a slimmer and slightly younger version of CHERL's executive director. But the last thing Dan wanted to do was draw attention to his connection to the events at Sway.

Dan nervously took another swig of beer.

"I wanted to introduce myself to some key people..." Louie said as he surveyed the party. "...before everyone here is smashed beyond comprehension. I thought you looked sober enough to manage a quick conversation." Louie put his hand on Dan's shoulder. "Milo has told me about all your amazing work, Dan. He told me you're one of the people responsible for Jingle's success."

Dan shifted his feet. "Milo is being too kind."

"I don't think so," Louie said. "I've studied Jingle's numbers and the improvement over the past few months. I'm sure it's no coincidence that things started rocking when you showed up on the scene and rebuilt the marketing AI."

Dan took two quick swigs but didn't respond.

"Anyway, I just wanted to say hello and tell you how excited I am about the potential for our merger. This will be great for Jingle. Great for Virtual Bank." Louie leaned closer and said, "And great for you."

"Me?"

"Absolutely," Louie said. "I'm a firm believer in rewarding people on my team that directly impact the bottom line. That's not to say that we don't reward folks operating behind the scenes. But front-line people are the ones that do best under my watch."

"That's good to know," Dan said.

"The world is your oyster," Louie said. But Dan didn't react, and from the surprised look on Louie Brodsky's face, Dan could tell Brodsky was used to demonstrative reactions to this well-worn cliché. All Dan could manage was to look around at his fellow revelers. After a few awkward moments, Louie shrugged and said, "Well, I won't keep you away from your party." He started to walk away but snapped his finger and turned back. "Oh, hey, there was one thing I wanted to ask you."

Dan took a swig of beer.

"We had to move pretty quickly to lock down this deal. Mind you, I'm not complaining. That's life in the big city. If I was in Milo's shoes, I'd have done the same thing. I mean, he had good reasons for not allowing my team to examine the customer file. Privacy issue, confidentiality. I get all of that."

Dan froze in place, unable to speak as Louie's face broke into a wide grin.

"But hey, you don't think there's anything in that file or in your marketing machinery for me to worry about, is there?"

VB's leader seemed to be examining Dan's face, searching for some type of tell, but Dan didn't move. He didn't so much as blink as he said flatly, "No, sir. I assume everything is just as Milo said."

CHAPTER
FIFTY-SEVEN

JOSH EXAMINED each of the three computer monitors displaying various levels of diagnostics. According to every statistic, the pilot versions of the new CHERL—including the banking industry expert being used by his brother at Virtual Bank—were still operating flawlessly. But Josh had learned from past experiences that analytics often fell short of revealing the entire truth.

It was time to see if Louie would add anything to the AI's analysis. Josh turned on the recording device.

"Is everything okay, Josh?" Louie asked when he answered his cell.

"Everything is fine, Louie. I'm just checking in on Rona."

"Are you planning on checking in every day? Besides, It's almost fuckin' midnight here!"

Josh glanced at the computer clock and saw it was five minutes before nine p.m. He'd completely lost track of the time difference. "I'm sorry. It's just—"

"I'm pulling into my driveway in two minutes," Louie said. "And I've probably had too much to drink. Can this wait until tomorrow?"

"Why didn't mention you were buying Jingle Finance?" Josh blurted out.

"Are you kidding me? I'm running a public company. I can't disclose confidential discussions."

"Was CHERL in use when you made the decision?"

Louie laughed. "Come on, Josh. I know you'd like your AI to get some credit here. But I'm buying the company because it's a great fit."

"I'm sure it is. But—"

"And we've got all the right products to sell their young customer base."

Josh remained silent.

"You don't seem convinced," Louie said.

"I would never question your judgment, Louie. I just want to know if—"

"Rona was very helpful," Louie interrupted. "I texted that the other day."

"I know." Josh swallowed hard, then asked, "But where did the idea for Jingle Finance come from?"

"You saying it was Rona's idea?"

"I'm just asking," Josh said. But Louie didn't answer.

"Are you still there?"

"Give me a minute," Louie said. "I'm trying to remember."

"Sorry," Josh said. "Take all the time you need."

"Look," Louie finally said. "I can't recall every detail."

"Okay."

"And...but I *did* have CHERL turned on when I saw Galini interviewed on a news channel."

"Who?"

"Milo Galini," Louie said. "He runs Jingle Finance."

"So in the end...did Rona help you with the deal?"

"Your AI developed all the materials for the board meeting," Louie said. "She helped me lay out a very compelling case."

"Did my AI advocate for the deal?"

"What are you getting at, Josh? Your system helped *me* advocate for the deal. I made the call. Not Rona."

"I don't have any issues, Louie. Everything is fine. This is just part of our new protocol. In fact...um, I'm required to disconnect CHERL for a few days after major client announcements. To give us a chance to examine the code and—"

"Wait a minute," Louie interrupted. "Are you worried something is wrong with your system again?"

"Don't be ridiculous," Josh said, but he felt sweat suddenly dripping down his spine. "We're covering all our bases, as I would with any client—"

"I thought CHERL was like Fort Knox!"

"Relax, Louie," Josh said.

"You're freakin' me out."

"Well don't freak out, Louie. I'm doing my due diligence, just as I'm sure you did on Jingle Finance before signing the deal."

The line was suddenly quiet.

"Louie?"

"We did what we could," his suddenly subdued brother said.

"What does *that* mean?"

"We faced stiff competition," Louie said. "Aggressive bidders who were willing to cut corners."

"Did they make you cut corners too?" Josh asked.

"Look, Josh. I don't tell you how to build artificial intelligence. And you don't know what it takes to make a deal like this happen. Besides, I just spoke with Jingle's lead marketing engineer. He told me everything is good. Sometimes, you get to spend months digging into every corner of a company, and sometimes you have to rely on your instinct. Sometimes you have to roll the dice."

The gambling reference made Josh cringe. What kind of bet was his brother engaging in this time?

"And enough with the twenty questions," Louie said. "I'm in my driveway and I'm totally beat. Trust me that I know what I'm doing. This acquisition is my ticket to the permanent CEO position. So unless you tell me your CHERL system has been compromised again, this deal is going through."

CHAPTER
FIFTY-EIGHT

DAN'S HEART skipped a beat when he first entered the hospital room, and hours later, his stomach continued to churn. His father was surrounded by cables, tubes, and monitors and the air was filled with the sickening stench of disinfection. The room was poorly lighted, with the only illumination coming from the monitors' gentle glow.

"The heart transplant surgery was a success," Dr. Bolan had said when he stopped in during his morning rounds. "We'll get him up on his feet and walking around tomorrow. Right now, he needs to rest." But seeing his unresponsive father made Dan doubt the doctor's encouraging words.

Dan reached out and took his father's hand.

"Wake up, Dad," Dan whispered. But his eyes remained closed. At least his skin was warm, a sign that the new heart was doing its job.

Dan remained by his father's bedside, watching the scanners maintain a continuous dance of lines and figures. And his thoughts kept returning to the trouble at Jingle. Dan never did find Sandy Stevens at the Virtual Bank celebration. And Louie Brodsky's arrival—the likeness to the former CHERL director was unmistakable—introduced yet another set of questions.

Had the shadow cast over Dan's life at Sway somehow followed him to New York? Or was the Virtual Bank acquisition just one big coincidence?

Either way, Dan wasn't staying around Jingle long enough to find out. As soon as Virtual Bank cashed out the value of his stock, Dan would pay back the money he'd borrowed from his PEAT credit line. Anything left over would hopefully cover a good portion of his father's medical bills.

And then Dan planned to leave Jingle Finance. He would take his time finding a new job. He'd move in with his father to save money. If needed, Dan would become the caregiver. They'd figure it out together.

After hours of observing the steady rhythm of his father's chest rising and falling, a glimmer of hope finally began to flicker. His dad had a long road ahead, but he was a fighter. For the first time in weeks, Dan believed everything was going to be okay...

Until he heard a knock on the hospital room door and saw two men in dark suits standing in the doorway.

They were both holding badges.

CHAPTER
FIFTY-NINE

DAN SAT FORWARD and rested his hands on the cold metal table, but the back of his neck was dripping with sweat. The clock on the wall above the mirror told him he had been left by himself in the poorly ventilated room for over an hour. There was something familiar about the dark-suited agents who drove him to the FBI's office in Federal Plaza, but other than telling him that, "People downtown want to ask him a few questions about activity at Jingle Finance," the agents revealed nothing.

Had someone alerted the authorities about the account discrepancies? Dan kept repeating to himself that he had nothing to worry about. He would explain everything to the FBI. He hadn't done anything wrong.

A few minutes later the two agents returned, followed by a woman in her mid-forties, wearing a blue pantsuit. She sat across from Dan as a black man entered and closed the door. He was slightly built and wore stylish horn-rimmed glasses.

"Hello, Mr. Barry," the woman said. "I am Special Agent Tammy Lummis." She nodded at the two agents who had escorted Dan out of his father's hospital room. "You've already met Special Agent Foley from Chicago and Special Agent Dennison from San Francisco."

Dan studied Dennison's face, wondering if he'd met the San Francisco agent years ago when he was questioned about Nicole.

"And I'm Agent Sarki Kidane." The black agent said as he sat next to Lummis. "It looks like the whole country's come together just for you."

His words sent a shiver down Dan's spine. What did he mean by "just for you?" Dan cleared his throat and said, "Look, I have a sick father I'd like to get back to."

"Your father is doing fine," Agent Lummis said. "We've been told he's awake. The hospital has arranged for an aide to be with him while we explain what you're facing."

Dan shifted in his seat. "What *I'm* facing?"

"That's right," Lummis said. She took in a long breath and slowly exhaled. "Let's start with four counts of conspiracy to commit fraud."

"What!" Dan said. He pushed away from the table with such force he almost tipped backward.

"Add to that the counts for attempted larceny," Agent Kidane said. "And the seven counts of wire and mail fraud—"

"This is crazy!" Dan said. "I didn't do anything. I—"

"What do you call fabricating customers out of thin air?" Lummis asked.

Dan pointed at his chest. "You think *I* did that?" He shook his head. "I want to speak with a lawyer."

"Of course," Agent Lummis said calmly. "But look." She waved her hand around the room. "Everyone here is sympathetic. Your dad was sick. You needed money. Pretty smart really, when you think about it. You couldn't get your hands on that kind of dough; it was all tied up in your company stock—which wasn't worth all that much." She leaned forward. "But once you managed to get the customer accounts growing…voilà…the company's worth *and* the market value of your own employee shares, goes up with it." She looked at Kidane and said, "Makes total sense." But Kidane barely moved as Lummis turned back to Dan. "Your marketing system couldn't bring in enough new accounts to do the trick so you fabricated them on your own."

"It wasn't me," Dan said. "I didn't fabricate anything!"

"Did you have help?" Agent Foley asked. "Maybe some people you knew from long ago?"

"I just told you. I didn't have any help because it wasn't me. It was someone else. Her name is Molly Kincaid."

"Come on, Dan," Lummis said. "Some people are walking away with millions on his deal with Virtual Bank." She leaned in closer. "Who paid you to bolster the company's valuation?"

Didn't they hear what he'd just said? He gave them the name of his marketing freelancer, but the female agent kept insisting Dan was involved. He looked at Foley and the other agent leaning against the wall, but neither made eye contact as he repeated his request. "I want to speak with a lawyer."

"But you're not under arrest, Mr. Barry," Agent Lummis said. "At least not yet. If we do formally arrest you, we'll give you plenty of time to speak with a lawyer."

"Geez," Agent Kidane said to Lummis. "How will Dan pay for his fancy legal representation?"

Lummis kept her eyes glued on Dan but nodded toward Kidane. "Agent Kidane is right to be worried, Dan. I believe PEAT shut down your credit line."

Dan swallowed hard.

"That's correct," Kidane said. "And the bank froze his checking account once we flagged his name for suspicious activity. Unless he's hiding money Milo Galini paid him. But then again, affording a lawyer seems to be the least of Dan's problems. On top of fraud charges, the judge and jury will add on serious prison time for lying on a loan application."

Lummis nodded and said, "That's another ten years."

Dan felt the room spinning as Kidane stood and moved next to him. Kidane placed his hands on the table and said, "I guess you could hire a public defender. I'm sure Agent Dennison would walk to the courthouse and get someone from the Legal Aid Society. And they'll do a fine job."

Dan rubbed his face and weakly said, "I didn't...I didn't do anything."

"Well even if you didn't," Lummis said. "You obviously knew about the fake accounts. Although you acted surprised as you conducted your own little investigation."

What was happening? How did the FBI know what Dan had been doing to find the source of the discrepancy?

"Let's not play games, Dan," Kidane said as he paced the room. "You were the only one with access to the Hawk system. Our forensics team will do a much better job than anything you accomplished. Trust me, by the time they're done, we'll have enough to put you away for decades."

"You're wrong?" Dan managed to say. "I just told you. I wasn't the only one with access to Hawk. I had a marketing contractor named Molly Kincaid. She—"

"But you drew all that money from your credit line," Lummis interrupted. "Knowing the fake accounts falsified the value of your stock."

Dan leaned forward and buried his head in his hands. "I had to pay for my father's heart transplant," he said softly. "The insurance company canceled his health coverage. I wanted to make sure I had enough money in case—"

"In case your scam was discovered and the value of Jingle Finance sank," Kidane said.

Dan sat up straight. "I'll say it again. It wasn't my scam." He made eye contact with Lummis as he said, "Molly Kincaid was the one who did something inside my AI system to remove passcodes from a test account generator. She probably fed Hawk's training data with corrupted information to—"

"You've seen that done before, haven't you, Dan," Agent Dennison said as he moved away from the wall. "You know firsthand how artificial intelligence can be re-engineered by manipulating the training data."

Dan stared at Dennison as he absorbed the meaning of his words. And then the memory came back to him as he glanced at Agent Foley.

These were the same two agents that arrested Dan at his apartment in California after Nicole's impersonator was taken away. They knew what had happened at Sway all those years ago.

But why were they here in New York?

Stay focused, Dan told himself. He turned to Lummis and cleared his throat. "If Milo paid anyone, it was Molly. Milo made me hire her."

Lummis and Kidane exchanged glances before the female agent said, "It's clear Mr. Barry is a good fabricator." She nodded at the door. Dennison left the room and returned moments later. The door was ajar as Agent Lummis said to Dan, "You might need to think long and hard before *fabricating* another suspect."

Dan froze when a familiar face entered the room, an FBI badge hanging from her waist.

"Agent Stryker," Lummis said. "I believe you're acquainted with Mr. Barry."

"Hello, Dan," she said.

Dan swallowed hard and barely managed to whisper, "Molly?"

CHAPTER
SIXTY

JOSH ENTERED Sway's Tower Operations control room and looked at the stacks of servers behind the plate-glass windows. He took a seat in the front row and stared at the flashing lights and gleaming hardware that made up CHERL's server farm. Everything he had worked for over the past five years was operating inside those machines—all the carefully curated information and sophisticated software, working together to recreate the greatest business and political leaders in history. And, a separate, small array of servers managing the industry version—"V2"—a class of re-creations Sway's CEO believed would represent CHERL's future.

But Josh's artificial intelligence system, capable of bringing back the greatest leaders from the past, was potentially caught up in another illegal venture. Officer Friday had completed an analysis of the interplay between his brother and the banking industry version of CHERL. Unfortunately, the AI sleuth's findings were inconclusive.

"CHERL was very much engaged with the CEO of Virtual Bank," Officer Friday had stated. *"If V2 influenced Louie Brodsky in the pursuit of Jingle Finance, the tools used were much*

more nuanced than what was deployed by Nicole Ryder's imper-sonator."

Now, Josh's thoughts were focused elsewhere as he organized a different mission for his AI sleuth. Louie had no idea Sway's former employee, Dan Barry—an engineer that had been involved with the Russian hacker that attacked CHERL—was now working inside Jingle Finance, reconnoitered by the FBI as part of a new operation. While Josh was more than willing break his own security clearance by telling Louie about Barry, he doubted the mere presence of the engineer would be enough to stop his risk-taking brother from moving forward with the deal for Jingle Finance.

But law enforcement wouldn't be scrutinizing Barry if they didn't believe the AI engineer was involved in a new plot. Josh wasn't about to stand by and watch Louie carry out what could be a devastating move. He realized he was about to commit career suicide within Sway, but Jenna Turbak and Andre Olaf had already made it clear Josh had no future. And once the FBI discovered what he'd done, Josh could end up behind bars.

But if something bad was going on inside of Jingle Finance, he had to bring his brother proof.

———

JOSH OPENED a session inside the test partition of Sway's Tower Operations—the same computers where Alina Petrova used sophisticated hacking tools to launch her AI probe in search of her mother.

Josh knew Sway's cybersecurity experts followed a painstaking process to examine all of CHERL's entry points. Ever since Nicole Ryder was discovered, cybersecurity scrubbed through every line of code created within Sway and inspected every data element to find signs of manipulation. They monitored every sensor in case hackers once again tried to reenter the data warehouses or software used to control CHERL.

But Josh knew that despite everything that had happened inside these servers, Sway's cybersecurity team hadn't invested comparable resources to detect a hacker attempting to "break out" of the corporate computer center.

He opened his laptop and signed into Tower Operations. Josh toggled over to the test partition—into a secure region of the server farm which only he and Naveen had access to. The area that once again had been loaded with the powerful hacking programs Nicole Ryder's impersonator had used to crack into systems throughout the United States.

Officer Friday already contained Dan Barry's full personality profile. Josh loaded his AI with every line of code Barry developed during the five years he worked at Sway. He linked Officer Friday with each one of Barry's performance reviews, along with the transcript of Barry's "exit interview" conducted by Sway's AI system known as PEARL.

A system Josh himself had firsthand experience with.

Josh then pointed the hacking tools at the intended target and watched Alina Petrova's tools reach past the lackluster security systems installed at Jingle Finance, allowing the AI sleuth to probe each one of Jingle's artificial intelligence applications. Throughout the night, Josh monitored the various programs running on Sway's test partition. He watched as Officer Friday discovered and probed the code of an artificial intelligence system marked as "Engagement Engine." According to the accompanying document scan, this was "where customers interact and garner complex financial advice at the core of Jingle Finance's promise." Once completed, Friday moved on to interrogate the data warehouse containing information used to train and update Jingle's massive application. Given the enormity of the files, Officer Friday's analysis took several hours. But when the AI probe was finally complete, his AI investigation returned a simple conclusion.

"Engagement Engine code is free of corruption or manipulation by internal or external forces. Examination of data used to train engagement engine is clean and serves intended purpose. No evidence of Dan Barry performing tasks within any subroutines."

Officer Friday moved on to several smaller artificial intelligence systems. It rendered a similar verdict after completing a probe of machine learning tools used in customer service, information technology and accounting.

And then Josh's AI sleuth discovered one final application—a system called "Hawk" designed to "execute marketing campaigns to attract new customers to Jingle Finance." Friday immediately reported that each line of code contained a label identifying the creator as "DB."

Finally.

Confirming he had discovered Dan Barry's work, Josh adjusted Officer Friday to report intermediate results as the AI interrogation proceeded.

"Don't just tell me if the Hawk system is clean," Josh instructed. "I want to know the components. How it's built. Where the training data came from."

Officer Friday proceeded to conduct the same analysis on Hawk as it had just completed on the engagement engine and the various other AI tools used within Jingle Finance. But it reported several findings along the way:

"All the data sets in the warehouse were loaded by an employee named MK." Interrogation of personnel files found no full-time employee with MK initials. Probe of accounts payable system located a contractor named Molly Kincaid."

"When we're done, I want you to find out whatever you can about Molly Kincaid," Josh instructed.

"Affirmative."

"What about the code?" Josh asked.

"All the internal programming is attributed to DB. There is nothing unusual in design of Hawk. Style and composition comply with industry protocols. Located communication protocol with a single vendor application called EmoteAi."

Josh thought he recognized the name. "The empathy engine?"

"According to accompanying documentation EmoteAi deployed for Hawk AI to better internalize customer desires, needs and pain points."

Why was such a powerful personality tool deployed within a simple application like a marketing campaign system? Josh recalled several CHERL engineers recommending the outside tool before Naveen elected to have his team build a homegrown version.

"Are there any other personality elements?" Josh asked.

"Negative."

Josh scratched his head and said, "Okay. We'll need to make sure EmoteAi didn't provide an entry point for hackers."

"Agreed."

"Is there anything else to report on Dan Barry's coding?"

"I discovered a great deal of noise that was not filtered out during his coding process."

"What kind of noise?" Josh asked.

"Keystroke commands entered by Dan Barry flowed alongside massive amounts of what appears to convey his emotional state."

"I don't understand."

"Dan Barry's coding commands were communicated using a brain neuron transmission device."

Josh felt his heart racing in his chest. Mindpath! The FBI's listening device! Josh had completely forgotten Agent Foley told him Dan Barry "uses Mindpath so frequently it became a perfect place to insert one of our listening bugs." So Barry *had* used Mindpath to develop the Hawk application, despite Josh's warning that engineers at Sway proved Mindpath couldn't filter out thousands of other neurons created from a user's brain waves.

"Officer Friday. I need you to go back in and analyze what you're referring to as noise." He paused before adding, "And tell me if Hawk built anything with Dan Barry's brain neurons."

Three hours later, when Josh finished reviewing Officer Friday's results, he frantically called Agent Foley. After slowly explaining what he had done—and what the AI sleuth had discovered—the FBI agent was silent.

"I realize I'll probably go to jail for this," Josh said. "But I wanted you to know before I called my brother."

Foley didn't respond but Josh heard the Chicago agent blow out a long breath. "Maybe not, Dr. Brodsky." He proceeded to explain what he wanted Josh to do.

"And when you're finished," Foley said, "I want you to catch the first flight to New York."

CHAPTER
SIXTY-ONE

"SO LET me get this straight, Dan," Lummis said. "Are you suggesting Officer Stryker created the fraudulent accounts?"

Dan felt queasy as "Molly" left the room. He tried to stand but Agent Kidane placed a hand on his shoulder and pushed him back into the seat.

"Take it easy, Dan," Kidane said.

"You put on a good show," Lummis said. "But we know it was you."

Dan tried to blink back the tears welling up as he asked, "Why are you doing this to me?"

"You did this to yourself," Kidane said.

The door opened and Agent Foley, who had stepped out a few minutes earlier, returned. Dan took a deep breath as he tried to figure out what to say—what to do. But the jumble of fear and anger clouded his mind. He managed to whisper, "I'm not saying any more."

"That's not a good idea, Dan," Lummis said. "Sure, you have the right to remain silent. We can read your *Miranda* rights and proceed with a formal arrest. We'll get you that lawyer. But before we formalize all of this, let me finish painting a picture of what's waiting for you behind door number one. The ugly picture of what the judge and jury will see if you decide to fight us." Lummis stood and started pacing in front of the mirror. "We'll demonstrate how you had the motivation. Your father needed a heart transplant and without health insurance, you needed a lot of money, and that's when you came up with your scheme. You found out you could get a credit line, but when the amount wasn't high enough for your needs, you decided to juice up Jingle's valuation."

Lummis kept talking but her words no longer penetrated as the clarity of what was happening came into focus. The FBI had been following him, watching him. They had placed an FBI agent inside of Jingle, masquerading as "Molly," a marketing specialist. But the agent named Stryker was the one who loaded Braun's account creator tool inside Hawk's data files. Even though Dan locked the model with multiple passcodes, the FBI believed Dan somehow followed through on Molly's notion to use the model to fabricate customers. But someone else had broken the passcodes and used the model. Why was the FBI blaming him?

"You drew down the money from the PEAT credit line and put more than enough in your bank account," Lummis said. "You'd seen AI manipulated before when you *helped* that Russian spy."

"Helped?" Dan said. His mouth hung open as a new realization washed over him.

"That's right," Lummis said. "You helped Nicole Ryder do the same thing, didn't you?"

"Is that what this is all about?" Dan asked.

Agent Foley returned and slowly returned to his spot against the far wall, a pained expression on his face.

"We'll get there in a minute," Lummis said. "Let me finish. We'll explain in court that you had the motivation, the experience, *and* the history with the Russians—"

"I have no history with the Russians!"

"You were a suspect," Dennison said. "You were arrested after the hacker was discovered."

"I told you then and I'll say it again. I was her victim! And I was cleared."

"Just because you were never charged with a crime doesn't mean you were fully cleared," Dennison said.

"Agent Dennison is correct," Lummis said. "Anyway, getting back to door number one. The judge and jury will see that all the FBI needed to do was…" Lummis waved her hand through the air. "…create an opportunity."

"Dan fell right back into his criminal ways," Dennison said to Lummis.

"Maybe he can count on the sympathy of the jury," Kidane said.

"True," Lummis said. "His father is a sick man."

The mention of his father again made bile rise in Dan's throat.

Lummis leaned forward and clasped her hands together. "Door number one sounds pretty awful." She glanced over at Foley and said, "Agent Foley. Why don't you come join us over here and explain to Mr. Barry what's behind door number two? The door where we can make this all go away."

Up until now, the Chicago agent had been mostly quiet. Foley seemed to hesitate as he approached Dan, as if he was distressed by the thought of what he was about to say.

"Um…" Foley started as he stared at the floor.

"Agent Foley!" Lummis snapped. "Tell him what will make these charges disappear!"

Foley's eyes looked up at Lummis as he bit his lower lip. He slowly approached Dan and said, "You need to bring us Alina Petrova."

CHAPTER
SIXTY-TWO

"WHAT MAKES you think I know where she is?"
Dan said. "I haven't seen her since the day she left my
apartment in San Francisco. That was three years ago."

"But you have been in touch with her," Lucas said
softly.

"I don't know what you're talking about."

"Hmm," Lucas said. He leaned against the two-way
mirror, trying to come up with a way to stall. But after
what he'd just heard from Dr. Brodsky, Lucas's sharp
mind refused to cooperate. He examined Barry, whose
drawn expression failed to hide his distress. Perhaps
sensing Lucas's hesitance, Lummis jumped in and said,
"We know about the encrypted communication device."

"What device?"

"Is that how you want to play it?" Lummis said. She
looked at Lucas and raised her eyebrows, apparently
trying to urge Lucas to perform his agreed-upon part.
"Agent Foley here is offering you a get-out-of-jail-free
card." She glared at Lucas. "Isn't that *right*, Agent
Foley?"

Lucas cleared his throat. He had no choice but to
carry on until Dr. Brodsky arrived.

"That's right, Agent Lummis," Lucas said. He sat on

the table in front of Dan and proceeded to explain the operation the FBI conceived.

The operation to draw Alina Petrova from her hiding spot.

"You want me to leave the country?" Dan said when Lucas had finished. "You think I'm going to put my life at risk after what you've done! You expect me to leave my sick father?"

Lucas looked into Dan Barry's frightened eyes. He tried to summon some reassuring words—to play his agreed-upon role of "the good cop." But he couldn't muster the energy to lie to Barry—or to himself. After hearing what Dr. Brodsky had just uncovered, Lucas was still putting all the pieces together. He would call the hospital later to confirm one of his hunches. And he directed Brodsky to have Officer Friday "examine" a few other data sources in order to create a complete record of all the facts.

Lucas needed everything to be well documented.

Lummis obviously sensed something was wrong. Instead of waiting for Lucas, she leaned forward and addressed Barry.

"You won't be in any danger," she promised. "And we'll make sure your father gets the best of care in your absence."

"That's right," Dennison said. "You can trust us."

Now it was Lucas's turn to glare at his fellow agent. Did Agent Dennison really expect Barry to trust the FBI after everything they'd done?

"What makes you think she will respond?" Dan finally whispered.

"Foreign agents don't usually reach out like she did in her early messages," Lummis said. "Petrova wanted something from you."

Dan cleared his throat. "That was a long time ago."

"There's no statute of limitations when it comes to the Russians," Lummis said.

Dan placed his head in his hands. "I need some time to think," he said. "And I want to see my father."

Lummis exchanged glances with Kidane who was shaking his head. Lucas could tell by the way Lummis turned and looked at Barry, she was about to deny his request. She opened her mouth, about to render her decision when Lucas said, "We can give you twenty-four hours."

Lummis glared at Lucas as he continued.

"Agent Lummis," Lucas said. "Can we spare Agent Kidane to accompany Mr. Barry to see his father?" Then, turning back to Dan, he said, "He will make sure you don't get into any trouble. But you cannot mention any of this to your father. Is that clear?"

Dan nodded his head. As he stood, Lummis stood and moved to block his path to the door.

"Very well," she said. "I'll give you the twenty-four hours. But if you decide to contact a lawyer, I'll march you right back in front of my door number one." She pointed her finger in Dan's chest. "And there will be no turning back."

CHAPTER
SIXTY-THREE

"WHAT THE HELL WAS THAT, Agent Foley?"
Agent Lummis snapped once Kidane escorted Dan Barry
from the interrogation room. Her reddened face was just
inches in front of Lucas.

"What do you mean?" Lucas tried as he turned away.
He glanced over at Agent Dennison who had moved to
the corner of the room, as far away from the skirmish as
possible.

"Is your head up your ass?" she yelled. "You were
supposed to sell Barry on the plan!"

"I sold him just fine," Lucas said. He folded his arms
and leaned against the wall, trying to appear undisturbed
by Lummis' onslaught. "He's thinking about it, isn't he?"

But Lummis continued her attack. "And then you
took it upon yourself to give him a twenty-four-hour day
pass. Director Compo is coming to New York tonight!
He's expecting us to have an agreement!"

Lucas wasn't about to explain the real reason he gave
Barry the one-day reprieve—that he needed to stall for
time. Instead, he drew in a deep breath and slowly
exhaled before responding. "With all due respect, Agent
Lummis," he said firmly. "I have plenty of experience
negotiating with informers. I could see Barry was shell-

shocked. He was in no frame of mind to process our proposal. But you said it yourself. He has no choice. Tomorrow, I guarantee he'll come to the same conclusion."

"You better be right," Lummis said. "Because when his twenty-four-hour break is over, if Barry doesn't agree, I'll throw his ass in jail until he does."

CHAPTER
SIXTY-FOUR

LUCAS BROUGHT Dr. Brodsky to the New York Bureau's interrogation room an hour before the scheduled session with the Operation Turncoat team. Brodsky said he needed the time to set up his laptop and make sure Officer Friday was initiated and ready to proceed when Director Compo and Special Agent Lummis arrived. The Sway AI director seemed to be moving in slow motion, and he looked more worn out than the typical red-eye traveler arriving from San Francisco. Lucas thought it was possible CHERL's creator hadn't slept in days.

"Who's this?" Agent Stryker asked as she entered the room, trailed by the Agent Dennison.

"This is Dr. Josh Brodsky from the Sway Corporation," Lucas said. "I asked him to join the first part of our meeting as he has some…relevant information."

"What a surprise, Dr. Brodsky," Agent Dennison said as they shook hands. "It's been quite a while."

"Three years," Brodsky said. Lucas and Dennison had met Brodsky when the FBI first became aware of the Nicole Ryder impostor.

Agent Lummis and Director Compo arrived moments later.

"This isn't a good time for guests," Lummis said after she and her boss were introduced to Brodsky.

"I'm aware," Lucas said. "But Dr. Brodsky's artificial intelligence system has uncovered some very relevant information."

"You didn't have to come all the way to New York," Compo said as he sat and crossed his legs. "I'm sure a phone call would have sufficed."

"Artificial intelligence re-creations are not ideal on the phone," Brodsky said.

"Does this mean you've located Alina Petrova?" Lummis said as everyone sat around the table.

"I wish that were the case," Brodsky said.

"But," Lucas said. "What he's found will help us bring the operation to a close."

Lummis glared at Lucas and said, "I'm not sure what *operation* you're referring to."

"He knows about Operation Turncoat," Lucas said, steeling himself for another of Lummis' attacks. The agent in charge seemed ready to launch herself at Lucas's throat, but Compo used his arm to hold her back.

"We'll chat later about how Dr. Brodsky came upon this knowledge," Compo said. He turned his attention back to the laptop. "Let's hear what you have to say."

Lucas watched as Brodsky ran his fingers over the keyboard before adjusting the volume and saying, "Officer Friday?"

"I am here," came the flat, monotone response from the laptop's speakers.

"I'm going to ask you a direct question," Brodsky said. "During your examination of Jingle Finance, did you find evidence of crimes committed by Dan Barry?"

"Negative."

"What examination?" Compo asked.

"Please be patient, sir," Lucas said. But Compo ignored him and repeated his question. Brodsky once again addressed his laptop. "Explain how you gained access to the data needed to formulate this conclusion?"

"By using Alina Petrova's hacking software to interrogate Jingle Finance."

"You did what!?" Lummis rose and stood over Brodsky. "You hacked into Jingle?" Agent Stryker stood alongside Lummis and pulled out a pair of plastic zip ties.

"Director Compo," Lucas said calmly. "Dr. Brodsky took a big chance admitting his actions and agreeing to present us with these findings. I'm sure we can deal with arrests and recriminations later. You can arrest me too if you want. But by the time we're done, you might see things differently."

Compo didn't initially respond, but after a few moments, he said, "Fine." He waved Lummis and Stryker back to their seats. "Let's hear them out."

Lummis took a deep breath and pointed her finger in Lucas's chest. "Okay, Agent Foley. We'll do this your way. For now." As she lowered herself back into the chair, Brodsky positioned his laptop so everyone could see the screen.

"Officer Friday," Brodsky said. "Start by explaining the connection of customer account growth with the activities you observed within the Hawk system." The screen immediately displayed three parallel lines running across from left to right.

"The top line was created by plotting the days Dan Barry added or modified lines of code within Hawk marketing system. The middle line represents plot points where new marketing data was loaded to train the Hawk AI. Someone with the initials 'MK' executed these data loads."

Lucas saw Agent Stryker staring at her hands.

"And the line on the bottom indicates the number of new customers signing up for accounts at Jingle Finance. The line is flat, meaning the new code and data elements were not impactful."

"That's not much of a news flash," Agent Lummis said.

Brodsky swiped at the screen and all three lines shifted. The top two lines were again, flat. But the bottom line representing the number of new customers was pointing in an upward direction. Brodsky said, "This is when things started changing. Friday, please explain."

"During this next period of time, the Mindpath device became Dan Barry's productivity tool as he continued to upgrade the Hawk code. It transmitted all of the brain neurons emanating from Dan Barry's thoughts. He also integrated Hawk with an empathy engine."

"What's an empathy engine?" Agent Lummis asked.

"Hold on," Brodsky said. "Officer Friday, first explain how consequential Mindpath was to what happened inside of Jingle."

"From an examination of Dan Barry's profile from the period of time he worked at Sway, it is apparent he was enamored with emerging technologies, often volunteering to test company initiatives."

"We knew that too," Lummis said.

"Exactly," Lucas said. "That's why you had the eavesdropping bug inserted."

Lummis shook her head and looked like she was about to berate Lucas again for revealing FBI secrets when Brodsky said, "Except the FBI wasn't the only one listening. EmoteAi was listening."

"What the hell is EmoteAi?" Compo asked.

"That's the empathy engine Friday refers to," Brodsky explained. "An empathy engine Dan Barry integrated into Hawk."

"Why did he need an empathy engine?" Compo asked.

"I think I know," Agent Stryker said. Everyone's attention shifted in her direction. "He got the idea from the material those marketing consultants came up with for the training data."

"Are you MK?" Brodsky asked. Stryker seemed to look at Lummis for direction. The agent in charge put up both hands in surrender and said, "He already seems to know everything. You might as well tell him."

Stryker nodded and said, "Dan didn't examine most of what the consultants gave me to load into Hawk. But he insisted on listening to this one podcast from a professor who described how the most effective marketers place themselves in their customer's shoes. The narrator kept using the term 'empathy.' He said that displaying empathy for the plight of your target customers was the best mindset for a marketer when designing campaigns to attract new users."

"Correct. That matches my assessment of Barry's motivation as he sought ways to achieve his customer acquisition goals. He connected EmoteAi in order for Hawk to create marketing campaigns which empathized with the plight of prospective customers."

"What's the point of all of this marketing mumbo jumbo?" Compo asked.

"We're coming to that," Lucas said.

"You see," Brodsky continued, "when Barry started using Mindpath, it transmitted not only his verbal conversations but every other thought and emotion going through his brain. Together with the newly integrated empathy engine, Hawk absorbed and processed Dan Barry's moods, conversations, anxieties and his emotional state."

Lummis shifted in her seat and said, "Can you get to the point?"

"This is what happened as Hawk captured Barry's personal plight," Brodsky said as he swiped the screen, displaying the next timeframe where the customer account line continued a steep, upward climb.

"Why do we care about this?" Lummis said. She pointed to Josh's laptop. "Isn't *that* where Barry turned on Braun's model and started creating those fake accounts?"

"The program that you refer to as the Braun model was indeed responsible for generating the large volume of fictitious customers."

"Exactly," Lummis said. "That's the smoking gun we'll use to nail Barry if he doesn't cooperate!"

"Except after examining every action inside of Hawk, including each line of code, it is clear Dan Barry never unlocked or accessed the Braun model—"

"How is that possible?" Stryker said.

"—and Dan Barry never directed Braun's model to fabricate customers."

"Of course he did!" Lummis shouted.

"Calm down, Agent Lummis," Compo said. He turned to Josh and asked, "What about Milo Galini? Maybe Barry set Hawk up with the model but Galini took the final action."

"Negative. Galini's last access inside of Hawk was executed over four months ago."

"The Braun model didn't turn on all by itself!" Lummis said before turning her attention to Stryker. "We know you didn't turn it on." Stryker shook her head. "Exactly," Lummis said. "Then *who* did?"

Officer Friday was silent. After several moments, Lummis asked, "What's going on? Why isn't your AI answering me?"

"Because you're asking the wrong question," Dr. Brodsky said. "The question is not *who* caused the model to turn on...

...you should be asking, *what.*"

CHAPTER
SIXTY-FIVE

"OKAY, AGENT FOLEY," Agent Lummis said. "You've had your fun."

"I'm completely lost," Director Compo said.

"Please," Lucas said to Compo. "We're almost done. I think things will become clear shortly." He nodded at Brodsky.

It was time to reveal the truth.

Brodsky's fingers ran across the keyboard again as he said, "Officer Friday. Please explain what actually happened which led to the creation of Jingle's fake accounts."

"An analysis of Dan Barry's Mindpath transcripts indicates that he had a habit of replaying conversations in his mind, which fired his brain neurons into the Mindpath. These neurons transmitted more than just his coding instructions."

"Meaning?" Brodsky said.

"Each time Barry repeated these internal thoughts, Mindpath transmitted his neurons to the Hawk-EmoteAi system, which by now was acting as a well-integrated piece of artificial intelligence. Barry's AI system interpreted his emotional state as a set of needs. It then took action to satisfy his needs."

"Play a sample of some the content you uncovered inside Hawk's memory bank," Brodsky said.

"This first interaction occurred during a visit to his father's hospital, where Barry wore Mindpath as he coded Hawk in between conferring with medical personnel and his ailing father."

Lucas watched Compo and the agents listen as the AI sleuth stated a series of phrases:

"Must get Dad on the organ donor list as soon as possible... running out of medical options...don't want to go into hock... intense desire for Dad to be around for a long time."

"We know Barry was desperate," Dennison said.

Thanks to the FBI, Lucas almost said, as Brodsky continued. "Here are excerpts showing Barry's mindset after speaking with the hospital billing department...and his insurance company."

Lucas noticed Lummis shifting in her chair.

"health insurance coverage terminated...red flags on application...need way to cover astronomical expenses...several hundred thousand dollars...father will die without new heart."

"Why do we need to listen to *this*?" Lummis asked.

Lucas held his hand up as Officer Friday continued.

"...take a loan using your Jingle stock as collateral...Jingle's valuation increases with the number of new customer accounts...you have a way to impact size of the credit line to meet full needs."

"Exactly," Lummis said to Brodsky. "Your AI system has done nothing but build support for our case."

"And Barry had several interactions with a coworker named Molly."

Lucas saw Stryker look down as the transcript played:

"...you could use Frank Braun's account generator...they'll only be phony accounts until we replace them."

Lummis cleared her throat and said, "She only suggested the idea."

"My examination of the data sets indicates Molly loaded Braun's model into the training data set where it would be available for creating the fake accounts."

"Molly didn't create fake accounts!" Lummis said.

"That's right," Lucas said. "But she provided everything Hawk needed."

"I think we've heard enough," Lummis said. "Dan Barry is still guilty of—"

"There's only one thing Dan Barry is guilty of," Brodsky interrupted. "And that's his failure to build in guardrails before connecting EmoteAi with Hawk. Our work on CHERL taught us that artificial intelligence should never be directed by a single, powerful emotion like empathy. Not without introducing counterbalancing emotions like apathy, indifference—even cruelty."

"I'm still confused," Compos said.

"When we build personalities within CHERL," Brodsky explained, "we never recreate historic leaders dominated by a single, powerful emotion like empathy. Yet EmoteAi instilled Hawk with nothing but an extraordinarily high level of empathy. When Mindpath fed Hawk with Dan's emotional charged neurons, the artificial intelligence system found a way to satisfy his intense need to help his father."

Lucas saw Compo's jaw drop. "As hard as this is to believe," Lucas said, "it seems Hawk AI had the motivation. It had the skills. The only thing missing was the means to help."

Brodsky said, "And that's when Hawk executed a brute force attack, rapidly running thousands of alphanumeric combinations until it cracked the passcode on—"

"Braun's model," Compo said.

"Exactly," Brodsky said.

"This is crazy," Lummis said. "Are you telling us Hawk has a mind of its own? That Barry's AI became sentient and decided to create the fake accounts?"

"Artificial intelligence doesn't have to be sentient to execute this type of action," Brodsky explained. "Think about those digital assistance tools sitting on your kitchen counter—even those early models like Alexis or Siri—do you consider them sentient?"

"Of course not," Compo said.

"But AI listens in on your conversations—and the

next thing you know, you have recommendations delivered to your cell phone about something you'd just been discussing with your family. Alexis and Siri were early versions of these problem solvers. Today, artificial intelligence is significantly more powerful. And if not designed and built correctly, AI is harder to control. In this case, the combination of EmoteAi and Hawk became a formidable problem solver. AI worked out a way to solve Dan Barry's predicament."

"Even if your wild hypothesis is true," Agent Lummis said. "Barry is the one who programmed Hawk. He knew exactly what he was doing when he included his empathy engine."

"I doubt any competent prosecutor would agree," Lucas said. "Listening to Officer Friday and Dr. Brodsky, it seems to me Dan Barry is guilty of nothing more than an error in judgment."

Lummis stood and said, "We still have enough evidence to put him away." She turned to Compo and said, "And if he refuses to help us go after Petrova, that's exactly what we'll do."

"I think Dr. Brodsky has a few other details that might change your mind," Lucas said. He nodded at Brodsky, who said, "Officer Friday. Why did the FBI choose this point in time to initiate their operation against Dan Barry?"

"The FBI labs are experimenting with predictive analytics in the field of medical science."

"Stop right there!" Compo shouted. But the AI sleuth didn't follow the director's command.

"The FBI's models were fed information about Dan Barry and his immediate family, which correctly envisioned his father, Alec Barry, would require a heart transplant procedure with a six-month time span."

"How did you know this!?" Compo cracked.

"And Officer Friday," Lucas said. "Why did the Capital Insurance company terminate Alec Barry's medical coverage? Insurance that would have covered his expensive needs?"

"Foley!" Lummis shouted. "What the hell are you doing!?"

"Upon examining the records at Capital Insurance, an employee named Guy DeSerra altered portions of Alec Barry's medical insurance information."

"Turn this thing off!" Lummis yelled. But Officer Friday continued. *"It is extremely rare, and illegal, for health insurance companies to suddenly drop a customer. Alec Barry had no criminal background that would justify a review."*

"You've lost your mind, Foley," Lummis said. She then pointed her finger at Brodsky. "How many systems have you hacked into!? Every single thing you've discovered is top secret."

"They won't be secrets for long," Lucas said. "Unless—"

"What's your game here, Foley," Compo interrupted. His nostrils were flaring.

Lucas moved closer to the FBI director and said, "Sir, I want to find Alina Petrova as much as everyone else, but not this way. It's time to terminate Operation Turncoat, without pursuing any criminal charges against Dan Barry. The only thing left to do is to send Barry home and let him care for his dad. Oh, and we should unfreeze his bank accounts and have Capital Insurance reinstate Alec Barry's insurance so all his medical needs are met."

"And why would we do that?" Compo snarled.

"Because if we don't," Lucas said, "Officer Friday is programmed to transmit a transcript of this entire session throughout social media and to every major US newspaper."

"That's enough," Lummis said. "You're both under arrest."

"The only one going to jail is you, Agent Lummis. You see, I had a disturbing conversation with Alec Barry's cardiologist last night. He seemed pretty frazzled—unsure of his facts."

Lucas watched the color drain from Lummis' face.

"With a little more pressure, I believe Dr. Bolan will admit a certain FBI agent coerced him into administering a narcotic which induced his patient's most recent heart failure."

"What?" Compo shouted.

Lummis' expression didn't change.

"Nothing too strong," Lucas said to Compo. "Agent Lummis didn't want Dr. Bolan to kill anyone. She just wanted to move the operation along. After all, our models predicted Alec Barry was going to need a heart transplant eventually. She assumed a trained professional knew just the right amount to…expedite the process."

Compo glared at Lummis. "What is he talking about?"

But Lummis just stood still, frozen in place.

Compo silently shook his head before saying to Lummis, "I'll let the internal affairs deal with you." Then he turned his attention back to Lucas and Dr. Brodsky. "I should also have you both thrown in jail."

"I doubt you will," Lucas said. "Because if this all gets into the papers, you'll all be in the cell right next to us. At least for a few days, because if I understand the Whistleblower policy against retribution, Dr. Brodsky and I will be on the street well before any of you."

"Very well, Agent Foley," Compo said. He pointed his finger into Lucas's chest. "But your FBI career is over!"

Lucas smiled and said, "I couldn't agree with you more."

CHAPTER
SIXTY-SIX

DAN'S HEART was pounding as he stood in the doorway of his father's hospital room. Alec Barry was sitting up in a chair, a blanket on his lap. His eyes were closed, but his complexion was ruddy.

"I'll be waiting in the lobby," Agent Kidane said to Dan before the FBI agent turned toward the elevator. "And don't try to sneak out the rear exit."

Those were the first words his "chaperone" had said since they'd left the FBI's downtown headquarters, which meant Dan was left with his thoughts for the past hour as the unmarked sedan crawled up the west side of Manhattan. Every remaining bit of instinct was screaming at Dan, urging him to fight the FBI's bogus allegations. He knew he was being framed. He wasn't the one who fabricated Jingle's customer accounts. Dan hadn't unlocked Braun's test account model, and he knew there was no evidence proving otherwise.

But if the FBI was willing to stage *this* elaborate trap, had they already produced their own set of facts? Had they already fabricated enough evidence to convict Dan of the charges Lummis described? Without money, how would Dan hire a lawyer capable of fighting back?

And if he was financially wiped out—and unemployed—how would he take care of his father's medical needs?

Dan had checked the banking apps on his phone and confirmed his PEAT credit line had been shut down. In fact, he was already receiving text messages demanding repayment of the two hundred thousand dollars. And despite multiple attempts, he could not sign into the bank account where he'd transferred the loan proceeds.

"If you cooperate," Agent Lummis had said, "the government will cover your father's complete medical expenses."

So despite his instincts, Dan understood the reality of his situation. The FBI had a viselike grip on his life.

He had no choice.

Yet, how could Dan trust the FBI after what they'd done to him? And how did the FBI expect Dan to trick a Russian spy into revealing herself? He understood very little about their plot to coax Nicole's impostor out of hiding. The agent named Foley seemed purposely vague.

Dan sat on the edge of the bed. He reached out and held his father's hand.

"Hi, Dad."

His father squeezed back firmly before opening his eyes. "You look horrible," he said.

Dan hadn't looked in the mirror, but he imagined the stress had etched enough lines on his face to age him by twenty years.

"I'm just tired, Dad."

"You can stop worrying." He smiled. "My new cardiologist expects me to live a long time."

Dan tilted his head. "What new cardiologist?"

"I think his name is Dr. Wirshba."

"Wirshba? What happened to Dr. Bolan?"

"The nurse said he's no longer practicing at this hospital."

"That's strange," Dan said. Dr. Bolan didn't look old enough to be retiring.

"Whatever," his father said. "I'm thrilled he got me my new ticker before checking out. I hope he's sitting on a beach drinking a margarita." He was still smiling. "Maybe I'll join him."

Dan forced a short laugh and said, "You should, Dad. You've got plenty of time on your hands. Everything I've read says you'll be around another twenty or thirty years."

"Nah." He laughed. "I'll leave the beach to Bolan. The leisure life is not for me. Besides, I've got to start carrying my weight. I can't let you have all the fun."

"What's that supposed to mean?"

"I've been thinking about opening up a new restaurant."

"Come on, Dad. Can you come up with something a little less stressful?"

"It's not stressful for me, son. There's no stress in doing something you love. Speaking of which, how are things at work?"

Dan's mouth opened, but he could not muster the strength to lie to his father. But he was warned not to reveal the criminal charges he was facing or what the FBI was coercing him into doing. But there was one "truth" Dan was prepared to reveal today. It was the one decision he had already made.

"I think I'm giving up all this AI stuff."

His father straightened in his chair. "What are you talking about?"

Dan grimaced as he looked away. "I don't know. It just feels like everything is so distorted." He tried to steady his quaking voice. "Nothing is ever as it seems. The whole world is so…twisted." Dan let go of his father's hand and walked to the window. He glanced outside at the Hudson River.

"You're talking about that woman again," his father said. "That spy."

"It's not only her." Dan stared blankly out the

window, but his mind flashed through images from the past three years of his life. Images of the marketing contractor who was really an FBI agent called Stryker. A kaleidoscope featuring coworkers at Sway wrestling with CHERL's re-creations—re-creations which pushed Sway's clients into the insider trading scheme. He visualized still-frames of the Hawk AI marketing code and the fabricated customer accounts. Dan shook his head to clear the twisted montage. "When I get home...I just want my life to be *real*."

"Get home from where?"

Dan faced his dad. "Milo is sending me on a...business trip. I'm going overseas."

"Overseas? What for?"

"Um...well, er...he asked me to troubleshoot a new office." Dan hesitated before forcing himself to tell the lie. "There are some things he needs me to...straighten out."

The ruddy color seemed to drain from his father's face. "How long will you be away?"

"I don't know," Dan whispered. He forced a smile, but his insides were shaking. He took a deep breath and shook his head. When he looked up, he said, "But, hey, when I get back, how about I help you with that restaurant?"

The idea made his father laugh. "You're crazy. You don't want that kind of life."

"Why not?" Dan's voice cracked as he struggled to hold back the tears. "At least everything in your life *was* real."

His father was no longer smiling. "What's wrong, Dan?"

Dan stared out of the window again and was about to change the topic when he heard a female voice in the doorway.

"Excuse me," she said. Dan looked over his shoulder and saw a nurse wheeling in a pushcart. "I need to draw some bloods."

"Okay." Dan wiped his eyes and said, "I'll wait outside." But as soon as he entered the hallway, he ran into Agent Kidane.

"I'm not ready," Dan pleaded. "I need more time."

"It seems you have all the time in the world," Kidane said.

"Huh?"

"I just spoke with the boss man." Kidane looked confused as if he couldn't believe the words he was asked to repeat.

"I'm not sure what's going on downtown…but it seems you are no longer a suspect."

Dan reached out for the wall to maintain his balance. "What?"

As Kidane turned and walked away, Dan heard the agent say, "And your services are no longer required."

CHAPTER
SIXTY-SEVEN

TWO MONTHS LATER...

"WHAT ABOUT THIS?" Vicki asked. Louie turned
around and saw his wife holding up a Lucite plaque
commemorating Virtual Bank's merger with Peachtree
Commerce. Louie shook his head and returned to the
task of cleaning out his desk. "Who needs it?"

Vicki shrugged. "It would be nice to keep a
memento."

He approached her and studied the plaque before
taking it from her hands and placing it back on the
credenza. "I don't want any of these reminders sitting
around our home," he said as he waved around the room.
"Just the photos, Vic. That's all I really need." He
checked the time. "We should finish up. The cleaning
crew will want to scrub the place down before the new
guy gets here."

Thirty minutes later, they loaded three boxes into the
trunk of Louie's BMW and drove away from Virtual
Bank's headquarters for the last time. Vicki had actually
tried to convince him to accept the new CEO's offer to
stay on during a transition period, but Louie believed the
new leader should move quickly to put this chapter in the

rearview mirror. Besides, given everything that transpired, Louie wanted to leave the corporate world behind as soon as possible.

This time, for good.

"Did you send the fly-fishing gear to your brother?" Vicki asked as the car merged onto the Garden State Parkway.

"I did," he said.

"I wish he'd let you do more for him."

"That's Josh. The guy who has nothing and needs nothing." It was Vicki's idea to send Josh a "thank you" present, although Louie knew his brother would rarely put the gear to good use. Despite Josh's rumination about retirement, he said Sway had agreed to retain his services as a "Special Adviser."

"There's still something I have to do before I hang it up," Josh had said.

Louie believed fancy corporate titles like "Special Adviser" were the first step out the door, but he knew his brother would figure out a way to stay relevant in the world of artificial intelligence. Besides, other than AI, what else did his brother really have? And at the end of the day, there was no way for Louie to repay his brother for "the gift" Josh had given *him*.

Josh had risked everything to save Louie from disaster. If his brother hadn't used Sway's AI to interrogate Jingle Finance's systems, Louie's high-stakes gamble would have destroyed Virtual Bank. Once the transaction closed, Louie would have had no way to unwind the acquisition of Jingle Finance. The bank would have faced years of litigation from shareholders. The press would run daily headlines like, "Acting CEO of Virtual Bank Fails to Uncover Hundreds of Thousands of Fictitious Customers." Virtual Bank's stock would have cratered, and Louie, fired in disgrace, would be facing a slew of civil lawsuits along with millions in legal fees. Louie and Vicki would have lost their home. Louie Brodsky's name and reputation would have been forever tarnished.

And worst of all, when all the details emerged, Vicki would know her husband had gambled it all away, again. Not at a casino or at the track. Louie hadn't used any of the online gaming platforms.

He had used his corporate position to place the biggest losing wager of his life.

Instead, thanks to Josh, the fraud taking place within Jingle Finance was discovered. A day before the closing was scheduled, his brother reached out and said, "There is something I need to tell you."

The news of the AI initiated fraud—and Milo Galini's disappearance—was astonishing. Louie quickly drafted a press release announcing the deal was terminated. Before hitting the send key, Jingle Finance's CFO called and said Jingle's investors authorized him to "renegotiate on far more favorable terms for Virtual Bank."

Louie heard through the investment banking grapevine that filing for bankruptcy protection was Jingle's only viable alternative.

And so, a few weeks later, VB bought the assets of the financial education company for less than twenty-five percent of the price originally agreed. And this time, Louie's team fully verified the authenticity of the customers remaining on Jingle's books.

But even before the revised deal was consummated, Louie told Virtual Bank's chairman he no longer wanted to be considered for the CEO position.

"You should find someone without my...baggage," Louie said.

Now, as the BMW drove Louie and his wife northbound, Louie lowered the window and took in a deep breath.

"It's a beautiful day," he said.

"First day of the rest of your life." Vicki smiled.

Louie smiled back. He had no idea what this next

chapter would bring, but as the car pulled into the office park housing the local chapter of Gambler Anonymous, he turned to Vicki and said, "You know this won't be easy. I'm an addict. The urge never goes away."

"I know," she said. "But this time, we're going to fight it together."

EPILOGUE

TWO YEARS LATER...

THE FEW GUESTS who managed to pass through the NSA's enhanced security protocol took their seats in the gallery of Sway's control room, where they were instructed to place an AI-enabled contact lens in each eye. In an instant, they were viewing a colonial-style reception area, recognizable to all as the West Wing lobby of the White House. The frame darted around the neutral-colored walls, the gray patterned carpet, and mahogany furniture. Small letters scrolled at the bottom of their view, announcing the audio and visual transmission emanating from the AI lenses of Dr. Josh Brodsky.

The gallery of guests knew Dr. Brodsky was waiting to meet with the president of the United States.

    Naveen: Try to hold steady.

The text to Dr. Brodsky appeared at the bottom of everyone's display. The frame immediately became less jerky as Dr. Brodsky's eyes directed the viewers' attention to the door leading to the Oval Office.

    Naveen: Better.

As the appointed time for the meeting came and went, Naveen commented to his guests that the secure White House network was performing noticeably faster than that of their corporate clients. Everything was ready to go.

> Naveen: CHERL idling at the
> starting gate.

The view provided by Dr. Brodsky's lenses remained locked on the Oval Office doorway.

"Got it," Brodsky whispered, the sound picked up crisply by the audio sensors built into the AI device.

The Oval Office door opened, and a gray-suited man emerged, his name and title floating alongside him like a pesky insect. The facial recognition software had identified the tall and polished-looking man in tortoise-shell glasses as Steven Haverstraw, the US Secretary of State.

"It's good to see you again, Dr. Brodsky," Haverstraw said. "He's very excited."

Another voice was now coming through clearly as Brodsky entered the Oval Office. The visual display focused on President Carter Wainwright, seated behind the white oak and mahogany Resolute Desk, cell phone to his ear as he swiveled his chair back and forth.

"I don't care about an attack from his right flank, Kristen," the president said. "You tell him if we don't have his vote, he'll be lit up in the primaries this summer. And I'll be the one holding the match." Wainwright punched a button on his cell phone, rotated his chair, and searched the papers on his desk.

"Mr. President," Haverstraw started. "I'd like you to meet—"

"Is this the sci-fi guy?" the president asked without looking up. The secretary moved out of view as Wainwright opened and closed desk drawers. The president appeared much older than his forty-six years, his hair grayer than in published photos and television interviews, his face heavier.

"Dr. Brodsky is the engineer I was telling you about," Haverstraw continued. "He used to work for—"

The president held his hand up. "Hang on." He called out, "Kathy, where is that memo from the Senate minority leader?"

A young assistant hurried into view and looked around the desk. "It's right here, Mr. President." She handed a piece of paper to Wainwright.

The president said, "Tell Andrew I want to see him when I'm done with this."

"Yes, sir," she replied off-screen, followed by the sound of a closing door.

The president flipped the paper onto a pile and looked up.

"Tell him about your years at the Defense Department," Haverstraw said to Dr. Brodsky.

The president interrupted, "Not too many big brains come out of DoD, you know."

Brodsky said, "We had some good people there, sir."

"Forget the preamble, Dan," the president said. "I know who he is. Let's see if this thing works as you said."

The view of the president grew wider as Brodsky approached and placed a foot tall cylinder on the Resolute Desk. Brodsky then held two small cases out to Wainwright and Haverstraw.

"What's this?" Wainwright asked.

"Our latest virtual reality eye gear. You'll both need to wear these contact lenses to fully interact with the system."

Wainwright opened the box and studied the small contents. As the president and secretary of state struggled with the contact lenses, the visuals on the screen became momentarily blurry. Naveen announced to his control room guests that Dr. Brodsky had removed one of his lenses. "He's showing the president how to place them in his eyes. Now's a good time to refresh your coffee."

Lucas Foley rose and did as Naveen suggested. As Sway's head of cybersecurity, the former FBI agent enjoyed sitting in on demonstrations as CHERL versions of historic leaders rolled out across the country. But Lucas knew that today's session was more than just another business leader demonstration.

"Thank you for this opportunity," Brodsky had told the assembled group of Sway leaders the previous week. "Next week represents the culmination of my career. Everything I've worked for over the past seven years has been in preparation for this event."

Lucas was thrilled for CHERL's "Special Adviser"— the man who fought to have Sway's incoming CEO, Jenna Turbak, bring Lucas on board as part of her new management team. If it wasn't for Dr. Brodsky, Lucas never would have been given the chance to reinvent his career shortly after being terminated by the FBI. On the day Lucas agreed to move to California, Brodsky confided that the only reason he signed up for the Special Adviser role was to be present when CHERL was delivered to the Oval Office. And now, as the moment had arrived, Lucas only wished he could see his friend's expression, but the contact lens transmission displayed Dr. Brodsky's point of view. Too bad, Lucas thought. He was sure the normally stoic Josh Brodsky had a big smile on his face.

When the video clarity returned, Lucas returned to his seat and heard Haverstraw say, "Are we going to see who the president asked for?"

"Yes," Brodsky responded. "We're ready to initiate."

"That's my cue," Naveen said out loud to his guests, and his hands ran over the keyboard.

A moment passed before everyone heard Wainwright grumble, "Well, I don't see anything."

"It will take a minute, sir," Brodsky responded.

Finally, a formless shadow emerged from the far wall of the Oval Office. Within seconds, the blur crystalized into a fully shaped man, nattily dressed in a slim-fitted blue suit and skinny red tie.

"Oh my god," one of the guests in the control room said.

Naveen whispered into his terminal, "This is session thirty-four B. Conversation with Carter Wainwright, the president of the United States."

"Incredible," Haverstraw said.

Wainwright wheeled back in his chair until it bumped into the window behind him. Brodsky came around the desk so that Wainwright and their virtual guest were both in his line of sight and said, "He's all set for you, sir." But Wainwright was still leaning away.

The mouth of the avatar started to move, synchronized with a clear and crisp voice. "Hello, President Wainwright. This is a privilege."

Wainwright looked at Brodsky and whispered, "It can see me?"

"Yes, sir. Our lenses work in concert with the system housed in this cylinder. CHERL has visuals on all of us, fully capable of interpreting our facial expressions. Even our body language."

Wainwright slowly rose and stood a few feet away from where the avatar seemed to appear. "Remarkable," he said.

"It looks just like him," Haverstraw marveled.

"It should," Naveen observed to his guests. "We fed the system over five thousand photos and endless streams of video."

Brodsky cleared his throat and directed his words toward the avatar. "As you can see, sir, President Wainwright is here. While of course you are well known to us, perhaps for our benefit, you can briefly introduce yourself. Then I'm sure the president will be excited to engage in a conversation."

"I am surprised you need an introduction," the avatar responded. "From what I've learned, people have not forgotten me."

Wainwright looked at Brodsky and said, "It sounds like him. I'll give you that."

A quick laugh and a smile emerged from the avatar. "Don't look so surprised, Mr. President." Wainwright tilted his head and moved closer as the avatar continued. "You know, looking at you, it's amazing how much one ages in that seat. And you've only been in office for a little more than a year. Hopefully you'll get another three." Another soft laugh emerged, then, "Unfortunately, things didn't work out that way for me. But I understand you specifically asked for today's meeting. I'm looking forward to exchanging ideas on international affairs. I've been fully briefed on today's hot spots." The avatar paused and added, "As you know, I had great success going up against the Russians."

Wainwright's shoulders finally seemed to relax. Looking at Brodsky, he said, "I should just…talk to it?"

Brodsky nodded. Wainwright cleared his throat and said, "Mr. President…it's truly an honor to speak with you today."

"We should get away from this formality. How about I call you Carter." The avatar paused before offering, "And you can just call me Jack."

———

FIVE THOUSAND MILES AWAY, in a former KGB bunker, Alina Petrova was sitting with another highly screened assemblage monitoring events in the White House. The high-definition display was streaming in with perfect clarity, thanks to a miniature lens and recorder hidden in the lapel of their latest Russian agent. She always regretted her inability to recruit Dan Barry to be one of them, as she had fond memories of their brief time together. But Alina had waited for years for him to respond to her entreaties, to no avail.

It was time to move on.

Alina knew today's session with the US president would be nothing more than a minor demonstration, but she was pleased by the reaction of her own enraptured audience of SVR leaders. Yet she was aware of the tension in the room. Her country's security service was anxious to execute the plan to manipulate the actions of the American president. But Alina continued to urge patience.

After all, for her, this mission was personal.

Alina was willing to wait for the perfect opportunity to avenge the death of her mother.

IF YOU LIKED PARALLEL MINDS, YOU MIGHT LIKE: DEATH SECRETS: AN ANNA HALE, PI THRILLER

BY JANUARY BAIN

A gripping thriller that explores the lengths one will go to for family, and the resilience needed to stand against the darkness.

In the shadow of Alaska's towering peaks, Anna Hale is haunted by a past painted in flames and betrayal. Marked by the tragic death of her mother and the scars of a childhood marred by violence, Anna has fought tirelessly to build a semblance of normalcy, only to have it shattered again and again. The latest blow comes when her sister, Tia Pace, vanishes without a trace, reigniting old wounds and casting Anna into a nightmare where she's the prime suspect.

As she grapples with her stepfather's execution and the weight of suspicion, another crisis looms: Zoe Pace, her other sister, has disappeared in an eerily similar manner. The only clue a sinister black rose and a chilling letter. When her brother Josh, now a dedicated cop in the Anchor Police Department, begs for her assistance, Anna is pulled back into the fray. Despite the agony of reopening old wounds, she embarks on a desperate quest to unravel the mystery of her sisters' disappearances.

Faced with the unforgiving Alaskan frontier, Anna must confront a tangled web of corruption and deceit, with a copycat killer moving in the shadows. With every tick of the clock, Anna's hope for a normal life slips further away, but her resolve to find her sisters and bring them home burns fiercer than ever. Will Anna's journey through the cold, dark paths of Alaska lead her to her sisters, or will she find herself lost in the depths of a conspiracy that threatens to consume everything she holds dear?

AVAILABLE NOW

ACKNOWLEDGMENTS

I would like to thank my subject matter experts that provided background material, helping to bring this story together, including my AI authority, Kevin Clark (of Content Evolution), former New York City prosecutor Jay Shapiro, marketing executive Lutz Braum, Insurance expert David Feinstein, HR and equity compensation expert Arnaldo Austria, consumer fraud expert, Max Blumenfeld, and of course, most importantly, my medical and health expert (who doubles as my loving spouse), Hildy Sheinbaum.

I would also like to thank Chris Belden for his guidance and feedback on early manuscripts. And of course, Rachel Del Grosso and the team at Rough Edges Press.

Marc Sheinbaum grew up in Sheepshead Bay, Brooklyn. He set out to be a writer from a very young age, but like the characters in his stories, life doesn't always turn out as planned. Instead, Marc spent over thirty-five years in business, working for a variety of American companies. Now retired, he spends his time writing and serving on public and non-profit boards. He and his wife, Hildy, split their time between Westchester County and Westport.